Gracie's Babies

Beth Durham

ISBN: 978- 1705877845

Original Cover Artwork by Dany Zamora

Chapter 1

As Gracie Berai strode away from the little white church building, she walked with direction and purpose, scarcely noticing the haying wagons in the field she passed or the attention the young men paid her. Her ebony hair was loosely contained in a knitted snood beneath a wide-brimmed straw bonnet. While her dress properly touched the dusty road, she had sewn the skirt more slender trying to imitate the latest bustled style without sacrificing the ease of movement required of workday clothes on the mountain farm. The overall affect was mesmerizing to the boys who were tasked with forking loose hay beneath the searing summer sun. The pair of big horses plodded slowly along despite the worker's inattention.

"Whoa," called one of the men, realizing the wagon had moved away from the frozen workers.

"Boys, you're gonna have to catch the nags now, just look at all this good hay you've left. She's a beauty, but you'll have to wait 'til Sunday morning to admire her. Now git on back to work."

As the words faintly reached Gracie's ears, she was thankful for the floppy straw hat that would hide her blushing cheeks.

Her determined pace quickly carried her away from the still-peeping eyes and she was soon beneath the shade of overarching trees. Turning on the Elmore road, she relaxed a bit and breathed deeply of the summer smells. The sweet scent from the creeping rose mingled with the earthy hay, even the sunbeams seemed to offer their own contribution.

Gracie was smiling as she stepped through the front door. No one questioned her for she was often smiling. Not a giddy girl, Gracie had rather a serious nature. Her keen chin and sharp nose would have seemed harsh had she not always had that pleasant smile to soften them. The Italian heritage she inherited from Philip Berai was obvious in her every feature, and Grandma often told her she was the spitting image of her father.

She had to take her grandmother's word on the family resemblance for she had never seen her father – well, not since she could remember anything about him. She'd lived on this little mountain-top farm with Grandpa and Grandma Elmore since her mother brought her and her sister here when Gracie was only three years old.

Despite losing Margaret Berai sixteen years ago, both daughters Gracie and Lottie felt they knew their mother far better than their father who still lived. Although he faithfully sent money, Philip Berai had remained in Chicago, leaving his children's upbringing solely to his in-laws. Through the years, Grandma Elmore wrote regularly to her son-in-law and encouraged her granddaughters to do the same.

Margaret, however, lived in their memories. Scarcely a day passed without some mention of the vibrant dreamer who ran away to the big city only to learn that her heart was still firmly planted on Tennessee's Cumberland Plateau.

Now, Gracie was thankful to her mother for giving her this life. She couldn't begin to imagine having spent her young life in the raucous noise of Chicago.

"Did you get the flowers in place Gracie?" Grandma sat at the kitchen table, a big bowl of green beans before her.

Gracie dropped her bonnet on the end of the table as she bent to kiss her grandma on the cheek. "Yes ma'am and the church house looks just beautiful with them. By morning the roses will have filled the room with sweetness."

The room seemed especially warm to Gracie after her walk in the sunshine. She dipped water from the bucket setting on the dry sink and wrinkled her nose at the warmth that touched her lips.

"I'll bring in some fresh water from the spring. Then I'll turn to helping Aunt Hettie with supper."

Grandma didn't look up from her beans as she answered Gracie, "Run on child, but Hettie and Lottie have gone to Matthew's cabin to do some cleaning."

With a shake of her head, Gracie headed out the back door with bucket in hand and Uncle Matthew on her heart. They were always trying to look after his cabin because he was certainly no housekeeper. She wondered what the cabin would be like if Aunt Lou had lived. But Gracie had never really known Matthew's wife for she died in childbirth the first year that Gracie lived in Tennessee.

There were plenty of girls in the community who would gladly have married Matthew, kept his cabin and shared his life. But whether it was the loss of Lou or the trauma of the war, Matthew had somehow withdrawn into himself. He shared supper with his family most evenings, but never when there were visitors. He attended church with them regularly, but he never stayed for fellowship.

Grandpa had often talked about the old Matthew; it seemed he missed him just as though he were still away at war – or worse as though he'd never come home. And now Grandpa was gone too. It was somehow different though because he'd gone home to heaven.

The whole family missed Grandpa but Grandma kept reminding them that they wouldn't want to keep old people forever – the young folks had to move on with their own lives, raising their own families. Still, it was obvious that part of Grandma had left with him.

You've gotta snap out of this Gracie or you'll make yourself sad. This is just too lovely a day to be sad. Despite all of the family surrounding her, Gracie often found herself in her own head, contemplating her own thoughts. Grandma said she'd taken that after her mother.

With a heavy bucket in hand, Gracie was just stepping onto the back porch when she heard Hettie and Lottie returning. Their friendly chatter seemed melodic as the breeze carried it to her.

"Well it's a good thing you've come back. Otherwise I was goin' to cook supper myself and make you eat it no matter how bad it was," Gracie called to them.

Lottie picked up her pace to nearly a skip as she raced to her sister. The seventeen year old was an adult for all practical purposes. But her jolly nature gave her a youth that Gracie wondered if she would ever outgrow.

"We've been to see Matthew you know," Lottie announced.

"Yeah, and it seems you've left Hettie to carry all of the washin' you brought back." Stepping away from the water bucket, Gracie reached to help with the burden.

Hettie thanked her, "Thanks Gracie. Don't chide Lottie, she's been lookin' for black berries on the walk back and I didn't want any of Matthew's things to get snagged on the briars."

"Blackberries? It's way too early for them."

Lottie was shaking her head, "Well I thought I might find enough for a pie. We have sugar in the house and it just seems like we ought to have pie."

All of the girls laughed at Lottie's enthusiasm and agreed the sugar was destined to be part of a summer treat.

As they entered the kitchen, Gracie drew their grandma into the chatter. "Grandma, this silly Lottie thought we could have blackberry pie with our supper. As though the berries would be ripe when she asked for 'em."

Grandma reached for Lottie's hand as though she'd protect her. "Well I've seen berries ripening not much later than this. When it's a real hot summer, they'll plump up and just beg to be eaten."

Lottie dropped into a chair and Gracie couldn't help but notice that her dress was too short and the tops of her boots peeked out from the hemline. "Well not today I'm afraid. I waded into every bramble between here and Matthew's house but the berries weren't even much red yet."

Gracie's concern for Matthew returned, "Did you find Uncle Matthew at home?"

Hettie had already begun bustling around the kitchen. She had truly become part of the family since she and Jesse moved in after Grandpa's death. They'd built a big addition but kept the kitchen just the same as Grandma always had and now Hettie made it her own. Uncle Jesse declared they needed the larger space for the family they planned to raise there. Grandma just rolled her eyes around the little house where she'd raised eleven children and two grand-children. However, she was happy to have her son making the home into a place his wife would love and claim for her very own home.

"Matthew wasn't there," Hettie explained. "I think he and Jesse are working the corn. We'll probably need to plan on helpin' with that next week."

Despite the quickly changing season, Jesse always said he wouldn't require the women in the fields. Still, they all took their turn with hoes. Grandma, Lottie and Gracie secretly laughed among themselves saying that any one of the women of the house could out-hoe both the men. Yet, it pleased them that neither Jesse nor Matthew ever expected them to be in the fields and never complained when chores in the house or garden kept them busy. By evening the horses' slow turn through the rows would have the field plowed through and the standing weeds would be waiting for their hoes on Monday morning.

Hettie stirred the fire in Grandma's big iron stove. Gracie had noticed two chickens ready for plucking on the back porch and she moved that way before she was asked. Grandma had finished the big bowl of green beans and was mixing cornbread for the iron skillet already warming on Hettie's fire. The first of the new potatoes would be the evening's treat and everyone was as excited by them as they would have been if Lottie had found blackberries.

This day was much the same as many others for the little farmstead. In fact, all of the summer of 1883 passed with the sweet familiarity to which Gracie was long accustomed.

Chapter 2

Gracie watched Grandma as she packed a small basket and prepared to go visiting. Now in her mid-sixties, Lottie always said she must be the oldest woman alive. But Gracie admired her as she moved about the kitchen.

"Where are we goin' today, Grandma?"

Grandma never slowed her preparations as she answered, "It's a tough walk, but I want to go see that young Turner girl. They don't have much and her time's about come to have that baby. We'll take her some of these fresh vegetables and some farmer's cheese. That will be good for her baby you know."

The screen door creaked as Jesse entered the kitchen and helped himself to a left-over biscuit from the stove's warming shelf. As he slathered molasses over the bread, he listened to his mother and niece.

"Don't you dare try to walk all the way to the Stock Road. I'll hitch the little wagon and Gracie will drive you."

Gracie smiled. Everyone in the household tried to take care of this woman who had cared for all of them for so very long and never asked for anything. Gracie wished she could drive her in one of the shiny buggies she'd seen in Crossville. But of course neither the Elmores nor any of their neighbors had such a thing.

By the time they were ready to leave, Jesse had their trusted old mare hitched alongside a young horse he was working and the rig was tied by the back door. Grandma took the liberty of carrying a second basket since they would not be walking and Gracie loaded both of them behind the board seat.

Jesse untied the rope and looked at his neice, "Now you watch Bob, he's young and still got a wild side. Cinnamon will keep him in line, you just have to keep an eye on things."

Gracie smiled at him as she climbed aboard, humored by the constant advice he had for her and thankful that he cared enough to always offer it. She took the reins with an expertise born of years behind a team. The little farm often required the young ladies to drive, freeing the men to fork hay onto the wagon, or manure off and into the fields. This too made Gracie smile as she thought how pleasant the drive with Grandma was compared to those chores.

Bessie Elmore let out a deep sigh as Gracie clucked to the single horse to begin their little journey. "I'll tell you child, I will never understand why I can get winded just gathering a few things in a basket and hopping on the wagon."

"Well Grandma, don't you suppose your legs are telling you they've walked an awful lot of miles?"

"More miles ahead of me Gracie." Grandma adjusted her straw hat and repositioned herself on the seat. "Just as long as the good Lord lets me live, I'm gonna keep goin'. Never seen nobody what sat down and gave up that come to any good."

Gracie answered only with a soft, "hmmm", but she was thinking how Grandma was always bringing good to those around her and never looking for a blessing herself.

Their chatter kept time with the jingle of the harness and wheels until they reached the little shack that George and

Nelda Turner called home. George worked for a farmer because he owned neither home nor land.

Nelda always had the door open before they could get out of the wagon but today there was no sign of her.

"Well she's too far along to have gone anywhere," Grandma pondered as she lifted one of the baskets.

Gracie was already at the door, knocking. "She's not coming to the door, but I can hear her inside."

Grandma grasped the doorknob and gently pushed; it swung open effortlessly.

The heat of the day was quickly building in the little house as the curtains had never been opened from the night.

"Neldie honey are you here?" Grandma called even as she crossed the threshold.

Only the weakest moan greeted the visitors.

Following the sound, they found Nelda drenched in sweat and writhing weakly on the bed.

Grandma practically threw the heavy basket onto the kitchen table and flew to the bedside. With one hand on Nelda's forehead and the other holding the girl's own hand, she began to ask questions. "Child, how long have you been like this?"

Grandma had to lean close to understand the weak girl, "Pain started at dawn but it's been gettin' worse all day."

"And George just left you like this?"

"No, no. I didn't tell him I was hurting. Just asked if I could rest a little while and he got his own breakfast."

Grandma looked to Gracie whose eyes had tripled in size; the girl was nearly paralyzed. Stepping away from the bed, Grandma spoke as sternly as Gracie had ever heard her, "Don't you dare freeze up on me Gracie. She's going to have this baby now and we're all she's got."

Gracie found her voice, squeaky though it was, "Do you want me to go for somebody?"

"Who would it be? You are probably too young to face this, but you're going to need to know and now's as good a time as any to learn."

Gracie didn't have an answer for the 'who' and Grandma never wanted to put off learning.

"Go stir up the fire and get some water as hot as you can stand to touch it. Call me when it's hot. See if you can find some clean rags too."

Gracie moved mechanically. She couldn't think, she could only follow orders. In the background she could hear Grandma encouraging Nelda and talking her through what seemed to Gracie like a dreadful situation.

There were very few coals in the stove's firebox but they had a good supply of corn cobs for tender and Gracie quickly had a little fire going. She checked the stove's reservoir and called to her Grandma, "The water's pretty warm in the reservoir."

It was a moment longer before Grandma crossed the cabin's single room and stuck the dipper into the tank. "It's almost warm enough. Fill that wash pan and set it over the open eye. We're gonna need the sharpest knife she has; if you see a file give it a swipe or two on the blade then put the knife in the hot water. Did you find any rags?"

Gracie pointed to a small pile on the table which made Grandma frown. "That won't do. I'm afraid she's going to bleed a'plenty. We'll use the sheets; just have lots of water boiling and we'll get them washed up as soon as we're done."

Done? Thought Gracie? She felt like they'd never be finished with this ordeal. She shook her head as she chose to shake off the fear. *What are you so scared of? Grandma has surely done this hundreds of times. It's just one more thing you really need to learn from her.*

With that, Gracie set her mind to complete everything her grandma pointed her to. In no time, she'd gone to the well and filled the largest pots she could find; they were standing ready to heat. She located Nelda's soap flakes and had them ready to clean the sheets.

By the time she returned from the well, Grandma was scrubbing her hands with lye soap. "Don't ever touch a hurtin' body without a good scrubbing. The good Lord didn't teach the children of Israel all that washin' for no reason, you know. You go ahead and scrub up too, I may need you."

Gracie had just finished giving her hands and arms the most thorough washing they'd ever known when she heard Grandma say, "Breech". What did that mean? Was it as awful as Grandma's voice made it sound?

As Gracie stepped closer, Grandma looked up at her and explained, "It's always harder when they're breech."

It felt like hours passed as Grandma coached and Nelda screamed. Whenever she could, Gracie sat at the girl's head and rubbed her damp hair. Finally, Grandma urged, "You've gotta really push hard now. His feet are coming and we have to get the rest out fast."

Nelda nearly broke Gracie's hand as she labored through the final moments of birth. Then, time was no longer dragging, but speeding by. Seemingly in the next breathe, Grandma held up the tiniest, purple baby Gracie had ever seen. She gasped, fearing the worst.

"Gracie hand me the knife now and take the baby while I cut the cord." Her hands moving like lightning, Bessie tied cords in two places on the cord protruding from the baby's stomach and then slit it in half between them. "Okay, now I've gotta take care of Nelda"

Gracie had seen several soft blankets Nelda had prepared for her new baby. Now, she grabbed one and wrapped him snuggly inside then pressed him against her own skin. He began to gurgle, whimper and then to actually cry. Gracie had seen birth many times on the farm. From baby chicks pecking their way out of their shells to calves that sometimes had to be pulled out by their legs, she always thought newborn creatures were both pitiful and perfectly gorgeous.

Now she looked at Nelda's baby and saw only his beauty. She wanted to bounce and admire the little baby but Grandma had more work for her. "Gracie, can you get him cleaned up, especially his face? We want to make sure he can breathe good."

She felt awkward trying to both hold him and dip the warm water to begin bathing him. She'd helped with her cousins and all of the babies at church, but this was the first time she'd held a brand new baby. By the time she felt he was reasonably clean, he was screaming and she knew that he needed his mother; he needed to eat.

Gracie moved toward Nelda's bed, but she was looking to Grandma for permission.

"Yeah, give him to his Mama, that's what a little one needs." Grandma had a pile of rags and sheets in her hands and moved toward the cook stove with them.

Nelda seemed too weak to even lift her arms but she was beaming as she took the little bundle.

"Will she be okay?" Gracie asked as she returned to Grandma's side.

"Oh yes, she's just all tired out. Why don't you go out to the fields in the wagon and see if you can find George. I'll wait here with Nelda and do this washing."

Gracie quickly found the new father and returned him to his family. Assured that Nelda's mother would be coming to them shortly, and with supper prepared, Grandma felt it safe to leave them.

The drive home was unusually quiet.

"Well, we've missed the first night of the protracted meetings. I'm sorry about that. I know how you young people look forward to it."

Gracie had to take a deep breath before she could answer. She felt like it was the first breath she'd taken in hours. "Oh Grandma, I wouldn't have missed this for all the young people in the world."

Grandma smiled and wrapped her arm around her little granddaughter. She knew Gracie was a woman now. Probably the young men were the ones who were disappointed tonight when they were deprived of Gracie's company. Bessie couldn't help but reflect that soon Gracie would surely leave them for her own home and family. Until then, she determined to enjoy every moment with her and certainly to continue to share these opportunities to teach her granddaughter. She looked anew at the girl who'd worked beside her all day and saw a gift she'd never known Gracie possessed.

God has a work for this one, I can see it now, she thought.

Chapter 3

There was a lamp burning in the kitchen as they returned to the familiar home. Grandma's first direction to Gracie was to change her dress and wash thoroughly. "Nelda keeps a good house, but it's a practice you need to always keep – when you've been helping with sick folk, you gotta clean up as soon as you get home."

Gracie had just finished her bath when she heard the rest of the family returning from church.

Lottie bounded in with her usual exuberance. "Gracie where have you been? I thought sure you'd meet us at the church. My but you missed it – there was a whole family from over 'bout Martha Washington visiting and the church house was overflowing."

Gracie hugged her sister and reminded her to slow down a little. "I can't understand a thing you are talking about. There was a good crowd I guess?"

Nodding vigorously, Lottie began picking at the bowl of popcorn Grandma had ready for everyone.

Jesse tried to help sort out Lottie's news. "The Ingle family came to the service; they live in Martha Washington. Well, I don't guess it was the whole family. The old man said he's got thirteen kids living, most of them right over there near him."

"But a whole bunch of cousins came too," Lottie added. "There was a young man named Daniel; he just laughed and grinned all the time. He would be a lot of fun, I think."

The whole family enjoyed a good chuckle but Gracie was left with a lingering curiosity about this family.

Her questions would be answered soon enough as the revival meetings were planned for at least a full week and the Elmores would attend every service.

On Tuesday the Ingles returned and Lottie was more than happy to make introductions for her sister. As soon as she saw the group from Martha Washington, Lottie grabbed Gracie's arm and nearly pulled her off her feet.

Waving Lottie called, "Joanna, Mandie Catherine, I'm so glad you could make it back." She took a deep breath after she arrived in front of the girls with their brothers and cousins gathered around. "My sister made it tonight and I wanted to introduce y'uns."

Gracie smiled, although she was feeling very conspicuous after Lottie's loud greeting.

Joanna Ingle was a full head shorter than Lottie and seemingly of a much quieter spirit. However, she gave them a bright smile and reached a hand out to grasp Gracie's. "I'm so happy to meet you. I'm Joanna Ingle. Your sister and neighbors gave us a wonderful welcome yesterday evening and we were eager to join you again tonight."

Under this warm greeting Gracie found her voice, "Hello Joanna, I am Gracie Berai. I'm sorry I couldn't be here last night; I was with my grandmother at a sick bed."

Compassion flooded Joanna's face, "I am sorry to hear that Gracie. I hope everyone is doing well."

"Oh yes, much better and improving steadily." Gracie dropped her eyes hoping they would not force her to explain the nature of the 'sickness'.

Lottie drew Joanna into conversation and meeting other neighbors. The younger sister, more shy even than the quiet Joanna, was left amid her brothers and cousins. Gracie smiled at her and reached out a hand, "Hello. Did my sister call you Mandie?"

The young girl nodded, "Mandie Catherine actually. Everybody calls me by both names."

"Well I think that's a lovely name."

Gracie's eyes darted among all the boys gathered around the girl and wondered if she ought to speak to them or whether that might not be proper.

Mandie Catherine read the question in her new friend's eyes and asked, "Do you know my brother Daniel?"

She reached for the boy's arm and Daniel Ingle turned his attention to the two girls. "Howdy," he greeted Gracie.

"This is my brother Daniel, and that's Andy yonder." She turned to her left side and pointed toward the next two she introduced, "Our cousins Stephen and Martin Todd. They live just up the hill from us. And let's see, our Uncle Bill is here tonight too. His wife Cathy is with him. She's new, but he had another wife before."

Gracie smiled enjoying the girl's descriptions and unable to find an answer to them. She looked to each of the family members to greet them.

Lottie's new friend Daniel was indeed jovial and Lottie managed to spend a few minutes cutting up with him before the music began to call them into the service.

Gracie noticed their cousin Stephen seemed a bit more serious and Gracie watched carefully as he spoke a few words to some of the men in the church and to some of the younger people too. He seemed older than the rest of the visitors and she tried to understand that. Surely he wasn't older than his uncle who Mandie Catherine had already declared was on his second wife.

Stephen wasn't as tall as Daniel and had a slighter frame. His dark hair hung low toward deep set eyes in a round face. His eyes were so dark they might have seemed brooding but a glint in them belied any darkness of spirit.

Lottie felt free to ask about each of the Ingles and Daniel's sister Joanna explained that Stephen only had one other brother besides Martin, who was visiting the church with the group. Martin still lived with his folks and worked on their farm while the older brother was married with a family of his own.

Stephen and Martin's parents were not along for the Tuesday service but Daniel's parents, George and Tobitha attended and all of the Elmores enjoyed them.

The older Ingles could not make the long wagon ride from Martha Washington every night of the revival. However, several of the young men did manage to make it either riding horses or walking. Both Stephen and Daniel attended each night. By Thursday Stephen managed to spend all of the time allowed for fellowship with Gracie's group of friends. He began to talk more, at least he was talking to Gracie.

Gracie's friend Paralie pointed out, "That Stephen don't have much to say 'cept when he's talkin' to Gracie."

Gracie blushed, "Oh Paralie, he just happened to be standin' near me, that's all."

"Yeah, he was standin' by you because everytime you moved he followed you. Why, he was a little like a puppy dog."

"Paralie," Gracie chided, "Don't tease like that. He's a very nice boy, don't you think?"

"Yeah he's nice, but he's too serious. Daniel's more fun, a'course he's only got eyes for Lottie. Guess the Berai girls caught all the attention that came out of Martha Washington."

Gracie was embarrassed by her friends ribbing, yet somehow she was encouraged that Stephen Ingle paid her special attention.

Just as Grandma had predicted on the first night, the young people were sad to see the services end both for the worship and the fellowship. They were serious services and many of the youth were serious about them. In fact, several were saved and others dedicated their lives to more earnest kingdom service.

As the group broke up on Friday evening the Ingles bade a final farewell to their new friends from the Elmore community. Lottie walked home with her head hung down, "I was hopin' Daniel would want to write to me. He didn't say a word though."

"Lottie you're too young to have a boy writing to you," Grandma declared.

"I am not. Mother was married by the time she was my age."

Grandma's eyes flashed open wide and Lottie immediately knew she'd said the wrong thing. "Lottie have you learned nothing about rebellion from your mother's stories."

It seemed impossible for her to drop her head any lower and now her shoulders drew inward as well, "Yes ma'am, of course I've learned. I would never run off or anything like that. Daniel Ingle is a nice boy from a good Christian family. Surely you'd be happy for him to write to me."

Grandma reached an arm around her granddaughter. "Yes Lottie, when the time is right Daniel is just the sort of boy I hope will court you."

Lottie's shoulders and head came upright and a smile lifted her face. "Well, surely some of the Ingles will stay in touch."

Gracie had remained quiet through the whole interchange and she kept the thought to herself; *I sure hope so Lottie.*

Chapter 4

After a week of protracted meetings upending their routine, the Elmore household had just begun to settle back into their normal evening pattern. Jesse came in just as Hettie pulled cornbread from the oven and Gracie spooned soup bones into a serving bowl. He hadn't washed yet so he stood by the door and tossed an envelope onto the dry sink. "Been to Isoline to get shoes for the ole' mare. While I's there I stopped at the post office and we had a letter. It's addressed to Gracie Berai."

"Is it from our father?" Gracie rarely received any correspondence, although Philip Berai continued to regularly send money to help with his daughters' upbringing.

Jesse grinned and pushed the letter across the counter where Gracie could see the return address. In bold, block letters, it read 'Stephen Ingle'.

Gracie froze after a sharp intake of breath, the steaming bowl in mid air. She knew she didn't want to read this in the kitchen with everyone there. Without another word, she slipped it into her apron pocket and carefully set the bowl on the table. Her hand went to the pocket as though to reassure herself the envelope was not a figment of her imagination. She searched her mind for an excuse to flee the kitchen out to the shady front porch where she could read it.

She looked up to realize the whole family was staring at her. Only Grandma spoke, "Child go read your letter. You won't eat a bite with it burning in your pocket anyway."

She smiled, "Thank you Grandma. I'll just go out on the porch I think."

Grandma waved her away and headed toward her seat at the table.

As the screen door squeaked shut and Gracie settled herself in a straight backed chair she heard the shuffles as her family sat down to their evening meal.

Gracie pulled out the letter and carefully broke the seal.

As she gently rocked and read the letter through again and again, she savored the words Stephen had written. His first line reassured her that he wrote with her Uncle Jesse's blessing.

Uncle Jesse! Gracie's heart shouted, *Why didn't you tell me Stephen asked to write?*

Stephen spoke of enjoying the revival service and appreciating the sweet spirit among her neighbors. He talked of his work on his father's farm and of dreams he had to improve it and eventually to own his own land.

A whole page, both front and back, were filled with a neat script recalling lines from the preacher's messages and quotes from her friends. He even reminded her of questions she had asked him and he said he'd thought more about the answers.

Gracie wanted to call out in her joy, instead she bit her lip and scrunched up her face trying to hold it all inside.

She thought of so many things she'd like to say to him.

Should I ask Grandma if I can write back to him?

No, she decided that would not be right. So she waited.

It was several weeks before Uncle Jesse made another trip to Isoline and Gracie longed everyday to ask him if he planned to go there. Somehow she managed to keep her questions to herself until he finally announced, "We're a'needing coal oil I'll go into Isoline today and get some. Grandma, do you need anything else?"

"No Jesse, I have everything I need around me," Grandma smiled as she cracked open another hull of beans.

Hettie spoke up without waiting for him to inquire of her, "I could really use a spool of sewing thread. Just natural color is fine Jesse."

He nodded and headed out the door.

Throughout the morning Gracie caught herself looking out the window or down the road; she stood quietly at the spring listening for the click of the saddle horse. Finally as Gracie and Lottie cleaned up the dishes from dinner they heard a horse's approach.

Gracie ducked her head close to the window pane and Lottie told her, "You know that's just Uncle Jesse comin' back from Isoline."

"Hmm, I guess it is," Gracie tried to dismiss her eagerness. By the time Jesse dismounted from his horse at the barn's door, Gracie could wait no longer. Grabbing the bucket she called behind her, "We need some fresh water Lottie. I'll be right back."

However she didn't head toward the spring house but went directly to the barn calling ahead of her, "Did you have a good trip into Isoline Uncle Jesse?"

"Hmm? Oh hello Gracie. Yeah, things are sure bustling there. There was a long train hissin' and lettin' off steam. Must've had a hundred cars of coal and lumber behind it."

"That many? How do they ever dig out so much coal?"

"Lot of men with a lot of shovels I'd reckon."

"Must be a hard life crawlin' in the ground everyday."

"I reckon it is Gracie." He was still shaking his head as he swung his saddle across the low stable wall and pulled the saddle bags from the back.

"Did you remember Aunt Hettie's sewing thread?"

"Oh yeah. I wouldn't forget that. Just like I wouldn't forget to bring your letter home to you."

Her eyes popped open wide and her voice squeaked out, "Letter?"

He chuckled as he handed her a small brown parcel which she knew instantly contained the wooden spool of thread and two envelopes. The envelopes he fanned when he handed them to emphasize the number.

Now she could only whisper, "Two?"

Both letters were addressed in the neat script she had memorized from the previous letter and both bore the return address, "Stephen Ingle, Clarkrange, Tennessee."

Gracie stared down at them for a moment before her eyes darted first to Uncle Jesse then to the porch, to the spring house and back to a big shade tree as she searched for a quiet place to read the letters.

Finally settled under the big oak tree where Grandpa Elmore had placed a sturdy bench many years ago, Gracie looked at the posting dates of both letters and carefully broke the wax seal with the earliest date. Stephen greeted her with 'My Dearest Gracie' and her heart seemed to melt into his words. He went on to tell her that he had been thinking of what to write since he sealed the last letter and that he had so much to tell her he feared his inkwell wouldn't last through all of the thoughts.

Oh Stephen pour out all of your thoughts, I want to hear everything. She looked up lest her thoughts had been spoken aloud.

He finished his letter by filling it with news from the Ingles and their Martha Washington community.

Stephen wrote about the land as though it were one of his dearest friends. He longed to see his sons working it by his side, just as he worked alongside his own father and brother now. Gracie began to learn about the great farm in Virginia where the Ingle family had raised four generations and how Stephen looked forward to the next generations of Ingles loving the Tennessee land as his father and grandfather had loved Virginia.

She smiled every time she re-read the letter where Stephen talked about raising his sons to walk with God. Every day Algurial Ingle had lessons to teach and re-teach his sons and understanding that repetition seated the lessons deeply in his mind and heart, Stephen planned to do the same with his own children.

As Stephen talked about his daddy's farm he yearned to own land of his own. The Ingles had been steadily adding to the lands Pappy Ingle first bought in Tennessee and while Stephen would certainly inherit a portion of his father's lands he wanted to continue the tradition of expanding their boundaries.

These letters Gracie kept in her trunk and pulled out almost every evening and she felt she began to see the future through Stephen's eyes. He even talked of his Pappy and Grandma sitting on the wide front porch of their home, watching for any of the grandchildren that might come running up the hill, of their working together even at the slower pace they kept in these later years. Stephen longed to have the love and friendship that pair enjoyed after nearly fifty years of life together.

Gracie looked so forward to these letters that even through the busiest summer months someone from the Elmore household found their way to Isoline at least once each week to retrieve the mail.

Chapter 5

The letters continued, although not as often as summer's work demanded more time from both Stephen and Gracie. As the summer crept toward harvest season Stephen mentioned a little house that stood near his parent's home. It was older now, having been built by his grandparents when they first arrived on the mountain. No one had lived in it for a long time but Stephen began to look more closely at it and found it to be dry and sound. He wrote of cleaning out the debris that had accumulated there and beginning to sweep it out. He pondered what kind of furniture would be needed to make it a home and whether Gracie might ever be satisfied living in the Martha Washington community. Gracie blushed at the unspoken proposal, reading the words again and again.

Just as the leaves burst into the red and gold beauty of fall, Stephen wrote asking if he might join the Elmores for church. Gracie approached her grandmother for permission.

"Grandma, you know that Stephen Ingle has been writing me since the springtime; we've talked about him some and you've let me write back a few times."

Grandma only nodded her head, never looking up from the mending in her hands.

Gracie took a deep breath and spit out all at once, "He would like to go with us to church next Sunday, what do you think about that?"

Grandma smiled; joy consumed her and she was forced to pause in her work. Throughout the summer months, Gracie had come to her with thoughts about this young man. While they did not know his family, Grandma certainly appreciated his approach to a courtship. She had been amazed that he had not made the trip across the creek before this.

Finally, she had to answer Gracie, "I think that would be just fine. Invite him to Sunday dinner too. We'll kill a chicken."

With a little bounce on her heels, Gracie went quickly to the writing desk to return Stephen's letter. She always tried to wait a few days before writing him back as she certainly didn't want him to think her forward. Grandma sometimes had even suggested that he might feel she didn't want him writing if she waited too long. But this letter, she would send right away.

When she was finished writing, Gracie realized since Uncle Jesse had been to the post office just today, he would not be returning for several more days. She decided to walk back there herself in order that the letter would go off promptly.

Grandma was still sitting by the window with work pants and socks piled in her lap as she attended the family's mending when Gracie came into the room carrying her wide brimmed straw hat.

"I'm going to take this letter to the post office. I don't want Uncle Jesse to think he has to make a special trip, but neither do I want it setting here for days either."

Grandma only nodded and watched as her precious granddaughter cut across the field toward the general store in Isoline which housed the post office.

Gracie knew that the Ingles received their mail no more often than the Elmores did so Sunday morning she didn't really expect to see Stephen. Still she found herself a pace ahead of the rest of the family as they approached the church house and she found herself squinting into the morning sun trying to identify each of the men standing on the little porch. Sure enough, there was a young man with wide shoulders and dark hair, his hat held between his two hands even though they had not entered the building. He was not looking at the other men but staring down the lane.

Gracie gulped and felt the butterflies take flight in her stomach. She smiled then looked down at her feet hoping he didn't see the glee she felt.

It took only another moment for the rest of her family to recognize the stranger among their closest neighbors and friends. Lottie hurried up to walk beside Gracie.

"Gracie, don't you see Stephen?" She asked her sister as she waved.

Gracie nodded ever so slightly, "Yes Lottie, I see him. You don't have to wave your arm off. We'll be there in just a minute."

"Well don't you want him to know you're glad to see him?"

"Of course I do, but not *that* glad."

They heard Hettie chuckling behind them and Uncle Jesse put a hand on Lottie's shoulder, "Give your sister some room with the young man Lottie. We'll do the same for you one day and you'll be thankful for it, I promise."

Lottie fell back into step at her uncle's side and joined his wife's giggles.

As they reached the dirt yard surrounding Clear Creek Baptist Church, Stephen stepped out to greet them. Gracie managed to look up and offer him what she felt was a properly restrained smile. "Good morning Stephen."

Stephen nodded as he twisted his hat brim. "Good mornin' Miss Gracie."

Uncle Jesse made a little cough to remind her the family was still there. Gracie blushed, realizing she'd simply been staring at him. Finally she found her voice and turned halfway around, "Grandma, do you remember Stephen Ingle? His family attended the protracted meetin's back in the spring?"

Grandma offered him her warmest smile, "Yes, of course I remember. Stephen, it's good to see you. Are your parents well?"

"Oh yes ma'am. They've been workin' hard but it's been a fine season, don't you think?"

"Mmmhmm, I do."

Gracie moved on reminding Stephen of each person's name, "This is my Uncle Jesse."

Stephen smiled and reached a hand out to him, "Yes, we talked some. It's very good to see you sir."

"Glad to have you here this morning Stephen. Did you walk or ride?"

"Rode. My mare's tied over on the west side of the church house."

"Good good. You'll come back with us for dinner I hope."

"Oh yes sir. Gracie mentioned that in the letter and I'm sure thankful for the invite. I hope I won't be no trouble to y'uns." He turned to Grandma and Aunt Hettie knowing the trouble of a meal would be squarely on their shoulders.

Grandma reassured him, "No son, we're eager to have you. Now we'd better get inside and find our seats."

As the group covered the last few yards, Gracie watched him and wondered if she'd described her family well in the letters they'd shared. She was certain she had mentioned each one of them. In fact she feared she may have said too much about them as she watched Stephen stand mute before them.

He wrote so freely and so beautifully, I wonder why he doesn't talk now?

Gracie determined she would make him comfortable with the Elmores as well as her church family.

Stephen, I'd like you to meet some of the neighbors."

Stephen followed as Gracie introduced the McCormicks, hesitating only when she came to Mary Belle who Gracie always thought was the most beautiful girl in the church. She led Stephen to Uncle Camel and Aunt Lizzie's seat where he had to bend down really close for them to hear anything he said. Then she found Paralie Dixon sitting on the very end of a pew and watching her friend.

"Stephen, this is my dear friend Paralie. I know I've told you about her in our letters. Did you meet her before?

Paralie answered for him despite hardly raising her eyes, "Yeah, we met."

Stephen smiled and nodded as Gracie explained, "She lives right behind our place on the Barringer Road. We've worn a solid path over that little hill walking back and forth the whole time we were growing up."

Stephen lifted his hand in a little wave to the young woman. "Gracie has written a lot about you. It's very nice to meet you now."

Paralie smiled and ducked her head, tendrils of curls tumbling free from her loose bun.

Gracie blushed at his reference to their letters, hoping that didn't sound like she was the main one doing the writing.

The service soon began and the circuit preacher made good use of his time, knowing he would not share God's word with these people again for many weeks. The sun was high and the temperature in the little church house grew uncomfortably warm as Gracie held the pew in front of her to keep from bouncing in her impatience.

Stephen led his big mare behind the group and Gracie walked beside him following her family by a few paces. The pair was silent as they walked and listened as Uncle Jesse commented on the sermon and the Aunt Hettie on the health of the neighbors. Grandma held Lottie's hand and Gracie wondered if it was out of affection or to keep Lottie from stealing back to walk with her and Stephen.

Gracie raised her head and looked up at the clear blue sky turning her head to take in the trees bursting with fall's colors that lined the lane. All of this was just to sneak another look at the handsome boy at her side. Afraid he'd catch her looking, she ducked her head and searched for something to say. "The trees are really beautiful this year, don't you think Stephen?"

He nodded and looked anew at his surroundings. "Yeah, they really are. The harvest is a lot of work, but the Lord blesses with beauty in this season too."

"Hmm. That's a beautiful thought Stephen. Do you dread this season?"

"Oh, no. It's what we work all year for ain't it? And if we don't have a good harvest the winter will be awfully tough. No, I'm glad for the hard work bringing in the crops and storing up the corn to feed the stock. Maybe I dread winter though. It's hard sloggin' through the mud to get in wood and care for animals."

Gracie nodded, watching her family ahead of her. "And winter is a tough time for old people and little babies too."

Stephen turned to look at her, "Do you worry about your Grandma?"

"I guess so. She's strong, maybe stronger than any of us. But me and Lottie have only ever known her as a mother and with Grandpa Elmore already passed on it just seems like we won't have anything if we lose Grandma."

Stephen lifted his hand to reach out to her but caught himself before touching her shoulder, "I don't want you to worry Gracie."

She smiled up at him, "Thank you Stephen. I'm not really worried, I just get to thinkin' serious-like sometimes."

"That's a good thing. Life is really very serious. We have to face it straight on that way."

She nodded as they turned down the little lane into the Elmores' home. Grandma finally loosed Lottie's hand and she bounded ahead of the whole group. Gracie shut her eyes tight hoping she could block out her sister's childish behavior, or maybe Stephen would just not notice her.

Opening her eyes she dared glance toward Stephen trying to determine whether Lottie was ruining everything. Instead she found him watching her and smiling.

She returned a shy smile and quickly looked away, "I'd better hurry ahead and help with the meal."

She rushed past Uncle Jesse who walked on toward the barn with their guest.

Dinner had been mostly cooked in the morning. Aunt Hettie stepped into her bedroom to lay off her Sunday hat while Gracie and Lottie slipped upstairs to remove hats and don starched white aprons.

"Lottie, please don't embarrass me with Stephen here. You talk too much and act all silly. I really want him to think we are a serious family like I believe his family is."

Lottie giggled, "I don't think they're so serious. His cousin Daniel just laughs and jokes all the time."

Gracie lowered her voice even more, "And you're too loud Lottie! He'll hear you. Anyway, Stephen is not like that Daniel. He writes me about his plans for the future and things he wants to do. You know we were just talking as we walked home from church about how life is serious."

"Well if you're always serious you'll never even enjoy life."

With her final word Lottie skipped down the steep staircase and Gracie heard her laughter the moment her feet touched the first floor.

Gracie shook her head and carefully made her way down to help in the kitchen. Grandma had the table set and several dishes already on the table. She had sent Lottie to the spring house for fresh cool water. Hettie cut the cake and Gracie dipped beans into their prettiest serving bowl. In no time the table was laid with a bounty that swelled Gracie's heart with pride.

Gracie thought fried chicken never tasted as good as it did with Stephen Ingle at the table. As he sat opposite Uncle Jesse, Gracie could only see him out of the corner of her eye. She purposely didn't look at him for she was sure a young woman ought not just stare at a young man as Lottie seemed to be doing.

Uncle Jesse bragged on the food before him, making a point to compliment the apple stack cake that Gracie had made and how light the apple filling was. To accompany the heavy molasses cake, Gracie had dipped into their precious supply of sugar to sweeten the dried apples. Through the meal, the family talked about the church service - commenting on the size of the crowd and wondering why the Martins hadn't made it in on such a pretty day. Jesse made Gracie smile as he gently questioned Stephen about his personal relationship with the

Lord and his commitment to reading the scriptures. He sounded like Grandpa and she knew that he was purposely filling the role of her missing father and grandfather.

Grandma sat across the table and Gracie watched her approving nods as Stephen gave the hoped for answers. She asked about his family, his mother's health after the cold winter and whether they had fruit trees blooming yet.

They learned that the Ingles had moved from Virginia after the war; things would never be the same in Virginia, he explained. Gracie remembered Grandpa Elmore saying the same thing and she was glad that Uncle Matthew had not chosen to join them. Somehow, she felt even the mention of the war's devastation would hurt him.

The sun was moving noticeably west before Stephen began to excuse himself. Everyone stood in the little parlor and Stephen stepped in front of Gracie, taking her hand. She thought for a moment he would kiss it as she'd read about gallant gentlemen doing. Instead, he held it for a long moment, giving a slight bow before saying a simple, "Goodbye Gracie".

Jesse followed Stephen out to the barn to saddle his horse and head home. Gracie watched from the door as the pair rounded the corner of the house and she marveled that they were in deep conversation.

She fairly pirouetted as she turned from the door, setting Lottie to giggling. The younger Berai daughter had held herself in check throughout the meal, but her exuberance could no longer be contained. She began to chatter, asking dozens of questions and moving on to the next observation with no chance for anyone to answer them. Gracie scarcely heard her sister as she moved into the kitchen to check whether anything was left undone from the noon meal. Hettie and Lottie had cleaned up, allowing Gracie to visit with her guest and now she felt she should do something to help them.

Lottie followed her into the kitchen and plopped into the nearest chair as she compared Stephen to his cousins and pondered whether he would be any fun at all on a picnic.

Gracie was about to shush her when Uncle Jesse returned from the barn. She questioned him with her eyes but received only a grin and a wink in reply as Jesse passed through the kitchen to sit with his wife and his mother.

Gracie couldn't help but follow him. By the time she'd dried her hands and re-hung the dish towel, she was several steps behind him. As she reached the parlor door, they were already talking and she stopped short of entering.

"…seems like a good boy," Jesse was saying.

Grandma suspected a bigger purpose and asked, "Well did he give you any idea of his intentions?"

Gracie wished she could see Uncle Jesse's eyes as she heard him say, "Ah, he asked if he could marry her, but he didn't say much else."

Amid the gasps of Grandma and Aunt Hettie, Gracie could contain herself no longer. In an instant, she was in the parlor jumping and hugging her family. Lottie overheard the excitement and came running to join in.

Grandma admired her granddaughter, happy that her normally serious nature had not stolen the fun from this moment. They would have their serious talk a little later.

Stephen Ingle was a fixture at the Elmore table throughout that harvest season. Jesse and Hettie wondered how he ever got any work done on his father's farm. "If he was working a public job, they would fire him for sure," they reasoned.

As the pair walked home on Sundays or sat quietly on the front porch swing, Stephen began to talk about the future. He was making plans for a married life and Gracie was thrilled to hear them. She thought surely he meant to share that life with her but she tried not to assume anything until Stephen actually asked her to be part of these plans.

It was late in the season and the air held a distinct chill before the rains came to drive away the last of summer's warmth and Gracie was wondering how many more trips home from church Stephen could make with them. The family walked ahead of Stephen and Gracie and Stephen seized the opportunity to speak quietly to her. "Gracie, we been talkin' a lot about a home and what we hope for our lives. I reckon I need to ask if you are interested in a life with me. Do you want to marry me?"

There was no way to hold back the smile that spread across her face. She stopped in the middle of the road and turned to face him. "Stephen Ingle, of course I want to be your wife. I decided that some time back and I've just been hoping that you were thinking the same thing."

"Well I guess I should'a asked before, it's hard though you know. I just kindly realized that I needed to hear you say you were willin' to marry me."

"You've heard it now."

He nodded and continued down the lane, still nodding.

As the weather worsened, Stephen's trips were less frequent. Gracie began to miss him and Grandma told her that was a very good sign. Grandma had tried to teach her granddaughters just as she did her daughters and since childhood they had talked about walking close to the Lord and reading his word every day. She read the Bible with them, and told them they must always read to their own children. As they reached teen years, Grandma urged both of the girls to study the model woman that the book of Proverbs described, and she prayed that they would strive to emulate that woman. Now, as her marriage drew nearer, Grandma spoke very directly to Gracie explaining the challenges of living with and loving a husband. They spent many hours quietly talking by the fire while Grandma mended for the family, and Gracie sewed new dresses and hemmed table cloths for her hope chest.

Chapter 6

For the rest of the household, the winter seemed to fit its normal routine. Only Hettie's world saw as much change as Gracie's. Late in December, on a night when the wind howled like a monster, Grandma went to check on Hettie who had been lying down most of the afternoon.

"Hettie honey, we've got supper on the table. Are you feelin' up to eatin' a bite?"

Hettie smiled up at Bessie and nodded, "Thank you for letting me rest a little. I am awfully tired lately."

Hettie swung her legs over the edge of the bed and Grandma moved her shoes into place for her to slip into them. "Every woman in your condition is tired child. I done it eleven times and it didn't get any easier carryin' them let me tell you."

Hettie pushed off the bed then put her hands to her back rubbing up and down.

"Is your back hurtin' now? You din' say anything about hurtin' before you laid down."

"Yeah it is. It's been kind of aching all day. To tell you the truth I didn't get much rest while I was in here."

Grandma slowly nodded her head, "It was a good thing you rested even a little 'cause I think it might be a long night."

The wind relentlessly beat against the old house causing the fireplace to flicker and chilling the floorboards. The family sat around the familiar table and Uncle Jesse returned thanks to the Lord for the meal.

"Lord God in Heaven, we thank thee for this food and the shelter thou has provided. We ask your blessing on our meal and our family through this night. In the name of our savior, Jesus Christ we pray, amen."

All of the family echoed his 'amen', raised their heads and reached for the pinto beans, fried potatoes and cornbread. Only Hettie kept her head down and Grandma was watching her closely.

"Hettie, it might be best if you didn't eat too much. Let me get you a glass of buttermilk."

"Thank you, I would take a piece of that cornbread."

Grandma handed her the glass of buttermilk and passed the plate of cornbread to her as she turned her eyes on Gracie, "Gracie, you be sure to eat good and don't dawdle. We've got a job ahead of us."

Gracie stopped chewing as understanding dawned on her. She reached for her water glass and gulped it down desperately trying not to choke. She finished in record time and carried her plate to the dry sink. She went ahead and made dish water from the kettles warming on the stove. Before Uncle Jesse and Lottie had finished Grandma joined Gracie, "Unless I miss my guess we'll have a baby before this time tomorrow. Why don't you go lie down for a little bit and see if you can get some rest. When she's in hard labor I'll come get you."

Gracie looked long at the wizened old woman until she finally had the courage to ask, "Do you think it'll be as bad as Nelda?"

Bessie Elmore's eyes popped open wide, "Nelda wasn't so bad. She recovered quickly, the baby is just fine and growing like a weed."

Gracie wondered if her grandmother might be losing her mind, or at least her memory. "Grandma, do you really not remember? You yelled, "Breech" and I thought that might be another word for death and you were moving faster than I've ever seen you move, and you wouldn't let me leave to go get help…"

Grandma interrupted her with a low laugh and vigorous patting on her back. "Child, it can be a whole lot worse than Nelda had it. I must've scared you and I didn't even know it. I'm sorry for that. No, I don't think Hettie will have any trouble but now it's her first one so you don't really know until it happens."

Gracie stared down into her dishwater, "And it happens so fast."

Now Grandma laughed louder, "I just hope you think it's all so fast when you're the mama."

Gracie couldn't help but smile now, realizing that she had not been the one suffering that day at Nelda Turner's house.

"Gracie you be faithful to the work the good Lord puts in front of you and He will always supply the grace to see you through it. Right now get yourself upstairs and rest a little."

Gracie truly wanted to obey her grandmother, not just because Grandma had raised her to be respectful and she always longed to please this woman who had taken her and given her such a good life, but also because she felt certain that Grandma knew exactly what was going on with Hettie and what would be required of them. Still, sleep did not come. Instead Gracie lay on her bed praying for Hettie and for the new baby that would join them. She prayed for Grandma and thanked the Lord for giving her to Gracie and Lottie and also for putting her in this place to help Hettie. As the wind raged outside Gracie confessed to God that no one would be able to get out on a night like this and that she understood Grandma would need help.

Lord I don't think I can do this alone, please give me the strength.

Gracie fell asleep praying and didn't know either when Lottie joined her in the bed or what time Grandma's cool hand on her cheek woke her.

"Child, come down and help me. Hettie needs us."

Gracie thought she could see the dawn breaking as she quickly peaked through the kitchen window on her way to the new part of the house. The stove was warm, and she wondered who'd opened the dampers and added the wood this early. Then she saw the coffee pot in the center and knew either Grandma or Jesse had been drinking coffee through the night.

"Grandma, how long have you been up with Hettie?"

"Really? All night. I wanted you to sleep as long as you could but she's been laboring ever since I sent you upstairs. It's gotten a lot harder and faster in just the past few minutes, so I know the time's a'coming."

Gracie took deep breaths silently reminding the Lord that she'd asked him to help her through this.

"What do you need me to do?"

"Just be ready is all I can say right now. Go ahead and wash good."

"Why? You know I'm clean."

Grandma shook her head and pushed Gracie back toward the stove, "It don't matter how clean you are, you always – and I mean always – you gotta wash good when you're workin' at a sick bed. You just keep a'washing. It'll save your life and hers too."

While she still didn't understand, she trusted her grandma and obediently scrubbed with the lye soap and hot water she was pointed to.

Grandma removed the lid from a small, steaming pan, "This is boilin' now, please get my sewing shears from the front room and put them in here. Leave it on the hot part of the stove so they'll get good and clean."

Gracie was no longer questioning her, she was only obeying now. And she could tell Grandma was speaking more quickly and offering no chance for discussion.

When Grace got back to Hettie's bedroom she saw a basket filled with rags at Grandma's feet as she sat on a low stool at the end of the bed and spoke softly to her.

"You're a'doing just fine. I can see his head. Everything is just the way it ought to be."

Hettie thrashed her head and moaned as she held to the iron posts of the bedstead. "I could curse the way things ought to be," she growled before she inhaled sharply and grimaced.

As she twisted her head she caught sight of Gracie, "Get out of here Gracie, you don't need to see this," she hollered.

Gracie was taken aback, Hettie had never once raised her voice to anyone in this household.

Grandma tried to calm her, "Shh, shh, I need Gracie. And I b'lieve she's got a gift for this." Grandma continued talking kind of low and very calmly; Gracie wondered if Hettie could even hear her – but Gracie heard every word.

"You know Gracie was with me at Neldy Turner's and I saw right away that she was good with Nelda. They weren't particularly friends before so you would've thought Neldy would've fought her bein' there but then again she was hurtin' pretty bad by the time we got there, and I guess she was a'wonderin' just what she was going to do."

Grandma looked at Gracie as she recalled the first time they worked together, "I guess Neldy was just glad to have anybody come in, don't you Gracie?"

Gracie nodded at her unable to find her voice. She stepped to Hettie's head instinctively and took one hand in her own.

"Hettie, you're doin' just fine. He's almost here now. I think if you'll give another good hard push I'll catch him…there you go… come on now you've got this thing licked."

Hettie squeezed Gracie's hand till she was sure it would never again be of any use. Gracie listened to Grandma's calm voice and thrilled at her command of the room as Gracie's heart pounded in her ears. Hettie stopped making any sound and only squeezed and Gracie jerked her head back fearing something was terribly wrong with her aunt. She found her face contorted with the strain and reddening from holding her breath.

Gracie's voice returned, "Hettie, you need to be breathing regular."

Hettie exhaled the tiny bit of air still left in her lungs and Grandma exclaimed, "There you go child. We have us a baby in the house and it is a boy."

A moment later the baby squalled and Hettie began laughing and crying.

"Listen to that, he's a strong one ain't he? Here Gracie, you take the baby and let me finish up with Hettie. Where's the shears?"

Gracie carefully laid the scissors on the end of the bed and took the tiny red creature on a waiting blanket. Grandma pulled a bit of string from her shoulder and deftly tied it around the cord extending form the boy's tummy. She repeated the process before picking up the still warm scissors and cutting between the strings.

"Okay, you get him bundled up good and be sure you've cleaned off his face and his little mouth. Hettie, I know you're tired, honey, but we've got just a little more work to do."

A weak voice responded, "Is my baby okay?"

"Oh yes, I think he's just fine. Don't you hear him hollerin'?"

She smiled and nodded her head slightly.

Gracie stepped away from the bed just a couple of steps and wiped his little face clean as she began to hum to him and gently sway in an effort to calm his crying. She kind of lost track of time watching this little baby come to life before Grandma called her back to reality.

"Okay Gracie, let's help Hettie get comfortable in this bed and then we'll get the baby bathed."

Gracie carefully laid the little boy in the waiting crib and helped Hettie get comfortable.

"Could I see him?" She asked.

Grandma was quick to answer, "You just wait till we get him cleaned up, it will be much nicer to see I assure you."

Hettie looked like she might cry and Gracie's heart broke for her, but she obediently followed her grandmother into the kitchen where they dipped warm water from the reservoir and tempered it from the waiting buckets to bathe the family's latest addition. Gracie thought it seemed like forever before the whimpering baby could be handed to his mother who shook in her joy.

Grandma turned to Gracie with one final job, "Why don't you run out to the barn and get Jesse. He'll be wantin' to see both of these two."

As she hurried toward the kitchen door she heard Grandma asking Hettie, "What'cha gonna call this boy?"

Gracie longed to wait for the answer, however, she continued on her way to find Jesse.

"Uncle Jesse, you out here?" Gracie called before she ever reached the barn door.

As though he'd had his ear pressed to the wall Jesse ran from the barn not bothering to close the door. "Is she okay? Is everything alright?"

"Yes everything is just fine. Hettie and your son are waiting to see you."

"My son." He began shaking his head and continued to do so as far as Gracie could see him in the pale morning light. Smiling she went to close the barn door and then hurried back inside the house.

As Gracie and Grandma later discussed it, Gracie explained her emotions. "How exciting to see a new life gifted from the hand of God."

Grandma chuckled softly, "Yeah, all life is a gift from the Almighty, but I wouldn't maybe call it that to Hettie for a day or two. I doubt she'd say labor was like opening a pretty package."

Gracie joined her gentle laughter and felt she did understand as well as any woman who had never gone through labor. She had thought she could feel Nelda's pains, and she felt she labored right along with Hettie as they worked so closely together to safely deliver her little boy.

Grandma sobered and looked directly into Gracie's eyes, "You were a blessing to me and Hettie both you know."

"I don't know how."

"Gracie, I can't exactly explain it, but you have a gift. You knew when Hettie needed you to comfort and support her.

You knew when I needed an extra pair of hands. Now I've been teaching you about healing for a long time, so, now it's up to you to remember that when you are called on you just need to trust in the Lord, and He's going to lead you. God has a plan for you, Gracie.

Chapter 7

Through the cold months of the new year, the ladies of the house spent their time in the preparations Gracie made plans for her marriage. By the time Jesse declared they'd surely had their last frost, her hope chest was full; she had new dresses, household linens, several quilts and a feeling of readiness to wed. Both Gracie and Lottie had been filling their hope chests for many years as they learned embroidery, quilting and tatting and they knew how to use these skills to make a warm and inviting home. Now Gracie looked over the precious items with fond memories of hours spent at Grandma's feet learning each skill. She imagined how her new home would look draped in so much love. Stephen had described the old farmhouse where they would live, continuing to write about it through the winter. Now she tried to envision the home she wanted to make for him there.

Due to heavy rains and nearly impassable muddy roads, Stephen had not been to visit in many weeks when he showed up the first Sunday in April. He'd found a bouquet of butter cups and held them up to Gracie as she opened the door.

"Oh Stephen, I didn't know when to expect you!"

Dropping his arm to look at her he explained, "Roads have been too bad to make it over here I'm afraid; we couldn't even get to Clarkrange to send you a letter. But you didn't forget about me, did you?"

Gracie placed her hand on his forearm and gently pulled him into the house, "Of course not you silly thing. What are you going to do with those pretty flowers?"

Stephen looked at them as though he'd completely forgotten he held them. "Oh, well they are for you. Found them at an old home place not too far from here and I thought you'd like them."

"I do, I really do. Thank you so much. Just let me put them in some water." She took a creamy-white vase from a shelf and hurried into the kitchen. She soon returned with the vase filled with the flowers which she carefully placed on the parlor table.

"Were you ready for church already?" he asked as he turned from the front window he'd been staring out while she was gone.

"Oh yes, I was just finishing up in the kitchen. But I'm all done now so we can talk for a bit before the family is ready to go to church."

"I was thinking I'd talk to the preacher today. Would that be okay with you?"

Gracie's smile was broad and genuine. "Of course it would be."

"I've been working on our little house and I guess it's as ready as it will ever be till you get there."

Stephen had told her a lot about the little house on his father's farm, but she still couldn't get a good picture of it in her head. "I wish I could see it."

"Well, if the preacher would be willing, we could say our vows today. Are you ready to be my wife?"

Gracie was shocked. She had been planning all winter to marry this man and yet somehow this seemed sudden. She studied the hand woven rug on the floor. Stephen moved slightly in the chair beside her and she realized he was waiting for an answer. Gracie said a quick prayer. She had already agreed to marry him; it wasn't as though she were debating whether she should. She really couldn't think of any reason not to do it today.

"I guess I don't know why not," she finally answered, raising her eyes to meet his.

"I don't want you to feel I've rushed you Gracie."

"Oh no, I don't feel that way. I don't know why it seemed hasty to me; I've been preparing all winter." She blushed slightly, wondering if that sounded like marrying him was a lot of work.

One look at Stephen assured her he was not offended. He was grinning from ear to ear and began bouncing his legs as though he could hardly hold himself in place. He looked to the doorway, knowing they could not leave until the rest of the family headed to church.

"I wonder if I should go early and speak to the preacher before the service?"

Before Gracie could answer him, Hettie entered with the baby well-wrapped in his blankets.

Unable to contain his excitement, Stephen poured it out upon the first person he saw. He spilled in one breathless sentence, "We'll marry today; I'm going to talk to the preacher, surely he'll let us say vows after the preaching, don't you think, I didn't know if Gracie would be ready but she says she's been workin' all winter long, and I have our house ready, and my family is certainly eager to have Gracie come to Martha Washington." With a deep breath he finished with, "What do you think?"

Hettie was speechless. She had just opened her mouth to try to form a reply when Jesse entered buttoning his coat.

"Jesse, I think Stephen and Gracie want to say their vows today."

Jesse looked at Gracie who looked just a little shocked but happy nonetheless. He looked at Stephen and remembered, from his own experience, the giddiness the boy was feeling. He looked at his wife and answered her as though the young couple were out of hearing, "I think we'll be well rid of her, won't we? She eats too much." He winked at Stephen as he teased his niece.

Gracie ran at her fun-loving uncle as though she would flog him with the handkerchief she held. He giggled and tried to tickle her. "Well you aren't going to be here for me to pick on anymore, what do you expect from me?"

For the first time since Stephen asked for her hand in marriage, Gracie felt a moment of homesickness – memories flooded of her childhood in this home, of Jesse really growing up with them, of Grandma and Grandpa teaching them and loving them all. A wave of tears washed over her eyes and she blinked to hold them in.

Jesse regained his composure and stepped to Stephen to shake his hand. This boy was passing into manhood as he took a wife and set his face toward raising a family. All of the men of the communities – both Elmore and Martha Washington – would give him a new respect.

The family made their way to the church house and shared the news with their neighbors.

Following the preaching, Gracie and Stephen joined Preacher Baisley and his wife along with Grandma in the preacher's little house. Before a warm fire on the chilly April morning, the preacher read the age old vows and Gracie never took her eyes off Stephen as she listened closely. With the "I do's" said, Stephen drove his wife and grandmother-in-law back to the Elmore farm.

Hettie and Lottie had hurried home to make a delicious lunch for the family. By the time they arrived, the table was laid with the best the family had to offer. Gracie was overwhelmed that her loved ones could share her joy so completely.

After the meal was finished, Grandma pulled Gracie out of the kitchen and away from the cleaning chores. She closed the door to the bedroom she and Grandpa had shared for so many years. Gracie looked around and realized that most of her personal things were missing from the dresser and table; she looked questioningly at her grandma.

"You and Stephen will stay here tonight. I'll sleep in the baby's room. Don't think I can quite make the climb to share with Lottie upstairs."

Gracie was confused and certainly didn't want to do anything to inconvenience her beloved grandma. "But why… I thought we'd go to Martha Washington… I can't take your room." Her words matched her scattered thoughts.

Grandma lightly rubbed her shoulder as she explained, "It would be awfully late by the time you got over there. Even though Stephen's been working on your house, I don't think any man would have it really ready to live in. It is best that you get an early start in the morning and you will have most of the day to put your house in order."

It made so much sense when Grandma explained it, Gracie wondered why she hadn't realized. "Does Stephen know we'll be staying here?"

"I think he does. He's seen a bunch of cousins marry off, and I'm sure they do things the same over there."

Gracie returned to the kitchen only to find Stephen and Jesse had escaped to the barn on the excuse of doing chores early. As the sun set on the clear spring day, the warmth quickly bled away and all of the farmers tried to have their work finished as early as possible.

The afternoon spent with her family seemed precious to Gracie. She knew this would be the last of such times and she wanted to savor every moment. Hettie put out a cold supper and the family was ready to retire much earlier than usual. Grandma pulled Lottie with her toward the baby's room in the "new part" as the added rooms were always called. With their goodnights said, Stephen and Gracie shyly retired to Grandma's room.

As she shut the door behind them, Gracie timidly smiled at her new husband. It was the first time she's really been alone with Stephen.

Chapter 8

Gracie awoke to the clatter of the stove door and movement in the kitchen. Someone was already hard at work on the morning's meal. Her first thought was to get herself up and ready for the day without waking Stephen, but a slight turn of her head revealed that she was alone in the bed.

She peeked out the window to try to understand what time it was and saw the wagon Stephen had driven yesterday already hitched to his big horses. One mare swung her head, worrying the bit in her mouth. Gracie knew she needed to get out as Stephen and Jesse would be wanting to load her things for the drive to her new home.

It took her only a few moments to emerge from Grandma's room, ready for the day and all it might hold. She saw that her heavy wooden hope chest already sat in the kitchen floor. Hettie turned to her as she entered the room.

"Jesse brought down your trunk. Do you have everything in it?"

Gracie knew exactly what the trunk held for she had looked through it so many times over the winter months planning the use of each embroidered decoration and warm quilt. "I just need to pack my clothes and things."

"I'll have breakfast on the table any minute. Do you want to go up and get those things before you eat?" Hettie asked without turning away from her hot skillet.

"Yeah, I don't know if I can eat anything this morning. I'm a little nervous."

Hettie smiled at her niece, "Well that's normal. Eat a biscuit with butter, that will sit well on your stomach. You can't leave without eatin' anything."

Gracie took the bread with her as she climbed the steep stairs up to the room she had shared with Lottie all these years. It was the same room and the same big iron bed that her mama had shared with Aunt Mary and Aunt Cathy.

Lottie was still upstairs and smiled shyly at her sister. Something had changed between them in just the hours since Gracie said vows before the preacher.

"Mornin' Lottie."

"Mornin' Gracie. Uncle Jesse took your trunk downstairs, did you see it?"

"Yeah, I came up to get my clothes and things."

Lottie looked to the end of the room where Grandpa had hung a line of strong pegs years before that would hold their dresses. "You've got more clothes than your mama and both of your aunts had the whole time they were growin' up," he'd fussed while he worked. He'd also been the one who often surprised them with a strip of ribbon or lace. Grandpa had brought home the first colorfully-printed-cotton sack he saw in the general store and offered it for the girls' use. It was a one-eighth barrel sized bag that held fourteen pounds of flour. Gracie smiled as she remembered Grandpa's joy in bringing a gift to the ladies in his home – flour for Grandma and printed cotton fabric for his granddaughters.

Gracie shook her head, bringing herself back to the task at hand. She carefully lifted each of her everyday dresses off their pegs. She was wearing her Sunday dress but she laid aside her best apron to cover it for she knew she would have a lot of work to do today and she certainly wanted to protect the precious garment.

Lottie helped her carry down the dresses and the plain boots she wore for her everyday chores. The Sunday slippers she now wore had been a precious gift the whole family gave her. All of the butter and eggs they could sell for the past months had been saved for the shiny black slippers. Carrying her boots down the steep stairs, she felt like a princess in the slippers yet somehow she also felt guilty that neither Lottie nor Hettie had anything so nice.

Breakfast was on the table, but the rest of the family had not waited for Gracie and Lottie to come down. As Gracie knelt at her trunk and tried to fit the rest of her things inside, Lottie joined the family to eat.

"It won't all fit," Gracie declared.

Grandma had a big split oak basket ready to scoot toward Gracie. "Put the rest in here."

"Grandma, where did this basket come from?"

"It's been under my bed for years. Grandpa bought it from a Cherokee family that passed through when we were very young. I think it will hold the rest of your things, won't it?"

Gracie nodded her head as she folded her dresses.

"Pull out one of your quilts to cover the dresses that way they won't get the dust from the road," Hettie suggested.

With the trunk completely packed, Stephen excused himself to load Gracie's things on the wagon.

Unwilling to let his family's routine be completely disrupted, Jesse pulled his bible from the corner shelf and announced it was time for family devotions. Stephen returned to the table and they stayed for what Gracie knew was the shortest prayer Jesse had ever said.

Then Mr. and Mrs. Stephen Ingle were on their way home.

The drive from Elmore Community to Martha Washington began as the most pleasant Gracie had ever experienced. The early morning air was still chilled from the night but the sun warmed her face and she was free to bask in the warmth of it with her husband at her side.

She found herself thinking of their home and planning what must be done first. Grandma and Hettie had packed a crate of food stuffs; Gracie didn't know what it contained but she was sure they wouldn't be hungry for a few days at least. She would have to get a garden in right away and she tried to think whether it was too late to plant any of the vegetables she was accustomed to having. Her hope chest contained a single iron skillet and she knew she could well make do with just that. There were also a few plates and forks that she had bought through the years.

"Stephen, I have so many questions about our new home. We don't have a cow, how will we get any milk? We don't have any stock, how will we get any meat?"

Stephen smiled and, holding the reins in one hand, clasped her hand with the other. "Don't you worry 'bout stuff like that, I'm not going to let you go hungry."

Clearly he had a plan but he did not further disclose it to Gracie. Her mind kept spinning. She tried to turn her thoughts to window curtains and straw ticks. "Oh, there is just so much to think about!"

Gracie had never been much further North than Rinnie and they were long since passed that little settlement. She knew they would cross Clear Creek although it was hard to imagine how that creek could wind around into their path again. The same water ran below the hill not far from the Elmore farm and as children Gracie's aunts and uncles had taken them down to it to wade and fish. There weren't many fish to catch, probably because there were always lots of little bare feet churning up the mud.

Gracie had no more begun to wonder about the creek when the little buckboard wagon started down the steepest hill she could imagine. The road turned first to the right then to the left and then back again. Gracie tried to look up at the morning sun to determine whether they were headed east or west but the curves were so sharp she couldn't tell. She saw that Stephen was practically standing on the brake and he spoke gently to his horse, urging her to keep calm as the shafts pressed her down the steep grade. Gracie braced her feet and held on to the low back of the wagon seat, and she prayed.

Looking ahead of the horse, Gracie could see the tops of trees seemingly at eye level and she might have thought they had miraculously taken flight except that the bone-jarring ruts and rocks reminded her they were on very solid ground.

When she thought neither she nor the horse could bear that hill any longer, the sound changed as the iron-shod horse stepped onto the plank bridge. On the north side of the bridge, Stephen stopped for a rest. "Whoa girl, we'll let you blow here before we try to climb the other side. You know Gracie I think it's as hard on her to hold the wagon back on the downhill side as it is to pull up the other side."

Gracie wondered if it would be as hard on the wife as it was on the horse going up the other side. But she took some deep breaths and didn't mention her fears.

After a few minutes rest, Red, as Stephen called the sorrel mare, began pawing with her front feet and Stephen declared her ready to try the hill. With a gentle cluck he told the horse he, too, was ready and they were moving again. The climb was just as steep and just as curvy but much slower, so Gracie didn't mind it so much. She could see the horizon ahead before she spoke again.

"Is this the way we will always have to travel when we visit my family?"

Stephen chuckled and winked at her as he said, "Nah, we can always walk, then we can cross the swinging bridge at the Ferry Bend."

Swinging bridge, Gracie thought, *would that be any better than this ride?* She began to realize this new life she had embarked on was going to be much different than her safe little world in Elmore Community.

Stephen was nearing his home turf and he became chattier with each turn of the wheel. He began to share his father's stories about coming to Tennessee from Virginia and the mountains they had to travel through. He talked about the farm in Martha Washington and all of the work the past three generations had done to improve the land.

Gracie listened carefully, as she had listened through all of his visits and she envisioned a lovely land and a comfortable home.

Stephen kept regaling her with these stories as they covered the last miles to Martha Washington. As they turned onto the little dirt road, Gracie's pulse sped up. She was almost home.

The road carried them through a low hollow and across another creek, much smaller than the dramatic crossing she'd already experienced. Then as they climbed a small hill with a dramatic bluff overhanging the road, Stephen pointed out the beginning of the family's farm. Soon, she saw the smoke from a chimney then a roofline then a wide porch.

"That's Dad's house," Stephen explained. "Our little house is just past it. It was the first house my granddad put up when he came to Tennessee. That was in, let's see 'bout 1870. Then they built the bigger house you see over there." He pointed to a two story home also with a big porch and two chimneys with wisps of smoke rising above them.

Gracie was preoccupied with the descriptions Stephen was giving her and didn't realize they'd reached the little house until the wagon came to a full stop. She turned her head and froze.

Before her stood a dilapidated shack with a sagging porch and crumbling rock chimney. There were dried weeds piled around indicating that Stephen had been trying to reclaim a bit of yard space. Two windows looked out on the porch, one with shutters, the other without. The board and batten siding was weathered nearly black and the batten part was missing in places.

Stephen swung to the ground and reached up to lift his wife from the wagon seat. "Welcome home Gracie Ingle."

Gracie was immediately repentant for her critical eye of the house. She looked at her new husband and saw the pride in his eyes. So rather than look at the ramshackle building, she wrapped her gloved hand about his work-hardened arm and allowed him to lead her into her new home.

"You'll have to tell me what you want me to do around here. I knew there would be things you'd want but just thought they'd have to wait for you to get here to decide what they were." The few times Gracie and Stephen had been together he was always very quiet and Gracie couldn't help but smile as she listened to him talking on and on about this home he wanted to create with her. She immediately liked this side of her husband and hoped she would see more of it.

"Let me get your things," he said as he disappeared out the still-open front door. He carried in her big hope chest, the oak basket and the crate filled with food. Each item he placed where Gracie directed.

She looked around the home, not sure where to begin. She well knew how to keep a home, but how should she start one? *Well, we're going to need to eat before long so let's get that kitchen in order.*

She turned to Stephen, "You said you have a well, right? Do we have a bucket?"

Stephen grinned, he knew that Gracie was getting started. "I'll bring you a couple of buckets-full of water right away. The well is a little walk from the house, I'll show you where it's at after while." With that he was off at a lope and called over his shoulder, "There's a good spring down the hill toward the creek; I'll show you that too.

Gracie stepped back into the kitchen laughing at her husband's enthusiasm.

There were signs that someone had tried to sweep the floor but there was still debris strewn about – *Is that hay that I keep seeing?* She could almost hear Grandma chiding her that, 'nothing will get done standing here'. So she picked up the worn broom she found propped in a corner and began by sweeping the piled dust off the table and the dry sink surfaces. She had almost finished this first task when Stephen re-appeared at the back door with two overflowing buckets.

"I see Mother and Betty comin' over the hill. They'll likely have dinner with them. I'm starved, what about you?"

Gracie's heart skipped a beat. She didn't even remember who Betty was and she sure didn't want her mother-in-law's first visit to her home to be in this condition.

Stephen noted the look in her eyes and wanted to reassure her. "They'll likely help us this afternoon. 'Many hands make quick work,' Mother will say."

Realizing there was nothing she could do – after all, she could scarcely wipe off the table before they arrived – Gracie took a deep breath and smoothed her hair.

It was only a moment before the Ingle women arrived at the front door. Just as Stephen had predicted, they each carried a basket. Mrs. Ingle had cold meat, fresh bread with jam and pickles. Betty's basket was loaded with brushes and rags for the afternoon's cleaning.

"Helloooo," called Katherine Ingle as she stepped over the threshold of the open door.

Gracie gave her sweetest smile as she greeted her new mother-in-law.

"Hello Mrs. Ingle. Welcome, welcome."

Katherine set her heavy basket on the little parlor table and reached for Gracie. She was a tall, stout woman. Hugging the slim Gracie she rather looked as though she might crush her. But she was expressing a genuine intention to love this newest member of her family.

"You know our Betty, don't you? She's married to our oldest boy, William. They live down the road a piece."

Betty was almost as tall as Gracie, but she was so round she appeared much shorter. Her cherub-like face fairly glowed as she stepped closer to Gracie to give her a hug.

Gracie was not really accustomed to so much hugging. But, she certainly felt this family was glad to have her.

After a quick meal, Mrs. Ingle dispatched Stephen to bring buckets and wash tubs filled with water, a fire was started in the big fireplace, and the cleaning really began.

"Gracie," Mrs. Ingle cautioned, "that's not your everyday dress, is it? It is lovely and you'll ruin it for sure in all this dust and dirt. Why don't you change?"

"Oh thank you. I thought of that as we were driving in, but then I got so excited about the house that it plumb slipped my mind."

When she returned from the back room, she fell in beside her new family, and before they heard cow bells, the parlor, kitchen and bedroom were scrubbed to a livable cleanliness.

Betty was the first to notice the time. "Law, I'll have to get on home. Now Gracie, you just get Stephen and come on up to our house for supper. I left a big pot of stew on the stove and if my little Mary's had the sense to stir it like I told her, we'll have a good supper waiting on us."

Gracie was so tired she could scarcely think of lifting a spoon, much less calling at someone's house for supper. But she didn't quite know how to turn down the offer. The two Ingle ladies were already talking between themselves and she understood that Mrs. Ingle was offering the remaining bread she'd baked this morning and promising to send Bud along with it shortly. Everything was planned and they had said their goodbyes to Gracie before she could catch her breath.

She turned a slow circle looking at the house that had been transformed from a filthy shack just a few hours before. While it wasn't the home she'd imagined for her family, she could certainly now picture it slowly filling that dream.

The evening with the William Ingle family was lovely despite Gracie's exhaustion. She and Stephen walked home in the chilly spring evening, hand in hand.

"You have a precious family Stephen."

"They are your family now, too, you know."

"Yes, I can really see that. Mrs. Ingle was so kind to me today and she worked awfully hard on our little house."

"You can't go on calling her Missus you know. She's Mother or Granny Ingle to everyone around here. She'll think you don't want to be one of us if you call her anything else."

"Oh, I hadn't thought of that. I surely don't want her to think I'm not thrilled to be an Ingle – I can hardly believe that I am."

Stephen smiled and wrapped an arm around her.

"You're warm," she smiled up at him. "It's nice, I was getting cold."

"I banked the fire good before we left so the house should be nice when we get there. It's just over there."

Gracie could smell the wood smoke and assumed it came from her house. "There's no stove, I was surprised by that."

"Can you manage with the fireplace? I'll be saving to get a stove. There's just so much to buy when you're setting up housekeeping."

"Oh yes, I can manage. Grandma taught us how to cook most everything on the open fire. Only, I'll hope to get some pans along the way. A deep one that I could cover with coals would sure be nice – like a Dutch Oven."

"Is that the first thing you'll want? I have some money saved and we can go down to Clarkrange tomorrow and get one."

"Yeah, I think so, only let's look around a little more and decide what else we might really need. I didn't even unpack the food basket Hettie sent since Mother Ingle brought our dinner to us."

Stephen smiled at her new name for his mother.

The fire was still burning when they entered the little house and Gracie was so happy for its warmth. She stood in front of it to enjoy the glow as well as the heat, but after only a moment she realized how terribly exhausted she really was.

"Stephen, I don't think I can hold my eyes open any longer."

"I'm pretty tired, too. We can finish up everything you wanted to do in the morning; it'll be here in no time at all."

She stepped just around the fireplace to the little bedroom – the only one on the lower floor. There was a small leather-covered trunk in the corner that she had not noticed before. *That must be Stephen's clothes,* she reasoned.

Betty had cleaned this room so Gracie hadn't spent much time in here today. This was the first chance she'd had to check the condition of the bed. One pat told her that the straw tick was completely useless. *This would be like sleeping straight on the ropes.*

"Stephen," she called. "We'll have to get straw first thing tomorrow for our bed. Do you think we can manage that at this time of year?" Ordinarily, women all re-filled these thin mattresses in the late summer when grain was being threshed or hay cut. There wasn't much grain grown around Elmore community, but with the Ingle's liberal use of flour Gracie had already decided they must be growing their own wheat.

Stephen stepped into their room before answering. "Sure, there's straw in Dad's barn, I'm sure he'll let us have enough for one little bed. Can we manage tonight?"

"I don't think we're going to want to sleep on that thing. Why don't we make a pallet with our quilts?"

Stephen smiled like a little boy. "That's a great idea. Do we have enough quilts?"

"I think so. Let me get them out of my chest and we'll see."

They decided to spread the quilts in front of the fireplace even though Gracie was terrified some of the family would come by and see them from windows that still had no curtains. As she nestled in the crook of her husband's arm, both her joy and the day's hard work reminded her she could have slept on a bed of rocks.

Stephen was up before dawn. Gracie heard him stirring up the fire and opened her eyes, squinting in the dark room. She looked across the flat hearth stone, seeing her husband silhouetted against the flames.

"Good morning, dear," he greeted her. "The cows will be waiting to be milked so I have to get out."

Gracie was not happy that he'd awakened before her again, *I don't want him thinkin' I'm lazy.* She stretched in the cold morning air and scooted closer to the now blazing fire. "Do you need me to help you?"

"No, I'm working as hired labor right now. When we have our own stock, I may take some help. Can you milk?"

"Of course. I can do most anything in the barn."

Stephen smiled. He was growing prouder of this little lady by the day.

"What are you goin' to do with your day?"

"Well the house is surely not finished so I'll keep working on it. You know Stephen, my purpose in every day will be caring for you and our family."

Stephen cocked an eyebrow as he questioned, "Family?"

This brought the blood rushing to Gracie's cheeks, "You know that we'll have children soon – surely by next spring. And lots more to follow, I hope. I pray that God will bless us with a houseful. And I've been praying most of my life that I will be the best mother ever."

He pulled her to her feet in a warm embrace, "Gracie Ingle, I just know you will be the perfect mother to our dozen little ones."

"Dozen?"

"Well you know, my grandparents raised thirteen."

"Oh. Could we start with just one and maybe work up from there?"

"Okay, one at a time." Stephen's laughter lingered as he stepped out the door into the dusky morning.

Gracie didn't waste another minute. She dressed in the work dress she'd worn yesterday and quickly had the quilts folded and stored back in her chest. The worn out mattress caught her eye and she knew that should be her first priority.

Just off the tiny back porch, she dumped the broken bits of straw from the ticking and then set out with buckets in hand to retrieve enough water to wash it. Stephen had pointed out the well's location during their evening walk. She was so accustomed to the spring her grandparents used that she was almost shocked by the sight of the steel casing protruding from the ground. A pulley hung above the well and the bucket waited on a hook in the upright post. Gracie didn't think twice as she dropped the bucket and began hoisting it back up by pulling the rope hand over hand.

With her two buckets overflowing, she walked slowly back thinking about her home. Since the ticking was all she needed to wash today, she just heated the water in the fireplace and scrubbed the ticking right in the house.

When she emerged from the house with the wet bedding and could find no clothes line, she draped it across the split rail fence to allow the sun to dry it.

By the time Stephen returned from the barn, with a small basket of eggs, Gracie had already emptied the food basket she'd brought from Grandma's house and proudly placed her few provisions and kitchen utensils on freshly cleaned shelves. Stepping back she thought to herself, *It almost looks like somebody lives here.*

Hearing her husband's step on the back porch, she turned her attention to his breakfast. She stirred up the tiny amount of flour she had with fresh butter Mrs. Ingle left and some milk then dropped little circles of the dough into her biggest skillet. With some good hot coals pulled out onto the hearth stone, she squatted before the fire to fry the bread.

"Now's when I wish I had that Dutch oven," she said thinking she was still alone in the room.

But Stephen had walked in quietly. "We'll try to get you one today Gracie. But there's an empty lard stand in the kitchen, Grandma used the lid to cover her bread. Do you think you could do that?"

"Well Stephen, you are brilliant," Gracie exclaimed as she hurried into the kitchen.

"Not me, I guess my old Granny was pretty smart though. She made do with little of nothing when they first came to Tennessee. I reckon they lost a lot in The War and she was just glad for the peace and quiet of this ol' mountain."

Gracie was hardly listening to him. She'd placed the lid from the lard can on top of her skillet and shoveled out a few more coals to cover it. She smiled proudly at her accomplishment and at the idea that she would serve her husband real biscuits instead of the fried bread she'd expected.

Chapter 9

Gracie settled easily into married life. She found the Ingles were an ambitious lot, having accomplished much in the fifteen years since they came from Virginia. Uncle Bill had a grist mill on Slate Creek which kept the family and the whole community in flour and meal – luxury items in Elmore community. Pappy Ingle, as the whole family called Stephen's grandpa, had bought a large tract of land when he settled in Tennessee and his determined sons had continued to add property as they were able. In fact, Gracie came to understand that land was a priority to this family and Stephen was teaching her of its value as he longed for his own farm.

Still, Stephen worked for his father and the young couple lived in the tiny, old house which Gracie tried to make into the home she dreamed of. Every feed sack that Stephen could get ahold of came home for curtains and table cloths, quilts and pillows. The pretty little prints were perfect for her household needs, but the farm produced almost everything the extended family needed so purchased items that came in cloth sacks were few and far between.

Both Grandma Ingle and Mother Ingle admired Gracie's strong work ethic and her devotion to their boy, Stephen. They proved this to Gracie one day when she happened in to visit Stephen's grandparents.

Seeing Pappy Ingle on the porch, she waved well before he could have heard her shouting. She quickened her steps and stood, smiling before him in no time.

"Good morning Pappy, ain't it a beautiful day?"

"Yeah 'tis. You just out for the sunshine?"

"Well that and a little visit with Grandma Ingle. What is she up to today?"

He casually threw a thumb over his shoulder, "Out in the loom house. Don't know why she's out there in the spring. Usually she does her spinning and weaving in the winter when it's too cold to get out and do real work. But I guess she had some cotton left over."

Loom house, Gracie wondered. She didn't even know that Grandma had a loom. She headed around toward the back of the house, following the general direction of Pappy's thumb. From the back porch, the direction became evident as she heard a rhythmic thump – pause – thump from one of the many little out buildings. As she drew closer to it, she heard her mother-in-law's voice along with Grandma Ingle's.

Gracie pecked softly on the door as she cracked it open to greet the ladies. "Good morning, can I come in?"

Mother Ingle turned with her right hand atop a tall spinning wheel and her left hand extended with thread she was pulling from the spindle. "Gracie! What are you doing here?"

Gracie took a deep breath, fearing she had entered where she was not welcome.

Before she could answer, Grandma Ingle scolded her daughter-in-law, "Katherine! You'll scare her to death with that tone. Come on in honey, we are just surprised to see you is all."

Katherine dropped her work and rushed to put an arm around Gracie's shoulder. "We were making you a surprise, Gracie, and I just didn't expect you to walk in."

"A surprise? For me? Why ever would you do that?"

"Well, you've been working so hard on that little shack and Stephen said you're wantin' curtains and tablecloths and the like. Grandma had some cotton and flax that she hadn't used up during the winter so we were just going to run you out a few yards of cloth to work with."

Gracie was speechless.

Grandma Ingle had not gotten up from her little bench in front of the loom and presently she resumed the thumping as she pulled fibers close together then paused as she threw the shuttle across for another row of weft fibers. As she talked, her hands and feet seemed to move all the faster. "We sure do admire the way you've thrown right in with the family Gracie. We want to support you any way we can. There ain't much I can do for young folk anymore, but I can still throw this ol' shuttle. 'Course we're just making you nutty homespun. Maybe you can embroider on it and make it a little prettier."

Gracie was still trying to understand what was happening in the tiny little building and her questions came in short bursts, "Nutty? Homespun?"

Grandma Ingle chuckled as she rocked back with the motion of the beater bar, "That's what I always call it cause the color is kinda' like peanut butter, or maybe lighter, more like chestnut butter 'cause it's a little more yellowy with the flax mixed in."

Gracie moved to Grandma's side to better see what she was producing. There at her knees was a growing roll of the most beautiful fabric she'd ever seen. Her hand involuntarily reached out to touch it and she pulled back, not wanting to disturb Grandma Ingle's work.

Grandma paused and adjusted a cog that rolled the fabric down toward her knees, "Go ahead, you ain't gonna hurt nothin'."

She secured the gear and then with another twist unrolled several inches of the finished fabric which Gracie caressed as though it were the finest silk.

"This is the sweetest thing I can imagine. Thank you. Thank you both for doing this for me. This must have taken an awful lot of your time."

Katherine had resumed her spinning and now spoke without looking at the other ladies. She stepped slowly backward, drawing out long threads of soft white cotton. "It was time well spent Gracie dear. But now that you know about it, you can help."

"Of course, what can I do?" Gracie moved quickly to her mother-in-law's side – only a couple of steps in the room that was dwarfed by the loom.

"I've about got the spindle full, we'll need to wind it off on one of those bobbins." Mother Ingle pointed to a basket of wooden bobbins and Gracie picked one up.

The Ingle ladies worked for the rest of the morning spinning and weaving. When Pappy Ingle stuck his head in the door asking for his dinner, they knew they'd need to stop for the day. Grandma began unrolling the finished fabric. "You can take what we have finished – let's see how much it is. A'course, we'll have to keep enough to wind it onto the warp beam."

After Grandma Ingle estimated what would be needed to secure the remaining, unfinished work, there was five yards of creamy, beige fabric that Gracie carried reverently home.

As she heated last night's meat for Stephen's dinner, her mind was spinning with everything she could do with that much yardage, and she made her plans carefully for best use in her home.

Gracie and Stephen were up with the sun, as usual. As Stephen drank a hot cup of coffee cut with chicory, he asked about Gracie's plans for the day.

"Mother Ingle has been telling me that she and Betty always go to the spring to do their laundry. So today they're gonna' take me along."

"Oh Gracie, I can't believe I haven't shown you the spring yet. It's the sweetest, purest water and bubbles right up out of the ground. I'm actually ashamed you've been drawing all of your water from the well."

"You don't have to be sorry Stephen. I imagine it's a lot more fun to do wash when you've got company anyway. Me and Lottie used to do it together. We'd get water everywhere when we first started, but Grandma kept sayin' we had to learn. I think that was one job she was glad to hand over to us because all of the mess was either on us or on the ground outside. Anyway, it will be a good day and I look forward to spending it with the other Ingle ladies while still knocking out an important chore."

Stephen was grinning by the time she finished with her story. "I like when you talk about your memories with Lottie. We'll get you over to Elmore to see them soon."

She turned to hug him, "Thank you Stephen. I really do miss them terribly."

"That's only natural Gracie."

"Still, this is my home now and I'm very happy here."

"I sure am glad to hear that."

He headed out the kitchen door and Gracie gathered all their laundry into the big basket Grandma had given her, placed a bar of lye soap on top and sat it all by the back door with a glance at the horizon to gauge the time.

Not good daylight yet so I'll get some time in reading God's word.

She sat at the kitchen table reading her bible until she heard Mother Ingle and Betty call to her, "Mornin' Gracie."

Engrossed in the prophecy of Jeremiah's concern for his sinful nation, she had lost all track of time and jumped at the sound of her name. With a shake of her head she closed the book and blew out the lamp that still burned from the morning despite bright sunlight now pouring through her kitchen windows.

"Come on in. I'll only be a jiffy," she called to the closed door.

Before she could store the bible and pick up her basket Betty gently pushed open the door. "You got everything together Gracie?"

"Oh yes, my basket is there by the door. I was just reading the bible and kind of lost track of the time."

"You just wait till you've got little feet runnin' all around you and three voices that are never quiet. Gracie I don't know where my time goes every day but it seems like I am up at dawn and the next thing I know it's dusk."

Gracie laughed at her sister-in-law as she always did when she spent time with Betty Ingle. Sure enough she could hear the little voices not far behind them.

"I can't wait to have my home filled with all of that joy."

Betty smiled with her, "They are a blessing for all of their noise."

With baskets settled between hand and hip the ladies made their way down the hill toward a stand of trees. As they drew closer Gracie saw poles erected with long clothes lines strung between them. The beautiful green grass of spring was worn low between the poles proving the repeated use this area saw. Noah, Harold and Donzie raced ahead until each of them in turn tripped on the steep hill and rolled the rest of the way down giggling louder with every turn.

Gracie laughed along with the children and said a silent prayer that she would see her own brood rolling and giggling on this hill very soon.

As the trio dipped and heated water then scrubbed and twisted the clothes, they talked, planned and dreamed. Gracie quickly saw that while Daddy-Jury, as Betty called their father-in-law Algurial Ingle, was hard working and wise in managing the land and stock, Mother Ingle was the one with a vision for their "new home".

She often talked of the old life in Virginia which had been so good before the war. Living on lands the Ingles had farmed since the Revolution and among people who they believed were as close as brothers, the family worshiped mourned and rejoiced with families up and down the Little Sugar Creek.

"Pappy Ingle din' never hold with ownin' another man and the good Lord blessed him with enough little ones that they could work that big farm by themselves. When I married Jury there was no question but that we'd stay right there among all that family. Just 'cause we didn't do things the same way didn't mean we didn't still love the neighbors that had a difference of opinion. We sat beside them in church and then the boys fought beside them in the Confederacy. Didn't make no difference when the Union won the war. The Yankees come down and the neighbors made like we were one of them."

"They treated you like the enemy?" Gracie couldn't help but ask.

Katherine handed her a balled up shirt to hand on the line, "Oh child, worse than an enemy. Some of 'em treated us like the devil himself."

"But their boys fought with the south."

"It didn't matter. Truth is, everybody was so beat down and hurt that things were bound to change no matter where your loyalties fell. It was hard to leave land that the Ingles had been on for a century but we knew it was the right thing to do."

"Hasn't Stephen told me that some of the Ingles stayed in Virginia?"

"Oh sure and they're certainly still family. One of the girls had a serious beau so she stayed on with her uncle. Jury's brother Lewis thought he'd stay but he's left for Ken-tuck now."

Gracie had stopped her washing and stood staring at her mother-in-law, "Mother Ingle, I can see how hard this has been on you."

Katherine stood up straight and drew her shoulders back as though she were preparing for the trip west to Tennessee again, "Life if often hard Gracie but you can't be lookin' back. You can remember, but you can't yearn for yesterday. We have a new life here and God is blessin' it."

Gracie smiled and turned back to her washing silently thinking how much like Grandma Elmore she sounded.

Chapter 10

While the young couple had little money, Gracie could not complain about Stephen's generosity. He faithfully saved a portion of the wages his father paid for the work on the farm and he often managed to buy things for their home. He relished every chance to surprise and spoil his wife.

Returning from Clarkrange, Stephen dropped a limp package on the table with his first trip in the door. Gracie turned from her work at the dry sink and reached out to touch it. Fingering the string on the simple paper wrapping, Gracie's eyes quizzed her husband.

Stephen answered her unspoken question with one of his own, "You'll want to make a new dress before we go see the Elmores, won't you?" he asked as he unloaded supplies from the buckboard.

"A new dress? Where would I ever find the dress goods?" She scarcely had the question out before the answer dawned on her and she drew a quick breath as she worked harder to undo the tight knot.

"Stephen, you shouldn't have. You know I have plenty of dresses. I think I'll save it. I'll be needing different clothes after…" She stopped herself too late.

Stephen froze with a heavy bag of cornmeal still in his hands. He looked around him to ensure none of his cousins were within earshot of this intimate conversation. Gracie raised only her eyes to meet his. "Gracie, are you… are we going to…. I mean… well, what did you mean?"

Gracie felt herself blushing as she dropped into a chair, "Oh, no Stephen, I'm sorry. I wasn't saying anything, only dreaming I guess."

He let out the breath he had unconsciously held and only nodded as he carried the bag into the little closet Gracie used as her pantry. When he returned with another armload of supplies just a moment later, he was talking about something entirely different.

Gracie looked closely in her husband's eyes, searching to learn the level of his disappointment but he gave nothing away.

She was giddy with the hope of seeing her family again and penned a short note right away. She sent the word out with the first Ingle cousin she saw that she had a letter to send along with anyone headed toward the post office. Then carefully saving the brown paper that had wrapped her dress goods she marked out the simple dress she would make.

Gracie smiled as she measured out yardage for a full skirt with little concern for the fashion demands Godey's magazine laid out. Even more than when she lived in her grandparents' house she knew she needed practical clothing that would serve her on her husband's farm and in her new community. Throughout the coming days she picked up her thimble and stitched on the dress every chance she could find.

Finally, the Sunday morning arrived when Stephen and Gracie would drive to Elmore Community to visit Gracie's family. They packed into the wagon food Gracie had worked on for two days, along with apples from their orchard, cabbages and walnuts. Best of all, Gracie had twenty pounds of what Uncle Bill called his very best flour. She knew this 'best' grade was still pretty coarse, but it would be such a precious gift to Aunt Hettie that she could hardly wait to deliver it.

When she thought the wagon could hold nothing else, she heard approaching voices. There were always Ingles around them – cousins dropped in all through the day, Stephen's brothers often followed him home for dinner and even Pappy Ingle was often seen poking about the garden or barn. But the hour was very early for Stephen had warned they wouldn't make church without an early start, so Gracie was surprised that any of the family was already stirring about.

Through the morning's mist, she saw cousins Daniel, Andy and Bruner walking toward them.

Stephen greeted them, "Mornin' boys. How're y'uns and how are Uncle George and Aunt Bithy?"

Gracie was quickly growing accustomed to the many members of her new family as well as their unique names. Aunt Bithy, she knew was actually named Tobitha. She'd noted that anytime a name ended with "a" it was pronounced as "y", thus Mrs. Tobitha Ingle was forever known as Bithy.

The boys chatted for just a moment with Stephen before subtly questioning where they were headed with a loaded wagon on a Sunday.

"We're goin' back to Elmore to visit Gracie's folks. I guess we've had her here all these months, she won't be tryin' to stay there today, do you think?" Stephen winked at his wife as he teased his cousins.

Gracie went about her preparations and left the boys to talk, trusting Stephen would finish his work and enlist his cousins wherever he needed them. When she returned to the wagon, wrapped in a warm shawl and adjusting her straw bonnet she was surprised the cousins were not only still there but in fact, they were seated on the rear of the wagon.

Stephen explained before she could ask, "These boys want to go along to Elmore today. You won't mind, will you Gracie?"

"No, of course not. But Daniel, weren't you just over there three weeks ago for the Clear Creek revival meetings?" Gracie was pretty sure some girl was influential in Daniel Ingle's hunger for religious meetings and she was eager to get back home to see which of her old neighbors might be following her to Martha Washington to live.

Daniel just dipped his head in answer to her questions and mumbled, "Yes Ma'am."

Daniel was only one year younger than Stephen. However, his jovial spirit made him seem like a boy compared to his more serious cousin. Gracie smiled when she thought of her own sister Lottie, who also seemed much younger than her age because she was always laughing, always full of energy.

The ride across the creek was made all the more lively for the addition of Daniel, and Andy. Before they rolled off the family property, young Bruner was evicted from the wagon for some annoyance he caused his brothers. The three cousins laughed and chatted. They included Gracie as though she had always been one of them. This was the way Gracie had been received by the entire Ingle clan and she breathed a prayer of thanksgiving for it.

As they approached the Elmore farm, Gracie had the briefest moment of homesickness. Everything seemed just as she'd left it five months earlier. In some ways she felt like it had been years since she'd lived here.

Hearing the harness' jingle, Jesse stepped from the front door. His white shirt shone brightly in the morning sun; he was already dressed for the morning's prayer meeting.

"Welcome, welcome. Well, you've brought our little Gracie home." He reached up to set her down from the wagon seat.

Wrapping her arms around her dear uncle, Gracie nearly cried, "Thank you Jesse. Oh, how I've missed you. Where is everyone? Is Grandma in the house?"

Jesse smiled and looked his niece over. She hadn't put on any weight, that was sure, but she looked well and happy enough. He just pointed toward the house with his thumb over his back and stepped forward to shake Stephen's hand.

Gracie hurried inside, ready to call for the women of the house, but Lottie was already in the front room, peering out the window.

"Lottie, what are you doing hiding in here? Why didn't you come out and greet me. Come here and give me a hug."

Lottie took one more look out the window and moved to hug her sister. "Gracie, I really have missed you."

"I knew that by all the letters you wrote to me."

Hettie entered the room with the baby in her arms, already wrapped in blankets and wearing his cap for the short walk to church. "Well, she's been posting a letter every week. If it wasn't her sister she was writing, I sure wouldn't know who it was."

Gracie looked at Lottie slightly puzzled, "Lottie, who are you writing?"

"Oh come on, Uncle Jesse told Daniel Ingle that he was free to write to me. And if a young man writes to you then he's expecting a letter back, don't you think?" With that, she returned to the window, moving the curtain very slightly for a better view.

Hettie and Gracie chuckled at her and Gracie realized she now knew the identity of Daniel's girl.

Grandma entered from her downstairs room, "Don't you girls tease little Lottie. She's grown up on us and will be looking to a home of her own I imagine." With a sideways look at Gracie, she added, "And the Ingles have been good to you, haven't they Gracie?"

Gracie could only beam a smile at her grandmother as she stepped into her warm embrace.

The church service was very brief. The circuit preacher was at another church today so there was only Sunday School then a time of prayer for the needs of the congregation and community.

After a delicious meal, Gracie enjoyed catching up with her family. She was thrilled that Jesse and Hettie's baby boy was growing quickly and the farm was doing well. She was greatly saddened to see how frail Grandma seemed to have become. There was little time to talk with her sister for Lottie and Daniel escaped to the front porch as quickly as Jesse would excuse them from the table. She wanted to question the family about them, but the glint in Jesse's eye when he spoke to Daniel answered everything she could have asked.

No one was surprised when spring's sun broke through the clouds, the fields began to green, and Daniel Ingle was ready to bring home a bride.

Gracie was never sure if he came to their little house that morning to get her blessing, Stephen's advice or just to escape the questions at home. She only knew for sure that she was thrilled to have Lottie coming to live so near her.

Daniel had grand plans for their life together; he explained they would stay with his family for a few months until they could build a home of their own. His father had given him a corner plot of the farm and the Ingles would work together to build a suitable home there.

"What part of the farm will you build on, Daniel?" Gracie questioned gently.

Daniel grinned knowing that the sisters would want to live as close as possible. "Southeast, right near the branch."

Gracie closed her eyes and pictured the little trickling branch that flowed down the hollow to run into Slate Creek just upstream of Uncle Bill's mill break. It wasn't the most practical piece of property that Daniel's family owned, but she could imagine the sound of the water from a back porch swing, thought of rocking babies to sleep to that kind of music.

She smiled and nodded her head as she assured Daniel, "I'm sure that Lottie will be thrilled to have a home there."

Daniel left them while it was still quite early. He was planning to walk to Elmore until Stephen cautioned him that it would be difficult to bring a bride home on foot. "What are you going to do with her trunk? You know she won't be coming to you empty handed."

The grin that lit up Daniel's face betrayed his excitement for the day. "I guess I hadn't thought of that. I'll have to go home and see if I can get the wagon for the day."

Stephen thought for just a moment, "Nah, we won't have the preacher today, so me and Gracie can do our prayin' at home. I'll help you harness and you can take my buckboard."

Gracie thought Daniel would skip to the barn. He stayed two steps ahead of Stephen's steady pace and kept his head turned backward to talk to his cousin. Watching them through her kitchen window, she shook her head wondering how the pair of lighthearted kids would ever make it together. "Their home will always be filled with laughter," she told the empty kitchen.

Daniel didn't return the borrowed buckboard until mid-day Monday. But when he parked it near the barn's hitching rail,

Lottie hopped down from the high seat and came trotting to see her sister. She was still dressed in her Sunday dress and seemed to glow in her joy.

"Gracie," she called as she cracked the back door open. "Gracie, are you here?"

Gracie hurried from the front room, Stephen's torn shirt still in her hand. "Land's sakes Lottie, I thought somethin' terrible must have happened. But I can see from that smile you're wearing that everything is right in the world."

Lottie wrapped her arms around her sister, "I'm married Gracie, can you even believe it. Daniel came yesterday and, well, we'd been writin' all through the winter. And he'd even talked to the preacher, I don't know how - he must have seen him somewhere when he was preaching at another church, but he had everything all ready and here he came yesterday and we said our vows. Aren't you happy?"

"Oh Lottie, I am so happy. Daniel is a good boy and I'm certainly glad to have you living in Martha Washington with me. Two Ingles, can you believe it? We were both Berais and now we're both Ingles."

The two giggled as they had when they were very young. The Ingles had been so welcoming to her that Gracie had scarcely known she was homesick until she had Lottie here with her and now the joy was almost overwhelming.

Gracie tried to bring herself back to reality and talk with her sister about the practical things of her new life. "So, you are going to stay with Daniel's parents for a little while?"

"Yes, Daniel says that his father and brother and… well, I guess all of the family, will start building the house as soon as the ground is dry enough to lay the foundation rocks. He's already cleared the brush from the spot – he pointed it out to me when we were drivin' here just now."

Gracie was getting a better picture of the morning the newlyweds had passed, "Then you've already been to see Uncle George and Aunt Bithy?"

"Yes, we went there and dropped off my trunk. I've just made the most beautiful things for our house, I can't wait to show you. But I think I'll make you wait until we are actually in our own home and you can see them when we're using 'em. Me, Grandma and Hettie worked all winter long. Only Grandma has slowed way down, you know, and she can't stitch anything like she used to."

Gracie couldn't help but grin at her little sister. She was a married woman now and Grandma had taught them that should make them be a little more quiet and reserved – after all they were taught to exude a meek and quiet spirit. Meekness came naturally but Lottie had always struggled with the quietness of spirit. When chastised, she used to remind Grandma that quietness was not a fruit of the spirit.

They heard their husbands coming in the back door, talking together. This moved Gracie to action as she wanted to offer them some refreshment. "Do you men want some coffee? I have a little cake made that would go well with something hot."

Daniel was quick to answer even as he sought out his new wife's side, "That sounds wonderful Gracie. Lottie, did you know your sister can make the best little cake you've ever tasted?"

Lottie was nodding but was calmer in her speech with Daniel and Stephen in the room.

Chapter 11

In only moments Gracie had the coffee pot hung from the iron hanger and swung over the flames. On the kitchen shelves she opened the little wooden box that covered the simple cake and served four generous slices.

"Lottie, it's a little coarser than the flour Grandma baked with, but we have a lot more of it. I'll get some apple butter to go on top."

The men seated themselves around the table and Lottie shyly took her place beside Daniel. Gracie was at the table in only minutes, and the foursome dove into the heavy, molasses-sweetened cake.

The men chatted about planting the fields, the horse that had gone lame last week, the cow that spoiled her milk in an onion patch and the leaking roof on Uncle George's barn. Lottie admired her new husband as though he were in command of every situation. Gracie simply enjoyed the picture.

Thank you Lord for bringing my family together like this. I never dared dream that Lottie could not only live near me but be part of my husband's family too. I can't wait to raise our children together, to watch those children enjoying their cousins. As precious as our years were with Grandma and Grandpa, there weren't other children really and with just one sister and no brothers, well, it seemed a little lonely. I'm just thanking you right now that my children won't ever have to face that. Lord, Stephen and I have been married for nearly a year now, and I'm ready to start giving him children. Of course, I know that is all in your time. But I'm ready...

"Gracie dear, where has your mind gotten to?" Stephen abruptly broke into Gracie's silent prayer.

Shaking her head slightly Gracie tried to explain, "Oh, I'm sorry. I was just thanking the Lord for this family and I lost myself in the prayer."

"Well, there's not a better place to get lost. But Daniel and Lottie have to leave. They've not done a thing to get Lottie settled and Aunt Bithy will be walking the floor to see them."

Everyone laughed, for all but Lottie knew of Aunt Bithy's penchant for good use of time. She would likely be standing on the wide front porch asking, "Whatever could they be doin'?"

Throughout the following months of spring, Gracie often saw Lottie. Of course all of the Ingle families attended church at Bruner's Chapel in Clarkrange. And on the Sundays when there was no visiting preacher, they would often meet together at Pappy Ingle's for prayer and a word of devotion from the family patriarch. The day would always include dinner with all the family's bringing what they had. This was a wonderful time of fellowship for brothers and cousins alike.

Pappy Ingle had thirteen children when he left Virginia right after the Civil War. More than half of them either came with him at that time or followed shortly after. Now, they were a huge clan when they all got together, but they were closer than many very small families. Continuing traditions like Sunday prayers maintained that closeness over the generations.

There were always plenty of young ones running about the place and none of the adults seemed to mind them being underfoot. In fact, Grandma Ingle who had fallen ill over the winter months and spent her Sundays in a soft chair, would beg each child to come sit on her lap and talk to her. She didn't mind if a dozen of them piled all around her.

These happy Sundays were interrupted in July when Grandma Ingle passed away. Again, all of the family gathered at the eldest Ingle's home. The family mourned, but their sadness was tempered by the sure knowledge that this saintly woman was at home with her Lord.

Amid the children's clamoring and adult's remembering Grandma, Lottie pulled her sister aside for a quiet moment.

"I was on my way to your house this morning when they came and told us about Grandma Ingle."

Gracie was always happy to have her sister drop in on her but today she looked a little troubled. "Well, we would have had a good visit. Too much going on here to visit much. How are you doing? Is it getting hard staying at Uncle George's house?"

Lottie was slowly shaking her head, "Nah, the folks are great. They give us plenty of space and anyway, our house is nearly finished. Daniel says we'll be moving by the end of the month."

"Well that's wonderful news Lottie." Gracie had watched the little house going up, taking a moment to stop in anytime she was walking past it.

"Gracie, we're going to have a baby. I just told Daniel this morning and I wanted to get to you right away. Isn't that just wonderful? But don't you know that I'm kind of scared too. Grandma is just too far away and too old to travel over here and I sure wish she could be with me. How many babies do you guess she's caught in her life?"

Whether it was the news or the July heat, Gracie suddenly felt lightheaded. She leaned her weight against the fence they stood alongside. She had to take a couple of breaths before she could respond to Lottie. She had missed the last half of Lottie's monologue and wasn't sure what the questions were. All she could hear was 'baby'.

"A baby?" was the only response she could utter.

"Yes silly, a baby. Isn't it wonderful?"

Pulling herself from her own thoughts, she wrapped her arms around Lottie. "Oh Lottie of course it is wonderful news. When do you expect it?"

"After the first of the year - February probably."

"Well, we'll just have to get your little house all ready for a family, won't we? And we'll get lots of sewing done for the baby after everything is harvested. And you know that I'll be with you. There is an old midwife out in Campground – her name is Reeder I think – several of Stephen's cousins say she's really pretty good."

Lottie let out a deep sigh and relief seemed to flood over her face. "Gracie if you'll promise to be with me, I just know I'll be okay."

Gracie put her arm around Lottie's waist as they began to walk back toward the rest of the family. "You know, you'll be just fine. Me and Grandma delivered Hettie and Jesse's baby by ourselves. And what about Nelda Turner? Why it'll be just like you had Grandma right there beside you."

Gracie's sweet nature and soft voice so completely reassured Lottie that she bounced off to the rest of the family as though she had never had a single care. But Gracie felt a great lump welling in her chest.

Gracie wanted to run, she didn't know where she wanted to go, she just wanted out of this crowd. She found Stephen sitting on the ground with his back against a shade tree.

"Stephen, do you mind if I go home for a while?" Gracie asked him quietly.

He put one hand on the ground to push himself up before he tried to answer.

Gracie stopped him with gentle pressure on his shoulder, "No no, you stay here. Pappy needs you, your folks need you and it's good for you cousins to all be together."

"Are you okay?"

"Oh I'm fine, just feelin' like I need to walk a bit. Is it okay with you?"

He nodded and settled back against the tree.

As Gracie walked she fought an inward battle.

Of course I'm happy for you, Lottie. Lord, you know that I'm happy for her. But what about me? Even Mother Ingle has been asking me about children. And Betty, well she only has two living, but she's mentioned that she had her first baby just thirteen months after she married William. Lord, is there something wrong with me? Will I never have children? I've always enjoyed such good health and Mama wasn't sick until after she had Lottie. I would think if anyone was going to suffer because of Mama's sickness it would be Lottie.

She'd reached her porch but couldn't make herself go any further. She fell down on the steps and cried aloud, "What about me, Lord?" Then the tears washed over her. She cried without restraint knowing that all of the family was at Pappy Ingle's house and would be for hours so her tears would not be seen, no explanation would be necessary.

When the tears would no longer fall, she picked herself up from the rough wooden step, straightened her back and smoothed her skirts. She walked into the empty house with the dignity of royalty. She had no answers, no audible word from God. What she had was peace in her heart for she'd poured everything out on the holy altar and at this moment, she knew it was in God's hands.

Chapter 12

By the time the gardens were harvested, Daniel and Lottie had moved into their home by the branch. The sisters were now living just across a broad field and small woodland. There was already a path but it would become well-worn as they travelled back and forth to each other's houses. Even as the winter months grew ever colder, and Lottie grew bigger with child, Gracie continued to make the trip to check on her sister.

The morning Lottie felt the first pains of childbirth, the gray sky threatened more snow. Her aching back had kept her from sleep the night before and Daniel returned to the house as soon as he had their cow milked and fed. Lottie questioned how he would ever make it to Campground to get the midwife. She was just asking whether Mrs. Reeder would even come out in such weather when Daniel turned from peering out the front window and announced Gracie was coming.

"I don't think I could be much happier if it were the good Lord himself coming over that hill," Lottie announced.

Daniel scowled at her flagrant reference to the Lord, but one look at the beads of sweat popping up on her brow warned him to remain quiet. He was not used to his jovial wife being ill in any way.

Daniel was on the porch when Gracie was within earshot, "Come quick Gracie, Lottie sure needs you."

"What's happened Daniel, is she okay?"

"I don't know. She's hardly slept, wouldn't eat anything for breakfast and she looks awfully pained in her face."

Gracie gave him a gentle smile. Men never understood the beautiful process by which they received their beloved children. She stepped past him into the warm room. The whole house was as neat as a pen, nonetheless Lottie was trying to move about the kitchen putting away dishes and setting a kettle to cook something for dinner. Gracie went directly to her and taking her by the shoulders directed her to the front room to sit.

With her feet up on a low stool and some cold water to sip on, Gracie began to question her sister to try to assess the situation. After only a moment she turned to Daniel, "Go get Mrs. Reeder."

Daniel's eyes popped wide and Gracie couldn't tell if he ran or danced out of the house.

Turning back to her sister she wondered, "Do you think he's that happy that the baby is coming or was he just glad to get out of the house?"

Lottie chuckled and began a retort which was quickly silenced by a wave of pain.

Very shortly, Aunt Bithy arrived with a basket on one arm and a baby quilt she'd just finished over the other arm. She shed her heavy woolen wrap and looked first to Lottie then to Gracie with an unspoken question.

Knowing Lottie could scarcely talk, Gracie answered her. "Daniel's gone for the midwife. She was hurting all night and the pains are fast now."

"Yeah, Daniel stopped at the house to get the wagon. He was going to ride a horse but I told him, 'Dan'l, how you gonna get that old woman on a horse to tote her back here to your wife? And then his Pa helped him harness up the wagon."

Even Lottie was able to smile at the continuing antics of her precious husband.

Daniel returned in what seemed to Gracie record time. Lottie had a different measure of the time. Still she was thankful when he returned, delivering Mrs. Reeder, the somewhat reluctant midwife to all of their community.

She entered the little house with lips pursed. "You think this baby's coming already? I'll betcha it's gonna be hours yet."

Mrs. Reeder made herself at home and began directing the Ingle women. They helped Lottie change into her night dress and got her into the bed. Daniel was expelled from his home and, trying to keep him busy, Gracie asked gently if he'd take word to Stephen that she'd be staying probably through the night.

"You might as well. It'll take us all night I'm sure. First babies come awful slow. It's gonna snow ag'in and I guess I won't see Campground for days," Mrs. Reeder grumbled.

Gracie tried to smile at the old woman and returned to care for her sister.

Contrary to Mrs. Reeder's experienced predictions, Lottie gave birth to little Ida Frances in record time. By lunch, the new mother was cleaned up, the sheets changed and boiling on the stove, and Ida was sleeping in the crook of Lottie's arm.

Gracie had not stopped moving since Lottie started pushing. From bathing her sister's forehead with cool water to fetching towels and rags as Mrs. Reeder needed them, Gracie had been a step ahead of the whole process. Mrs. Reeder stood amazed.

Rolling her sleeves down, Gracie explained to the other women, "I'm going to walk to my house and get Daniel. I know he'll be on pins and needles. I'll be back shortly and I'll stay with them tonight to help Lottie."

Mrs. Reeder gave a perfunctory nod and Aunt Bithy patted her back as she thanked Gracie for her help.

The walk across the snowy field felt good to Gracie. She breathed the cold air deep into her lungs as she praised God. *Thank you Lord for your care of Lottie. And thank you for Ida Frances – what a beautiful gift you've given to my sister! I don't know why I haven't received such a gift yet, but I know you will send my children to me in your perfect time. This is the most wonderful day. The sun on the snow is almost blinding yet I can't close my eyes to it; I wonder if that's what it's like to look at you? Grandma would chastise me for thinking of looking on the Lord. No man has seen God, but Jesus has declared him. Lord you don't need to prove yourself to me, but seeing a new life born certainly does prove you. Thank you.*

She prayed for the whole walk home and it seemed to be only ten steps from her sister's door to her own. She hadn't gotten the gate closed before Daniel erupted from her front door, Stephen stood in the doorway his usual calm self.

Poor Daniel couldn't utter the questions in his heart and Gracie didn't make him ask. "You have a perfect little girl."

"Lottie?"

"She is just fine. Mrs. Reeder and Aunt Bithy are with her. You can go home now but you must be quiet and let Lottie rest. I don't think she slept a wink last night, did she? And she's been through a lot this morning you know."

Daniel was nodding his head like a Tennessee Pacing horse traveling right. Gracie thought she must let him go before he got a permanent crick in his neck.

"I'll be back within the hour, just let me get some dinner ready for Stephen and then I'll stay the night with her. Lottie will need help tonight."

"I can ask Mother to stay."

"Nah, Aunt Bithy's got plenty enough to do and Lottie will rest easy with me I think. Run on home now and I'll be there shortly."

Stephen was smiling broadly as he reached for his wife, wrapping his arms around her waist. "He took you literally, he'll run all the way home. When do you think he'll remember that he's left Uncle George's buckboard here?"

They shared a laugh; it felt good to Gracie to laugh as she leaned against her husband's strong chest. He looped a finger under her chin, raising her face to him. "Are you okay? Was it hard work on you?"

Gracie smiled, thankful for his sweet concern. "No, Mrs. Reeder was really in charge. Although it's harder to work with her than it was with my Grandma. Grandma loved midwifing; she was honored by every baby she got to catch. This woman acts like she's the one in labor."

"Well, she's a sour old lady anyway. I hope Daniel remembers to pay her; she won't ask for it but if he doesn't give her something our name will be mud in Campground for weeks. Now I really want to know about you; I'm sure you never thought you'd be delivering your baby sister's children before you had one of your own."

Having moved into the little house, Gracie was working at the fireplace, pulling coals onto the hearth rock and preparing to cook Stephen's dinner. "I already heard Aunt Bithy asking Mrs. Reeder what they owed. So she'll probably handle that before Daniel even gets home. Do you want coffee?"

"Nah, I had some while Daniel was here. I'll just drink some milk. The coffee tin was feeling pretty light and I hadn't planned to go to the store for another week."

With the falling snows, Stephen stayed close to home. It was a miserable ride in freezing temperatures to go to Clarkrange on a horse and they didn't have a covered buggy.

"I'll write to Grandma so someone will need to take the letter tomorrow. Do we have money left for more coffee?"

"I think we can swing it. You didn't answer my question – what about you?"

Gracie had to stop; she stood up from her work at the fireplace and looked beyond her husband as though she were returning to the conversation she'd had with God while walking in the snow.

"Our babies will come in God's perfect timing. I want them right now but I'll be happy when he chooses to send them."

The tear that escaped the corner of her eye belied her brave front and Stephen didn't miss it. However, he chose to lighten the moment as he pulled her onto his lap, kissing the nape of her neck, "Well I'm ready for God's timing too you know."

She giggled and pulled herself free, smacking playfully at his hand. "Now you stop that or you're going to starve. Anyway, I've gotta be gettin' back to Lottie right quick."

Stephen shrugged his shoulders and kicked back still grinning as he opened the weeks old newspaper that lay nearby.

Chapter 13

With Stephen well fed, cold meat laid by for his supper and the rest of the stew in the buckboard beside her, Gracie drove the borrowed wagon back to Daniel and Lottie's house. She wasn't surprised to find Aunt Bithy sitting contently in the rocker by the fireplace and Mrs. Reeder pacing in front of the windows.

Mrs. Reeder greeted Gracie's return with more complaints. "That fool boy run off and left his wagon so's he couldn't even take me home. The works all done now and with Mizz Ingle sittin' here, I don't reckon there's anymore need for me." Turning her head toward the back of the house she yelled, "Dan'l you come on out here and drive me home. I'll catch pneumonia if we're driving after dark."

Gracie bowed her head to hide the smile she couldn't contain. She nearly asked whether Mrs. Reeder was concerned with Daniel driving home after dark, but felt it best to be quiet. As she busied herself in the kitchen, putting the leftover stew on the back of the stove and checking whether there was enough cornmeal for bread at suppertime, she heard Daniel leave with the midwife and the squeaking of the rocker stopped as Aunt Bithy moved into the kitchen.

"It's a pity we have to call on that woman when we have babies. She's the meanest thing I've about ever seen."

Gracie nodded, "I wonder why that is? She has the most marvelous work to do; she sees every miracle in the community."

Aunt Bithy had raised five children and lost five more. The smile she offered Gracie was melancholy. "Remember that not every child is as perfect as our Ida Frances and not every birth as easy as Lottie's. The old woman's seen her share of sadness serving us as midwife."

Aunt Bithy turned to walk out of the room but stopped with the parlor door in her hand, "She was impressed with you though. Said you'd make a fine midwife and maybe she could just retire now."

"Uh, what… why…," Gracie stuttered, unable to comprehend the obvious hint her husband's aunt had dropped.

Aunt Bithy smiled and gently closed the door behind her. She resumed her place by the fire until Daniel returned to drive her home.

Before Daniel got home, Ida awoke asking to be fed again. From the kitchen, Gracie heard Lottie stirring in the bed and she stepped into the rear bedroom to see if she could help.

"She's a good eater. Grandma would say that's the best sign, wouldn't she?" Lottie questioned Gracie as soon as she saw her.

"You're right. I sat down and wrote Grandma a little note earlier. Stephen will take it to the post office tomorrow morning. She'll be wanting to know how everything's gone. I don't guess Uncle Jess will try to bring her over until the weather warms a little though."

Lottie looked up from gazing at her daughter, "Yeah, she's just gotten too old and frail to be out in the cold, hasn't she?"

As much as they were comforted by living so close together, both girls missed Grandma Elmore. "We've been blessed to have her you know," Gracie said. "What would have happened to us if Mama had left us in Chicago?"

Grandpa and Grandma had told them many times how their precious mother used her last bit of strength to get her daughters home to Tennessee when she knew she was dying from consumption. They heard many stories about Margaret Elmore as they walked the path to the little family graveyard where they kept the weeds pulled and flowers blooming on their mother's grave. No ill word was ever spoken about their father Philip Berai who had chosen to stay in Chicago instead of traveling with his ailing wife. Somehow both Gracie and Lottie had come to understand how much better their lives were living in poverty with their grandparents in Tennessee. They had discussed it between themselves many times.

While Philip regularly sent money to the Elmores and would usually write a few words to his daughters, they never knew him. Nor did they know very much about his business, except that he seemed successful enough to care for them.

The winter of 1886 was brutally cold on the plateau. Gracie and Stephen found their little house a bit drafty, but Gracie used well the spare hours and sewed pretty curtains, lining them with homespun wool to keep out the cold wind. They had stocked their cellar well during the warmer months and now enjoyed the fruits of their summer labors. Even on the coldest days and despite the deep snows, Stephen made his way to his father's barn and did the chores he was paid for, milking, feeding, and ensuring the stock would not unduly suffer from the cold.

Despite the hardships that winter brought, Gracie enjoyed the slower pace and more time with her husband.

Lottie quickly regained her strength and Ida flourished as winter-borne babies rarely do. Whenever the weather was clear enough, Gracie made her way across the field to visit Lottie, Daniel and little Ida Frances. She held Ida, carried her to look at the bright yellow flowers that greeted the springtime, and talked to her as though she were a beloved friend.

Lottie treasured the time she had with Gracie and was thrilled that her sister loved Ida so much. She saw the longing in Gracie's eyes as she looked at little Ida Frances. She hurt for her sister as she'd grown a mother's heart in just a few months of loving her little daughter. She prayed that God would soon give Gracie children of her own.

The baby charmed everyone who stopped to visit, as the Ingles often did. Gracie regularly found one or more of Stephen's cousins, their wives and children in Lottie's little living room. Lottie was a gifted hostess, and had learned well Grandma Elmore's lessons. No matter how many people sat in her front room, Lottie greeted the next visitor before they made their way beyond her gate. Here Gracie saw how perfectly Lottie and Daniel were matched for he welcomed everyone and could put any stranger at ease with his jovial manner.

Stephen drove to Clarkrange as often as he could, and it was from one trip to the post office that he brought Gracie an unexpected letter.

She often received little notes from the Elmores. She and Lottie always made a quick visit to the other sister whenever one had such a letter. But this letter addressed in Uncle Jesse's familiar handwriting was very heavy. When she broke the seal another sealed packet fell out. This second letter was written on fine paper which Gracie held for a long moment, enjoying the feel of it on her fingertips. The hand that addressed it didn't seem to fit the quality of the stationary as the letters were shaky and the ink pressed deeply into the paper.

It was addressed to Gracie Berai and showed a return address in Chicago.

Whoever would write me from Chicago? The letters from her father were very rare and she would recognize his careful script right away. The thought that perhaps something had happened to him flashed into her mind with a surprising lack of emotion.

With a quick glance at the scant words from Uncle Jesse which assured all was well, the family healthy and the farm running smoothly, she broke the seal on the mystery letter and read:

Dear Miss Gracie,

I surely hope that this post will make its way to you. I only know a little about where Mrs. Margaret was from and where she took her children.

You see, I knew her and worked with her in Mr. Philip's dance hall – well I mean to say that I worked in the kitchen with her.

Your Mama was the best friend I have ever had and I have missed her these twenty years. I am able to travel a little now and would very much like to call on you and your baby sister. My husband and I will be in Tennessee the last week of March if the weather will permit it. I look forward to seeing you and Miss Lottie then.

Very Truly Yours,

Mrs. Thomas Bourke

Gracie held the letter for a long moment, not entirely sure how to react. The mother she could scarcely remember was this lady's dearest friend and now she was coming to visit. A pang that Gracie could not explain pierced her heart. There had never been a chance to feel sorry for herself growing up with her grandparents. Mama's name had been mentioned so often that one would have thought she'd just gone away for the week to visit family instead of dying when Gracie was only three.

Grandma Elmore carefully shielded Gracie and Lottie from the nature of their father's business until Gracie was old enough to ask pointed questions that could not be honestly ignored.

With a look to the western horizon to confirm she would not be caught out in another snow storm, Gracie slipped the letter in her apron pocket and began tying a woolen scarf about her shoulders. "Stephen," she called as she stepped out the back door, "I'm going to run over to Lottie's. I'll be back in time to put supper on."

Stephen was mending the corral fence and looked up with nails held between his lips; the nod of his head acknowledged he'd understood.

Gracie was moving quickly and had her head down, shielding her face from the icy wind. In this way, she very nearly ran into the wagon that had entered the yard.

"Whoa here Jewel," called a strange voice and caused Gracie to jump slightly. "You Mrs. Gracie Ingle?"

Gracie looked up at the man who seemed so demanding despite the fact he was standing in her own yard. She was trying to find her voice to answer him when Stephen answered for her. "Well Lafayette Baldwin, whatever brings you down here on a day like this? This is my wife, Gracie," Stephen put a hand lightly on Gracie's shoulder.

"Mildy's baby's a'comin and I gotta get help." He sounded near desperation.

"Well you need to go for Mrs. Reeder," Gracie finally found her voice to help the poor man.

"Been there. She's down sick and can't come. Said you'd be the next best thing."

Stephen was as confused as Gracie now, "Well, you ought to go get Aunt Bithy or even my mother. Wish we still had Granny Ingle – why after raisin' thirteen children, I'll bet she'd be a fine help."

"No." Lafayette was nearly screaming now. "Mildy's had troubles a'fore and Mrs. Reeder said to get Mrs. Gracie and no other. Won't you please come help us? I been gone more 'an two hours and I just gotta git back to her."

Gracie snapped into action. There was no more time to talk. She was climbing into the wagon before Stephen could even get his hands on her slender waist to help her. "Two hours? She's not alone, is she?"

Lafayette Baldwin was releasing the wagon's brake as he answered, "No, her mother is with her. But she's was with Mildy before – I mean the last time…I just don't think she can help her. We need somebody else."

With a jerk, the wagon was rolling north along the rutted Martha Washington Road. Gracie did not know where she was being taken, she didn't know this Lafayette Baldwin, the wife he called 'Mildy' nor where the family might live. Mother Ingle had mentioned a family by the name of Baldwin who lived down in a hollow north of Martha Washington, Gracie thought maybe that was their destination.

She had little time to worry about her endpoint for she was holding so tightly to the shuddering wagon that she could not engage her mind to think of anything but surviving this ride. She braced herself with her feet and still she was thrown against the stranger repeatedly.

"Mr. Baldwin, can we slow down some? It's probably a long time till the baby comes. When did your wife start hurting?" Gracie had to raise her voice much louder than she'd normally speak, hoping the man would hear her above the rattle of harness chains, the squeak of the wagon and the rising wind.

"She's been hurtin' all mornin'. Don't think she slept much last night either."

Seeming to sense their masters' urgency, the lathered horses didn't slow even as the road slanted steadily downward. The weak sunlight of the winter afternoon faded quickly as the trees seemed to swallow up the road behind them. Gracie longed to look back, to see if there would be a way out of this place but she was afraid to even know the answer. Gracie could feel the tension in LaFayette's muscles as she jostled against his shoulder. He hunched further forward and his foot rode on the brake pedal. The friction brake squealed as the wheel hub rubbed against the hard wood relieving some of the wagon's weight from the horses. The big animals leaned back into their breeching lest the rig overrun them and Gracie could see their wide eyes, hear the snorts as they panted for breath. They looked as panicked as she felt but somehow the driver kept them under control. He seemed to grunt comforting words to the team and she supposed they were used to his way because they did their job all the way to the bottom of the long hill.

The dirt road held even deeper ruts than the Martha Washington Road and the wagon seemed to fall off huge rocks, bouncing Gracie into the air more than once.

Gracie heard roaring water and felt cold air blast her face. She realized the trees had changed down here with the evergreen boughs of hemlocks and cedars further blocking the daylight. The air changed too, carrying a mixture of freshness from the river, piney accents and a hint of the pungent odor of decay.

Then she saw a patch of light where the trees had been cleared from a relatively flat area and a small house erected.

LaFayette didn't slow the rig until they made the turn into the Baldwin's home. Gracie realized how cold she'd gotten only when the heat from the big fireplace hit her face. *How will I ever help this poor woman if I can't even feel my hands? How I wish Grandma was with me.*

Rubbing her hands she reached toward the fire for a split second, trying to clear her head. A short, wiry woman stepped into the room, her lips pursed and brow wrinkled. "You the midwife?"

Gracie wondered if this family always spoke with such curt sentences or if it was just the stress of the moment.

"Mrs. Reeder was down sick so she sent Mr. Baldwin to get me. I'm Gracie Ingle." She offered a cold hand to the woman.

The lady ignored Gracie's hand and asked, "You ever done this before?"

"Well, yes a few times. Is Mildy your daughter?"

"Yeah, she's my middle girl. Got four other girls and five boys."

Gracie smiled trying to comfort this woman in some way, "My, ten children. Well I guess you're the expert here."

"I never had trouble like Mildy has. She's lost two already you know."

No, Gracie didn't know that and somehow the knowledge shook her confidence. *Lord God what have I gotten myself into?*

Gracie continued to try to put Mildy's mother at ease, "What is your name ma'am? We're going to have to work together, aren't we?"

"I'm Matilda Key. We'd better get back to her."

"Yes, I expect you are right, Mrs. Key. I just need to wash up. Is this the kitchen?" Gracie had removed her wrapper and pointed toward a back room. With a nod from Mrs. Key she went to the stove, whose fire was far too low. The reservoir held very warm water, and she dipped out enough to fill the wash pan. As she scrubbed her hands with the strong lye soap she found, she heard the back door open and Lafayette Baldwin stomped off his boots.

"Mr. Baldwin, I'm sure glad to see you. We need this fire stirred up. And, can you fill a couple of pots with water to heat?"

His only response was, "Glad to have my hands busy."

Gracie smiled as she left him to his kitchen chores and went to meet her patient.

Armilda Baldwin was a small woman. She appeared to be several years older than Gracie but somehow had a child-like, angelic face. Despite her pain, she smiled at Gracie and thanked her for coming to help.

After a few questions, Gracie checked her progress and could see no immediate problems. "Mrs. Baldwin, can you tell me what trouble you've had before?"

She had to blink to clear the tears that threatened to escape before she answered, "Honey, just call me 'Mildy' like everybody else. I've had two. The first one came early and he was blue when I had him. The second one was a girl and she looked good when she came out but she was awful small and it was right in the winter; she lasted just three days."

Now it was Gracie's turn to blink before she could speak. She had to try to work through this. That was what Grandma always said with the animals as well as with people, 'You've gotta know what's happened before.'

Well there doesn't seem to be a pattern exactly, Gracie thought to herself. She looked to Mrs. Key, "We need a lot of good clean rags, do you have those ready?"

As Mrs. Key handed Gracie the pile, Gracie noticed her fingernails were dirty. *Now how do I explain that we have to have everything clean? Grandma just told me to wash all the time, I can't say that to this woman who's twenty years my senior.*

"We need to make sure everything is good and clean in here. I've asked Mr. Baldwin to get the fire stirred up in the stove and have some extra water heating so we can clean up Mildy and the sheets and such afterward. I've already scrubbed real well so I'll stay with Mildy if you want to go wash up. Would you care to drop a good sharp knife in the boiling water and bring it when you come back? Do you have a ball of strong string?"

Mildy's eyes popped open at the mention of the knife and Gracie saw the fear.

"Don't worry, honey. We are going to have a screaming baby on our hands in a minute and I'll need to cut his little cord."

The sigh of relief Mildy breathed was interrupted by a strong contraction and Gracie turned her full attention to the birthing.

Mildy labored another three hours with Gracie talking softly to her, praying silently and trying constantly to relieve some of her pain. She was about to suggest walking when Mildy screamed, "Now!"

Mildy knew what she was talking about for a writhing, red little boy was shortly in Gracie's hands. With a skill that disputed her youth, Gracie cut the cord, turned the baby on his stomach, swept her finger in his mouth, gave him a firm pat on the back and wrapped him in a soft blanket. With a quick wipe of his face, she placed him in Mrs. Key's arms and turned her attention back to Mildy.

The blood seemed to be coming fast and Gracie was close to panic. But in moments the placenta slipped free with no effort from Mildy. Gracie quickly cleaned the new mother and slipped from the bedroom to send in Mr. Baldwin.

After gently urging Lafayette to wash in clean water before touching his new son, Gracie busied herself in the kitchen, boiling the bedding and searching for a bit of food for Mildy. She could hear the little family talking to their new baby boy and each other. It was the sweetest thing she'd ever heard. Yet, somehow it seemed melancholy to Gracie.

Lord, when will that be me and Stephen?

Gracie took Mildy a cup of tea with some buttered bread and while she ate, Gracie took baby Wyatt and bathed him properly. She talked to him as she worked and he was quiet except for the softest chirps. "We've gotta' get you cleaned up right here. Folks are liable to come see you as soon as word gets out that you've arrived and we want you ready to greet them, don't we?"

Mrs. Key brought Mildy's empty cup to refill, "That child has got the appetite of a horse. I never could eat after my babies were born. Can you Gracie?"

Gracie froze for a moment, her hand cradling Wyatt's tiny head. She blinked slowly and took a deep breath before answering, "Mrs. Key, I don't have any children."

Mrs. Key's face was no longer puckered and lined; she wore a smile that seemed to take years from her appearance and the smile didn't falter with Gracie's confession. "Well you did a fine job with Mildy and you handle that baby like you've done it a hundred times. I guess it's just how the good Lord's gifted you. Why, I think I'd rather have you than Mizz Reeder."

Gracie blushed slighty and dipped her head. "Thank you Mrs. Key, that's very kind of you. Of course, Mildy did all the work and God gave plenty of grace."

"Amen, honey."

With the baby cleaned, Mildy fed and the pair resting, Mrs. Key began instructing her son-in-law. "I'd imagine Mizz Gracie will be wantin' to get home now, wouldn't you?"

Gracie was still more concerned for her patient, "Won't Mildy need some help?"

"No, child, I'll stay with her. Fact, I'll probably stay till Fayette runs me off. I'm so happy to have that baby boy safely in the world that I can't stand to leave him."

Gracie looked out the small window that faced the family's barn. The early spring night looked inviting and she longed to walk in it. But she knew the temperature would be dropping soon and she really had no idea how far they'd driven and barely which direction her home lay from this hollow. Now that she was calming down, she realized how utterly exhausted she was. "Thank you. Mr. Baldwin, I will be ready to go whenever you are."

The drive back to her little home was much calmer than the earlier trip and Mrs. Key had the foresight to wrap a thick quilt about Gracie's shoulders before they left. Lafayette Baldwin wasn't nearly so curt as he was this morning, but he was still quiet. Gracie didn't mind as she was consumed with her own thoughts.

Stephen was sitting by the big fireplace when she walked in. Dropping into the chair beside him, she felt like she could fall asleep sitting up.

"Was it that bad?" He asked her. "Did you have any help besides Lafayette?"

Gracie giggled, "Oh no, once we got there, everything went very smoothly, for me anyway. It was a hard time for Mildy of course. Her mother was there, in fact she's staying with them. I'll have to wash. Grandma always taught me to wash up as soon as we got home; she said you never know how other women keep their house."

Chapter 14

The next day, Gracie had every intention of taking Daisy Bourke's letter to Lottie, but the time simply did not allow it. When Friday dawned bright and sunny, she could no longer wait to share the news with her sister and she left immediately after she'd cleaned up from breakfast.

Her walk across the quickly greening field seemed to liberate her heart. She had not realized how confined she'd felt through the winter months. Spring was always a welcome season and now she thanked God for his renewing of the earth each year. She heard the clanking of a cow's bell and watched as the little brown Jersey picked her way across the field she shared with Gracie.

Lottie was shaking rugs off the front porch as Gracie opened the gate. "Mornin' Gracie. Sure is good to see you. I hear you've been busy – had to catch a baby down in the Baldwin Gulf."

Gracie smiled and hugged her sister. "How did you hear about that?"

"Come on in here and have a hot cup of coffee. That sun sure is good to see, but it's still none too warm, is it?"

"Well I wasn't cold while I was walking."

With two steaming mugs in her hand, Lottie sat down at the table with Gracie, clearly preparing for a good visit with her sister. "Mother Ingle spoke with Tildy Key and she was telling her what a good job you did helping her daughter with the baby."

Gracie smiled, enjoying the compliment. "Well, like I told Mrs. Key, Mildy did all the work and God supplied the grace."

"Gracie, you are too modest. I can't help but wonder if this is your callin'. I know you were like an angel sent straight from heaven when I was birthing Idy."

"Speaking of the little darling, where is my niece?"

"She'll be waking any minute now, wanting to eat."

"Well, before she does, I want you to take a look at this letter that I got a couple of days ago. I was just coming over here to show you when I had to go rushin' down that holler to care for the young Mrs. Baldwin."

Lottie took the letter and carefully unfolded it. "This paper feels downright rich, don't it?"

"Yeah, I thought so."

Lottie read silently for a moment then looked up at Gracie, her eyes wide with disbelief. "Did this surprise you as much as it does me?"

Gracie nodded.

Lottie looked over her shoulder at the calendar hanging by the kitchen door. "Last week of March, that's just two more weeks."

"The letter came to Uncle Jessie so they'll have to tell her how to get over here to Martha Washington."

Lottie stood as she heard Ida beginning to stir, "Well, we'll just be ready for them when they get here, won't we? Daniel and I will be happy to have them stay here."

As she stepped out of the kitchen, Gracie looked around the familiar kitchen. Lottie had brightly colored curtains at the window and a similarly colored rag rug at the door. She had made their new house into an inviting home. They certainly had more room to keep a guest than she and Stephen did so she was happy to have Mr. and Mrs. Bourke stay with her sister.

Lottie returned with Ida happily nursing under a blanket. "I guess I never imagined we would meet anyone that knew Mother in Chicago, did you?"

Gracie remembered having the same thought when she first read the letter. "No, I never imagined. Why do you suppose she would want to come all the way down here? Even our father has never bothered to make that long trip."

"I just don't know. She says that Mother was her dearest friend. Maybe she still misses her, I know Grandma does."

There was no solving the mystery of this guest until they could meet her. So the sisters spent a couple more hours visiting and playing with little Ida Frances before Gracie left to allow Lottie to make Daniel's dinner.

She was enjoying her return walk even more than the morning because the sun had continued to warm the air. Seeing movement across the field, she recognized Betty and altered her course to speak to her sister-in-law. Betty's head was down, and she didn't see Gracie coming before she heard her cheerful calls. Raising her head, with the ever-ready smile, she returned the greeting.

"Mornin' Gracie. I'm out huntin' fresh greens. Do you want some? I think we can probably find enough for both."

"I'd better not tarry that long. I've been over to Lottie's and Stephen will think I've fallen in the branch if I don't get on home pretty soon. Do you need any help?"

Betty stood and kneaded her back. "Nah, I'll get it, just have to go slow because it's hard on the back after sittin' all winter."

The days flew by as Gracie and Lottie awaited their guest's arrival. With all of their anticipation, there was no question who was pulling into Gracie's yard in a shiny black surrey. Lottie and Daniel sat together in the back seat holding their baby with a stranger holding the driving lines and quite an elegant lady beside him.

Gracie held open the gate and the ladies stepped down from the carriage. Lottie beamed as Daniel handed her the bundle of blankets that kept Ida warm.

"Gracie, you see they've come. This is Mr. and Mrs. Bourke from Chicago."

Gracie smiled, suddenly feeling shy with these city folks. Still she extended her hand and tried to utter words of greeting.

Daisy Bourke immediately put her at ease. "You just call me Daisy. Your Mama wouldn't have thought of calling me anything else. And my husband is called Michael."

In moments the little party was seated around Gracie's kitchen table with coffee boiling and fresh bread, butter and jams before them. Michael Bourke was fascinated with the farm and peppered the Ingles with questions. Finally, the three men excused themselves to the barn to answer some of Michael's questions and to see to the stock there.

Daisy let out a long sigh, "I thought those men would never leave, didn't you? Now we girls can really have a visit."

Gracie and Lottie exchanged a little smile for they often wanted to escape to have their own chats.

Daisy continued talking as though she'd held it all in for too long, "I knew your mother, Mrs. Margaret as we called her, in Chicago. Course I knew your father too. But it was Mrs. Margaret who meant so very much to me."

Gracie unconsciously leaned toward this new friend. They felt they knew their mother from Grandma Elmore's stories. But there were no stories from her time in Chicago, nor from her marriage to their father.

As Daisy talked, the elegant lady seemed to peel away the layers of mystery to expose a sweet woman. "You see, I was sent to Mr. Philip's dance hall kind of by trickery. My own dear mother had passed on and my step-father didn't really want to be bothered by me. So he forced the Berais to take me. But it turned out to be the greatest blessing in my life. Mrs. Margaret, she took me under her wing and let me work with her in the kitchen. Me and her never had any dealings with the dance hall – we just cooked the food. Of course, we did have to serve the other girls who worked there."

As Daisy paused to sip her now-cool coffee, Gracie tried to breathe deeply. Grandma had said little about the nature of the business; Gracie always thought the Elmores didn't really know much about it. Gracie wasn't entirely sure what a 'dance hall' was but she'd been taught dancing was a sinful practice and Grandma had said enough about Mother's rebellion to make Gracie and Lottie understand that their father's business was not altogether honorable.

"Those other girls were never good to me, but Mrs. Margaret she was kind from the first day that I met her. Well, anyway, we always knew there was something sort of different about her. She wanted to go to church all the time and whenever Mr. Philip would agree to take her – mostly after little Gracie was born – then she would always invite the whole household. I was the only one who ever went, but I went every time they did."

Daisy looked around the little kitchen and stared out the window for a moment, "She talked all the time about her home in Tennessee. I never imagined I'd ever get to see it."

Gracie smiled at her, "Well, you know this was never actually her home. She always lived in Elmore. Did you go there first and did Uncle Jesse tell you how to get here?"

"Well no, that's what we intended to do but the most amazing thing happened when we got off the train in Monterey. Of course we had to hire the carriage and Michael was talking with the fellow working there and asking how to best get to Elmore. The man asked if we had family in Elmore and Michael told him we were hoping to see you girls. Then he tells Michael that you've both married into the Ingle family and they live in Martha Washington. Well, I heard that and I thought, have we come to the wrong place altogether? But he went on to explain that it would really be a better drive to come directly here. So, that's what we did and here we are."

Gracie and Lottie exchanged glances, each trying to decide which of their old neighbors from Elmore was now working in Monterey. Since the railroad was built from Nashville a couple of years ago, there was better work to be had there so really it could be anyone.

Determined to finish explaining the purpose of her visit, Daisy took a deep breath, a last sip of the coffee, and continued. "Anyway, after little Lottie was born, Mrs. Margaret just got weaker and sicker. Yet she seemed to have all of the energy in the world when it came to telling all the girls about the Lord. And we couldn't understand why she was so devoted to a God who was letting her be that sick."

Lottie dashed a tear from her eye and stood to bounce Ida who had begun to fret.

"She told me about the Lord so many times that I was thinking that I actually knew him, I mean personal-like the way you know the butcher or the milkman. Of course it wasn't until I met Michael – he was working for the grocer Mr. Philip bought from – that I began to really understand what it meant to accept Jesus as my savior and to have a relationship with him."

Gracie's heart began to flood with emotion and she wasn't sure she would be able to control the sobs that were trapped in her throat. Her emotion was written clearly on her face and Daisy moved to sit very close to her and wrapped an arm about Gracie's shoulder.

"Dear girls, don't you now see why Mrs. Margaret was the dearest friend I ever had. Why, I married the only other friend that was half as good as her. But for your mother and my dear husband, I would still be a hopeless heathen living in a dance hall."

The emotion could no longer be suppressed and Gracie bolted from the room with a half-croaked, "Excuse me".

Alone in her bedroom, Gracie pulled out a clean handkerchief, then another. This was going to require a good long cry and she couldn't abandon her company for that long. She began to take deep breaths trying to calm herself. The breathing only loosed the sobs and she could not hold them back.

In a few moments Lottie joined her. "Gracie, dear, hasn't Daisy brought us the most precious story of our mother? Why has it made you cry like this?"

Again, trying to consciously breathe, Gracie tried to put the myriad of feelings into words for her sister. "Yes, it is the most wonderful story. But don't you see how convicting it is that Mother was working for the Lord even as she was dying. Oh Lottie, do you think she knew she was dying when she was witnessing about God's greatness?"

Lottie gently rubbed her back, "Yes, I'm sure she knew that her time was limited at the first signs of consumption.

Don't you remember Grandma saying that she knew almost the minute they carried her into the house when we first arrived back in Tennessee? But Mother had work to finish before she could go home – either home to Tennessee or home to her Lord."

Gracie was nodding as the tears began to slow. "Then why am I here wallowing in my own misery when I have plenty of life before me?"

"Misery? What is miserable about your life Gracie?"

She couldn't even look at her sister as she answered, "Oh Lottie, I've been so jealous that you have little Ida and I've been married a full year longer than you and Stephen and I have no children. I begin to despair that we never will have any. And now I seem to be expected to help other women birth their own babies. I don't think I can bear it."

Lottie wrapped her sister in her arms as the sobs renewed. She gently rocked her and shushed her just as she did baby Ida. "Maybe God is giving you a chance to love all these babies – more babies than you could ever hope to raise."

Gracie sat up and looked deep into her sister's eyes. She blinked, trying to focus through the tears that clung to her eyeballs. She was speechless and Lottie seemed to understand it and offered only a gentle smile.

Lottie kissed her on the cheek and stepped out of the room as quietly as she had entered. Gracie knew her baby sister would be playing hostess as long as Gracie needed to compose herself.

Gracie smiled, thinking of the kind, sweet spirit Lottie always possessed. Lighthearted and jovial as she was, there were times that she seemed to express the wisdom of the ages. *Thank you Lord for this precious sister. You and I have a lot to talk about, don't we Lord? I promise to spend some good time alone with you just as soon as the people are gone from my house."*

The Bourkes left well before supper with Daniel, Lottie and Ida loaded into their rented carriage. Gracie promised she and Stephen would be at Lottie's house the following day for supper and more fellowship with Daisy.

As the carriage moved out of sight, Stephen seemed to sense that his wife needed time alone and he made himself quite scarce for the remainder of the evening. She stood in the center of her suddenly quiet kitchen and looked from right to left pondering what she should do. As though a voice in her head was calling, she found herself in her rocker by the window, Bible in hand.

Unable to read, she stared at the page until she shook her head and reminded herself aloud, "You are supposed to be talking this over with the Lord."

Her prayer preparations were interrupted by a soft pecking on the door which caused her to jump like a gunshot would have. She turned her head to the window and saw the backside of skirts at her door. *How did I not see her walking up? And who could that be?*

But there was no time to find answers to her questions for she had to answer the door.

The door opened to reveal a very young lady, a complete stranger to Gracie.

"Good afternoon," Gracie greeted the stranger.

"Howdy ma'am. Are you Mizz Gracie?"

At the nod of Gracie's head, she continued, "I live over in Muddy Pond and we been hearin' that you're catchin' babies now and my sister she asked me to come by and see if you would be willin' to come talk to her about helping when her time comes. She's expectin' to deliver in about a month. Would you come talk to her?"

This seemed a strange request and Gracie had never even been to Muddy Pond. Stephen had talked about the treacherous drive across the often raging Hurricane Creek to reach the hillside community but Gracie never imagined venturing there herself. Yet, this young lady seemed so earnest in her request.

"How did you hear that I would help in birthing?"

"Well Ma'am, I don't know just 'xactly who told us, but everybody knows that you done delivered Mildy Baldwin's baby boy, and after she done lost two before, and Mildy's Ma said no one could've done better than you did with Mildy.

This girl's compliments were certainly swaying her decision. At last she gave her answer, "Well if your sister isn't due for another month, I guess I have some time don't I?"

The strange visitor nodded her head vigorously.

"Okay, I'll come over there before the week is out. What is your sister's name?"

"She's Georgie Wilson, Ma'am and we certainly thank you. We'll be lookin' for you."

With that the girl turned and left. Gracie realized that she had not even invited her in the door and she felt awful to have treated a visitor like that. But she reflected that the girl scarcely gave her a chance. *What a strange young girl. I can't imagine what I'll find in her sister. Muddy Pond? How can I ever make it so far when a baby is coming? Wonder why they don't have a midwife over there?*

Her musings stopped when her eye caught the open bible on her chair. *Lord, I've still not spent any time with you, have I?*

She took her seat again with the precious book on her lap, but the words would not come. The sharp conviction she'd felt as she listened to Daisy Bourke was still fresh in her mind, yet she could not pray about it.

Her eyes sought the sun out her west-facing window and judged she would have a couple of hours before dusk. Without thinking further, the grabbed her wrapper and slipped out the back door. She chose to walk eastward, away from Lottie's house and as her feet trod the familiar cow paths, her heart began to open.

She lost all track of time and would have walked well out of the Ingles property had the big bluff overlooking Slate Creek not stood in her way. As she peered into the gulf, she felt she was looking deep into her own soul. Finally she was able to pray.

Alone in the vast woodland, she prayed aloud and permitted the tears to flow unchecked.

"Lord, here I have this wonderful husband and we live among all of his family and he comes from such a large family. I was sure I would be able to give him children. Grandma would probably say I'm fretting over nothing, and after all, we've only been married two years. Somehow I just know that you're trying to teach me something. Please speak to my heart and make me understand this lesson."

She sat on a rock outcropping and waited. Whether she was waiting for God's voice to echo out of the deep gulf or for an angel to appear beside her, she did not know. Somehow in the silence God did speak; he spoke quietly within her heart.

Thoughts and images passed through her mind – images of Mildy Baldwin, of the young Wilson girl appearing at her door, of Grandma attending Neldie Turner. She tried to channel her thoughts.

"Mrs. Bourke's testimony about Mother was beautiful. Will anyone have such a story to tell about my life?"

The silence stretched on as birds glided down toward the slow moving creek below. She heard in her mind the opinion Mrs. Key had spread through the community of her work with Mildy, of Lafayette Baldwin repeating Mrs. Reeder's direction to get Gracie and no one else.

"Father God, I am sorry that I cannot seem to focus on the matter at hand."

Somehow the apology fell back to her, she knew then that this was not just her mind wandering. "Lord, why do I keep thinking about these women?"

Again she heard Mrs. Key and Mrs. Reeder and even Aunt Bithy as they spoke of her skill and her gift with the babies.

"What about MY babies?" She cried out to God.

"*Gracie, if you will obey me I will give you more babies than any woman on this mountain.*" The statement was so clear to her she jerked her head from right to left trying to see the source. Had someone happened upon her? Had an angel actually appeared? But there was no one to be seen. No cloud hovered over the bluff. No loud thundering followed the statement. She knew that God had spoken to her heart, but spoken so clearly that she could not mistake the message.

"I don't know how Lord."

"*Trust me,*" was the answer. She knew it was all the answer she would get. It was all the answer she would need.

For another long moment she stared down toward the water then slowly rose and turned toward the setting sun to make her way home.

Gracie could see her little home sitting way across the field and saw warm light spill from the windows as Stephen lit a lamp for the evening. She picked up her pace knowing her husband would need his supper and regretting that she was absent when he came in for the evening.

As she opened the back door, Stephen knelt at the fireplace pulling hot coals to the front to warm the big kettle hanging from its iron hook. She smiled at him, thankful that he was always ready to help even in jobs she thought belonged to her.

Stephen crossed the room to greet her, "You're out late and I'll bet you're freezing. The spring temperatures drop fast when the sun goes down."

Warmed by the brisk walk she laid her wrap aside and began to put together a quick supper. "I was down at the bluff praying." Gracie's eyes darted to her husband to determine if this statement brought a negative response but none was visible. "I didn't realize how late it had gotten till I started home and saw the setting sun. I'm sorry you have to wait for your supper."

"Gracie, I'd be a fool to ever complain that my wife spends too much time praying. That's a beautiful spot the Lord's made, but you be careful, it's a long drop down to Slate Creek."

"Oh, I noticed that. There were birds diving down toward the water so that I was looking over them. It's really breathtaking. Is that still Ingle land that far from the house?"

Stephen had removed his boots and pulled a worn newspaper across the table but still seemed interested in talking with his wife. "Yeah, that's the eastern border of Pappy Ingle's land. It runs along the creek a ways and meets some of the Gernt land."

Gracie recognized the Gernt landmark. Mr. Gernt was a German immigrant who had moved into Fentress county in recent years and purchased all of the land he could. He was now the biggest land owner in the county although he neither occupied nor tended most of the land.

"Well it's a lovely spot. I'm glad I didn't wander anywhere I wasn't supposed to." She chatted with her husband as she quickly pulled together a meal of fried pork, potatoes and cornbread with a garnish of pickle relish.

By the time she had the meal on the table, Stephen had finished his paper and brought in the evening's buckets of water. As Gracie took her seat beside him he reached wordlessly for her hand and bowed his head to return thanks to God for the meal.

"Father God, we thank you for your generous provision for our family. Thank you for my sweet wife who rushed home from her prayer-perch to cook it for me. Bless her Lord and answer her every prayer. In the name of your holy son we pray, amen."

Gracie kept her head down just a second past the 'amen'. When she raised her head, she saw Stephen looking tenderly into her eyes.

As he reached for the plate of meat he sought to understand what burdened his wife. "Did today's visitors bring trouble to your heart?"

Gracie truly wanted to share this with her husband but she felt deep shame to confess her unwillingness to completely surrender to God. With a deep breath, she tried to answer his question. "No, not really. Mrs. Bourke – Daisy – she had a beautiful story to tell. It seems that my mother was a great witness for the Lord. Daisy says she would never have been saved except that Mother told her about Jesus so many times. I never realized – I mean, she was so young when she died and Grandma was always very honest that Mother left home without their blessing or permission. But Grandma also taught us that when she returned, she had repented of all that."

Stephen wasn't entirely sure he was following his wife's explanation. "Gracie, that is the best thing you could ever learn about your mother. Why has it burdened you so?"

She laid her fork gently beside the plate and took a long sip of water as she tried to collect her thoughts. "I guess I would have thought I was better than that – I never ran away and I married you only after Grandma and Uncle Jesse gave us their blessing. Now I realize that Mother was much more obedient to serve God than me."

"How do you mean? You are certainly serving me well." Stephen gestured toward the meal and the home.

The giggle escaped before Gracie could catch it. "Be serious Stephen!"

He placed a large, work-worn hand over her smaller one. "You're right Gracie. God has placed a call to service on each of our lives and it is the most serious thing that we yield to that call. Isn't it wonderful to learn that your mother was serving him so faithfully and now, all these years later, we see fruit from her work?"

Gracie was again moved to tears and stood to leave, but Stephen held her arm and drew her close to his chair. "Don't leave me Gracie, we need to work through this together."

"But I'm going to cry." In fact the tears were already streaming down her face.

Her husband reached ever-so gently to wipe away the tears and he lightly pushed her back into her chair. "Tell me why you are crying."

"Oh, I'm just emotional. You know how women can get."

Stephen smiled at her, enjoying the woman he'd married. "I'm learning."

Gracie paused for a moment, wondering if this over-abundance of emotion could be an indicator that she was finally pregnant. Even as she asked herself the question, something within her told her that was not the issue now.

"Stephen, I'm sorry I haven't given you a baby yet."

His face split with a mischievous grin as he said, "Do you think you're in control of that?"

"Well, I can't help but think that if you'd married someone else, you might have two children by now, maybe even more."

"Gracie, you do make me smile. We'll have children when the good Lord wills it and not a minute before. Your Grandma taught you all about birthing babies; did she never tell you who was in charge of it all?"

She saw the teasing smile, heard the lilt in his voice. Still, Gracie felt deeply chastised by his words. "Stephen, I am going to go to our bedroom now because I need to finish up something with the Lord."

"I'm never going to stand in the way of that. I'll clean up in here." He held up a hand to stop the protest before she could utter a word and watched as she slipped out of the room.

The bedroom was dark and cool; the floor hard beneath her knees. Gracie was driven to pray and noticed none of the discomforts. As she closed her eyes and sought the words, her heart seemed to pray for her.

Lord, I come. My mother served you far from home and in less than ideal conditions. Surely I can serve you living among this precious family Stephen has given me. Use me Lord to your glory.

For a long moment Gracie remained prostrate, believing she must say something profound to her Lord. No words came beyond the honest surrender she'd offered. And then there was peace in her heart, quietness and a joy. She knew God had heard and accepted her surrender.

Softly she whispered, "Thank you, Lord." Then she rose and returned to her kitchen where Stephen was busily washing the supper dishes. He stopped as she entered the room and silently wrapped his arms around her.

Chapter 15

Supper at Lottie's house was a sweet time of fellowship. Daisy and Thomas fit right in with the Ingles and both Gracie and Lottie enjoyed their new friend.

She answered numerous questions about Margaret and Philip, providing missing pieces to their family puzzle that both had wondered about through the years.

"Mr. Philip is a strange bird, if that's not too disrespectful to say since he is your father."

Lottie shook her head and Gracie added a smile and said, "No, no. We don't know him at all and we've always wanted to know more about him. All we've ever had were a few letters through the years. Mostly though, he just sent money to Grandpa in a single folded paper sayin' it was to help with the children."

Lottie chimed in, "Did he never marry again?"

Daisy shook her head but could not look them in the eye as she answered. "He's just lived in that dance hall all these years. Really he's kind of married to the business, I think that was his focus even before your mother left."

Gracie didn't want her new friend to be uncomfortable so she tried to learn more about her. "Where do you and Mr. Bourke live now?"

Daisy smiled as she began to tell them about her new life. "We're still in Chicago, only out on the edge of town. We have nice rooms in a family house. Thomas found the rooms for us before we were married. He was very eager to get me out of Mr. Philip's house – even though he knew I'd never worked in the hall itself you know."

"How long have you been married?"

"Well it's been just about six months."

Thomas had been standing near the fireplace talking with Daniel and moved toward the ladies now to add, "She's talked about Mrs. Margaret's children since the first day and finally I told her that we would find you if the Lord would allow it."

"Such a long trip, I never dreamed of making such a trip." Lottie looked off into the distance as though she was trying to see the end of such a journey.

Daisy nodded her head, "It was ever so long. I would never have the courage to do it alone, but your mother set off with two little bitty children. Lottie, you were still in a basket, and Mrs. Margaret so sick. I wonder now that any of us let her go off like that. And I just knew when we watched the carriage drive away toward the trains, that I'd never again see my dear friend."

Gracie laid a hand on hers as she reminded her, "Well you won't see her again in this world but she's waitin' for all of us up in heaven."

"Yes, amen." Daisy pulled her embroidered hanky from her sleeve and dotted her eyes – an action she seemed to repeat every time the topic turned to Margaret Berai.

Gracie looked up to Thomas, "Thank you for bringing her. You will never know the blessing you have given us in doing so. We know so little about our mother's life in Chicago and to learn that she was instrumental in Daisy's salvation just means all the world to me."

Daisy leaned forward as she added, "It weren't just me. She had an impact on all the girls workin' there at that time. And she surely had an impact on her husband too."

"I hope so Daisy, I surely do. I don't reckon we'll ever know him but I have prayed for him all these years to come to know Jesus as his savior."

They talked on until well after dark with Thomas telling funny stories from his days working for the green grocer until he was able to establish a drayage business after buying his own team and wagon. The picture the couple painted of the bustling city left all four of their hosts wide-eyed and Lottie and Gracie just a little frightened. Daisy assured them it was just the only life she had ever known and living out on this beautiful farmland seemed pretty foreign to her.

"So you will go back to Chicago?"

"Yes, we'll have to leave tomorrow. Thomas' customers will find another means to deliver their goods if he doesn't return soon. He has a good business but it cannot be neglected."

Thomas beamed at his wife's understanding of his work as Stephen and Daniel nodded as they saw the similarity of his business to the demands of their farm-work.

When Stephen began to yawn Gracie moved to end the visit. "My husband won't be able to make the walk home if we wait any longer I'm afraid."

With hugs all around Lottie, Daniel, Daisy and Thomas stepped onto the porch with them. Daisy promised to write them after she left the next day and Gracie walked away hoping she'd be faithful to that promise.

129

Gracie closed her eyes at the very thought that she would doubt someone's faithfulness made her close her eyes asking God to forgive her.

Lord, I'm the one I hope will be faithful. I've made a promise to you and I desperately want to keep it.

Gracie's decision would be tested within the week, when another strange man knocked on her door begging her assistance in a moment of need. It was mid-day and Stephen was just finishing his dinner. As Stephen talked with their nervous visitor, Gracie calmly draped her woolen wrap over her head and shoulders and emerged from the kitchen with her basket in hand. Stephen appeared to know the man and after brief introductions and a few questions about the expectant mother, Gracie followed him into the rickety wagon and was off to do this work that God seemed so clearly to be leading.

Chapter 16

Gracie sat a basket of clean laundry on the kitchen table and began folding. Stephen slipped silently in from the front room and she jumped a little as he wrapped his arms around her waist.

"Oh, I didn't hear you come in."

"I heard you humming and couldn't resist."

"Hmm, while I've done the wash today I've been thinkin' about that Wilson girl. Her sister said it would be a month but I can't help the feeling that I need to go check on her. Anyhow I told the sister I'd come by week's end."

Stephen nodded, "You better do it then. Muddy Pond's a fur piece to walk. Why don't you just ride Ol' Molly? You don't have to carry much of anything with you and without the wagon you could cut through Key Town and come out at a good place to ford Hurricane Creek."

"How'll I find it? I've never even been past Campground and she didn't really tell me where they live."

Stephen smiled, "Wilsons are like Ingles – you get across the creek and anybody can point you to 'em. It's dry so the creek's way down right now, you won't have no trouble a'tall."

With a nod of her head she declared, "Okay, I'll do it first thing tomorrow."

Stephen mirrored her nod, "Then I'll put the mare in the barn when I milk tonight so she'll be rarin' to go come morning."

The Lord blessed Gracie's decision with a bright sunrise and cloudless sky. She fried meat and potatoes and buttered Mother Ingle's day-old bread for Stephen's breakfast. By the time she'd cleaned the dishes he had the little mare tied by the back door. "I love you Gracie Ingle. You be careful out there nursin' the needy."

She smiled and stood on tiptoes to kiss him goodbye.

Gracie was as comfortable on a horse's bare back as she was in a saddle. She feared her neighbors would not approve of her riding like a man yet she reminded herself that she was following her own husband's wishes today. "Molly girl, we'll just have to take care of each other, won't we?"

The horse snorted at the sound of her voice on the quiet morning. Farmers tending to their morning's chores threw hands up to greet her and Molly paused where a spring muddied the dirt road. Through the trip Gracie prayed, asking God why she felt it necessary to visit this young girl before they sent for her. She heard no answer but she gave the horse a little bump with her heel as her own sense of urgency rose.

The Hurricane Creek was wide as ever but barely deep enough to cover Molly's hooves. Both horse and rider looked up at the steep hill they faced on the west side of the creek. As the terrain levelled out a girl turned in the road to watch Gracie approaching.

"Mornin'!" Gracie called.

"Mornin'."

"I'm glad I saw you. Do you know where Georgie Wilson lives? Am I close to the house?"

The girl nodded, her eyes sliding from Gracie's face to her skirts hiked up by the spread across the horse's withers. "Thur my cousins. Live behind my Granny just a little piece on down the road yonder."

Gracie smiled all the brighter for the girl's glum response, "I thank ya'."

"I'm goin' to help my Granny for the day. She can't do ever-thing the way she used to."

"Well maybe I will see you a little later then. I'll head on to see if I can find Georgie now."

As she walked the horse away she heard the scratching sound resume and knew the girl was following her and dragging her stick along the roadway` . Within a few minutes a farm appeared among the thick trees and sure enough a small log house sat behind the neat white farmhouse. Gracie slipped from the saddle and led the horse down a well-worn footpath leading straight to the front porch. Before she could step onto the porch the door opened scraping loudly against the floorboards and out stepped the same girl who had visited Gracie.

"You're Mizz Gracie. Wha'cha doin' over here?"

"Well hello to you. Do you know that you never told me your name? Only told me it was your sister Georgie what needed my help."

"I'm Margie. Sorry about that. Didn't mean no disrespect not tellin you who I was."

"It is very nice to know you Margie. I've had your sister on my heart and thought I ought to come talk with her."

Margie Wilson cocked her head as though she were weighing whether Gracie spoke the truth. "Georgie ain't feelin' good today."

"Well, then it's a good thing I've come."

Margie held fast her position in front of the open door. "Mizz Reeder said she wouldn't even come to catch the baby. Why would you come when we ain't sent for ya'?"

Gracie shrugged her shoulders, "Can't explain it, I reckon The Good Lord just puts it on me sometimes to check on folks."

"The Lord don't have no dealin's with us."

"Oh Margie, why-ever would you say a thing like that? God is here with you the same as he is at my house in Martha Washington."

"Oh I guess he's around here, just don't have much use for us Wilsons."

Gracie breathed a quick, silent prayer as she realized the sorrow here was far greater than labor pains. She flipped the reins from her hand over the short hitching rail beside the house and stepped up to join her new friend on the porch. "Will you let me talk to your sister now?"

Margie stepped out of the doorway without another word. The darkness of the cabin pushed back as Gracie stepped in from the bright morning. The smell of breakfast mingled with wood smoke and a sweet grassy scent that drew Gracie's eyes up to the rafters. Bundled handfuls of dried herbs waved slightly from their tethers to the exposed rafters. Beds built into two walls were topped with patchwork quilts and one of the beds held a mass that Gracie assumed to be her patient.

Glancing back at Margie she pointed to the bed, "Georgie?"

Margie only nodded.

Gracie spoke softly, "Georgie, my name's Gracie Ingle and I thought I'd come check on you."

The disheveled head that peeped from the covers was as leery as her sister. "Why you want to do that?"

Gracie smiled, "Don't know 'xactly, just thought I ought to. How are you feeling?"

"Well I'm huge and I'm tired of being penned up in this ol' house. And Margie ain't ever much company but she's worse than ever lately." She put both hands on her protruding stomach, "I just want this thing gone."

Gracie sucked in a deep breath, "Oh Georgie, you mustn't talk like that. The Good Lord will bring this little baby into the world in His own time."

"God ain't got nothin' to do with this. You just ask anybody you meet on the road whil'st you're gettin' yourself back to Martha Washington." With that, Georgia turned to face the wall.

"Georgie, your sister said it would be a few more weeks, but I'd like to try to figure when we might expect you to give birth."

Georgia wouldn't answer and made no sound, no indication that she could hear Gracie.

Gracie turned and saw that Margie had gone back onto the porch. She followed her outside.

Margie looked up from the bench she sat on without a word.

"I know these last few weeks carryin' a baby are hard. She will settle into motherhood when she can hold that precious baby in her arms."

Margie shrugged and stared back at the floor.

"Where is her husband?"

"Ain't got one."

"Oh. Where are your parents?"

"Ain't got none."

Gracie looked around. The cabin was small but the chinking between the logs seemed sound and the inside had been clean. She looked over Margie trying to decide her age. "It's just you and Georgie? How long have you been alone here? Is that your Granny's house?"

Margie nodded, "Pawpaw made us move out here when Georgie fell pregnant. They raised us but now Granny says she's failed and she's too old to do anymore. Says she can't raise another one."

"Did the baby's daddy not want to make it right?"

"Georgie don't go with nobody in particular. Just whoever pays her some attention. And nobody's paid her no attention since she started showin' with this baby. That's when she started bein' so mean."

Gracie stared at the floorboards just as Margie did. *Lord what am I to do with this situation?*

"Is that why Mrs. Reeder wouldn't help her?"

"Yeah, I reckon. Lot's of folk don't have much to do with us."

"What about your church? Don't you have friends there?"

The girl's head slowly wagged from side to side, "Don't go to church. Never have really. There's a church right up on the hill yonder."

Gracie straightened up, pivoted on her heel and walked directly back to Georgia's bedside. "Miss Wilson, God has laid you on my heart and I do not intend to ignore that. I will help you through this but you will have to help me. Now, have you done anything to get ready for this baby? Do you have diapers or blankets? Have you made any clothes at all?"

Georgia pulled the quilt down just enough to peer out at Gracie. "No."

"Well we have plenty of work to do, don't we? You get out of that bed and let me take a look at you."

Her eyes darted to the doorway, Gracie wondered if she was looking for her sister or maybe thinking of running away. Georgia swung a leg off the bed and planted bare feet before pushing herself off the bed with her hands.

A paper-thin dress with numerous patches covered a rail-thin body; it stretched taut only over her belly. Georgia turned sunken eyes up to Gracie and laid one hand over her abdomen.

"My dear what have you been eating?"

Her tone was gentler than when she first spoke to Gracie, "Why do you care?"

"I care because there is a new life here that we must care for. I care because God has put you in my path to care for."

"Do you really think God cares anything about me? Or this child that's come from my own sin?"

Gracie wrapped an arm around the thin shoulder, "Georgie, don't you know that the Bible tells us that God has loved us with an *everlasting* love? And he said he loved the whole world enough to send his own son."

Georgia hung her head, "I don't think that's talkin' about me."

"Oh my dear friend, it is talking about you and me and Margie… and your baby too."

Her hand absently stroked her pregnant stomach. Gracie took a deep breath as she sensed a heart opening before her.

"You said this baby came from your sin – does that mean you understand that you are a sinner?"

"Well I've been told I'm a sinner since my earliest memory."

Gracie turned to face her, "You need to realize that your sin is no different than mine or any of the rest of the world. Jesus had to die to pay for my sins just the same as yours. And his death pays for your sins just the same as mine."

She shrugged, "I don' t know about that. I been hearin' about you; you married one of the Ingles and you live on their farms with all that good cleared land and they have a mill and everything."

Gracie chuckled, "And I live in a house that was used for a barn last year! I have a great family and I'm thankful for it, but God certainly doesn't see any difference in me and you."

"Is that right?" Georgia cocked her head back assessing Gracie.

"Oh yes. He asks only that you admit you are a sinner and believe that Jesus can forgive you of your sins."

"Well I done told you I sure am a sinner. What if I do believe Jesus would forgive me?"

Tears welled at the corners of Gracie's eyes as she steeled her voice to clearly explain, "Then all that would be left would be to confess it all to him – if you prayed and told the Lord that you want to know Jesus as your savior then he would come into your life and you would be one of his children."

"Just like that? Right away? Then everything would be alright?"

"Georgie, it takes no time at all to be saved from your sins. As for everything else, God will walk with you through all the troubles of this world – including the troubles your own sins have brought on you."

"I'd like that. Will you help me?"

"I will but all you need to do is ask him to forgive your sins. Just talk to God like you're talkin' to me." Gracie sat on the side of the bed and Georgia sat beside her.

They joined hands and Georgia began to pray, "Lord I never knew you were there for the likes of me. You know I'm a sinner but I don't want to be. Thank you for sending Jesus to die to pay for my sins and I want him to be my savior if you would kindly forgive me of my sins."

She raised reddened eyes to meet Gracie's, "Is that the right way?"

Her words burst forth as laughter, "It certainly is right!"

Gracie lifted her face toward heaven but stopped short when she saw Margie watching the whole scene. The girl stood frozen, almost mesmerized. It was Georgia who finally broke the silence.

"Margie, I done got saved. Would you have ever thought that could be?

Margie just shook her head.

Gracie stood and moved toward her, "Margie you look almost scared, what's the matter? Do you understand what Georgie is saying?"

Margie bolted from the room and was completely out of sight before Gracie could follow.

"Mizz Gracie, you don't worry about her. I'll help her now that I understand."

Gracie grasped her hand, "Georgie, I know you will. You'll no doubt help a lot of people. Jesus said the one that's forgiven of much will love much. I always think that's more about the ones that realize how very much God has forgiven because we all have an awful lot of sin."

Georgia just nodded.

"Now, we need to get down to business of getting ready for this baby - and getting some weight on you."

She looked around the little cabin again, "How have you and Margie been eating? Do your grandparents help you with food? Is there any family that's supplying you with meat?"

Georgia shook her head, "We've scrounged up what we could through the winter." She dropped her head as the added, "It wasn't always right though."

"Well, I'd just take you with me except that I'm on horseback. Let me get home and see what I can work out and I'll be back in a day or two."

Georgia stepped out onto the porch with her, "Thank you Mizz Gracie. I b'lieve I'll take the pole down to the creek and see if I can catch a mess of fish for supper. And there's greens a'plenty now so I'll put Margie to collecting them."

"Georgie that sounds wonderful. We've got to get some good food in you – you'll need plenty of strength to give birth."

She laid her hand across her stomach again and for the first time she smiled.

Chapter 17

The tree lined path grew eerie with lengthening shadows as Gracie made her way back to Martha Washington. She tried to talk to the mare but found her thoughts returning again and again to the shack she'd left in Muddy Pond.

"Molly, I can't keep my head in this trip so it's going to be up to you to make the turn toward Keytown otherwise we'll have to go all the way to Campground and it will be pitch dark before we can get home."

The horse nodded her head either in acknowledgment of the assignment or in time with her steady steps and Gracie lifted her head to call out for God's help.

Lord you know I didn't go over there to lead that girl to you but I thank you for taking charge of the day. Now what? Surely you don't mean for her and that little baby to come home to you by starvation. But how am I going to feed her? Should I have brought her home with me? Will she be okay before I can get back?

The questions petered out as the heavens answered only with a distant call of the whippoorwill and chirping crickets. Gracie's heart seemed to keep time with the horse's hooves and her mind conjured Stephen's face.

"Thank you Lord," she whispered as she realized her husband would help her.

And thank you for giving me a man what supports this work you've called me to.

The lamps were lit in the Ingle houses as Gracie weaved through the neighborhood. She heard the creak of a rocker on one porch, the voices of children not yet called in to supper. Her eyes fixed on the single light that she knew Stephen would be sitting in front of and she didn't have to kick the horse to increase their pace.

Stephen met her halfway between the barn and house, "Glad you're home Gracie. It was a long day, huh?"

Nodding, she slipped from the saddle. "Long, but good Stephen."

He wrapped one arm around her waist as he led the horse into the open barn door and propelled Gracie along as well.

"Tell me all about it while I get this saddle off. Molly was settin' a good pace there on the end. We'll need to give her a good rub down."

"I'll help you. Did you get some supper?"

"Warmed up the beans. Mama brought cornbread at dinnertime so that was good with it."

"Cold though. Man should not have to be eatin' cold cornbread. I'm sorry Stephen."

"Shh, none of that. Tell me how you found the Wilsons."

Gracie paused her brush on Molly's neck, "I'll tell you every detail but let me start at the end. I didn't plan it and I don't really know how it happened, but Georgia Wilson got right with The Lord today."

"Well you don't say!" Stephen's voice rose as his grin widened. "I reckon you've had a regular prayer meetin' on that ride home."

She chuckled at his joy, "I should'a but instead I've been burdened for those two girls."

"Burdened? But Georgie's whole life will change now that she's got God in it. I don't know 'em much, but the Wilsons have the name of bein' a rough bunch. That little lady may do a work in the whole family."

"Maybe – I guess my faith is small. The thing is that she and Margie have been put out of their grandfather's home and I think they're about half starved. Georgia said they'd gotten by on whatever they could scrounge."

Stephen opened the back door and swatted the horse's flank. He turned back to his wife and nodded toward the house.

Gracie was accustomed to Stephen's quiet moments. She tried to give him time to work out the plan she knew was forming in his head.

She was suddenly starving and went straight to dipping some of the still-warm beans and filling a glass with milk. As she sat down beside Stephen she tried to probe him with here look. "What are you thinking?"

"Hmm?" Stephen inhaled deeply as though he'd been thinking so hard he'd forgotten to breath. "Oh, I guess I was wondering about hungry wintertimes. Spring's here for good now so the land will begin to feed us again."

"Yeah, Georgie was already saying she'd send her sister to pick greens and she was hoping to catch fish for their supper."

"Sounds like a good meal, don't it? Something 'bout the smell of spring makes me crave greens."

Gracie studied her uneaten food. She closed her eyes to pray, *Lord I thank you for this food. Please fill a plate for Georgia and Margie tonight as well.*

Stephen responded to her silent prayer, "I'll ask Uncle George if his youngest can go over there with some food stuffs tomorrow."

Gracie beamed, "Oh Stephen, thank you. I just know he'll let Jack and Mandie go and they'll be kind to the girls and oh, can we spare them anything you reckon?"

She stood to make preparations and felt Stephens firm hand pulling her back into her chair.

"We'll find 'em plenty of stuff to take but you have to take care of you first. Eat Gracie."

She smiled but didn't sit, instead she thanked her husband with a warm embrace. "I knew you'd have a plan, I think the Lord told me you would take care of everything."

Stephen was still pushing her back to her chair, "Then why were you frettin' so?"

"Just a lack of faith I guess. You know Stephen today's visit really shook my faith at first. I'm afraid when I saw that house and heard how the old man Wilson had put them out of his own home, and then Georgia had such an awful turn when I first met her that I was asking God, why her and not me?"

"What do you mean? Gracie there's just no comparison."

"No Stephen, I mean why would God give her a child when he hasn't given us one?"

"Well Gracie Ingle, but for that baby Georgie might not have met you and might never have been saved from her sins. That baby's doing great work for the Lord before he's even born."

"Oh Stephen, of course you're right. And I really do know that God's got a plan for us too – just wish I knew more about that plan."

Stephen let Gracie sleep late the next morning; she was just swinging the coffeepot back over the warming flames when he stepped through the front door.

"Got Jack and Mandie all loaded up with some potted meat, flour, lard and a jug of milk."

Gracie shook her head to clear out the last hint of sleepiness, "What time is it? Have I slept the whole day away?"

"No, no. If you tell my mama and Aunt Bithy that there's a chance to help somebody then you want to stand out of their way or they'll flat run over you gettin' stuff together. I had to stop them or they would've loaded the wagon to its limit."

Gracie smiled and breathed a prayer of thanksgiving for this precious family God had placed her in.

Chapter 18

Every week there seemed to be someone in need and they began to come to Gracie in droves. Gracie talked with Mother Ingle often and soon learned she could rely on Stephen's mother to comfort, advise or correct her.

"Gracie the neighbors are a-wearin' a path to y'ore house. What do they all want?"

Gracie took a deep breath trying to steel herself for a reprimand. "Well some of 'em have babies on the way and want to ask me to plan on catchin' for 'em. Sometimes they have pains or sickness in their family and they ask me about healing tricks. I don't know where they've all come from."

Katherine chuckled, "Gracie, honey the word had already passed around that Stephen had married you and brought you home from Elmore. The neighbors would mostly have waited to meet you at church or a funeral, but when you went down and helped lil' Mildy Baldwin well that news spread like a brush f'ar."

"Oh! You know folks were always comin' by for my Grandma's help; it was that way my whole life. I never thought about how it all got started." Gracie swung the hook bearing a simmering stew back toward the flame as she turned to her mother-in-law.

"Guess it's always the same. Sometimes the best way to help out a neighbor is to pass the word along when you hear somethin' helpful. Gracie, how are you feeling about all that company?"

She shrugged, "I worry more about how Stephen feels about it – and you and Pappy Ingle. Do y'uns think I'm not keepin' house the way I should or neglectin' my husband? My Grandma she was an old woman when she went around helpin' everybody. Her kids were mostly grown and there were lots of hands around to help with her work at home."

Katherine stopped with a bowl and dishcloth held in mid-air. "Gracie, honey, the good Lord has gifted you. It would just be wrong for me or Jury to criticize you doing what He's called you to do. You'll find a way to get your doin's done – and me and Betty and all the Ingle youngins around here will help out."

Gracie smiled at what was more an assumption of help than an offer. Then one word from Mother Ingle settled on her.

"Called?" She whispered the question but punctuated it with saucer-sized eyes.

Katherine cocked her head, "Sometimes it's easiest for people lookin' in from the outside to see the hand of God on your life. Yes, Gracie, you have a callin' on you to help and to heal. What you do with that is up to you but I'm not going to answer to my maker for hinderin' you."

"Do you think others in the community see that 'call' as well? Is that why they come to me instead of someone older and wiser?"

"Hmmf" Katherine sniffed, "Age don't mean nothin' when God's the one a'callin. How old was David when God called him? Or Samuel?"

"Well Mother Ingle, I'd hardly compare myself to those mighty men."

"Child, it's not the man I'm comparing, it's the calling."

Gracie smiled, finding no argument and wondered, *This is the wise woman, why don't people go to her with their questions?*

Mother Ingle was as good as her promise to help Gracie. She regularly made extra bread and brought loaves to Stephen and Gracie, hoping to save Gracie the day-long chore. She would arrive on Gracie's laundry day and cut the washing time in half by wringing and hanging every piece Gracie took from the boiling water.

The close relationship the Ingle family enjoyed wrapped itself around Gracie. She found herself as comfortable in Mother Ingle's house as she was in her own and she frequently stopped there when making her way home after a call.

On an unusually warm day in early June, Gracie made just such a stop. The kitchen door was standing open and she called as she stepped across the threshold "Mother Ingle, are you home?"

The voice surprised her as it came from behind, "Yes dear, I'm here. Been out to the cellar storing a run of pickles."

"What? Have you already put up pickles? My word, I'm behind. I don't even think I have enough cucumbers for a run yet."

"Well, you just don't worry about it. I reckon I'll have enough for both our households. Stephen don't much care for 'em anyways. Sit yourself down there and we'll have a sip of coffee together. Where you comin' from today?"

As she sat at the familiar table, Gracie suddenly realized just how exhausted she was. "I've been up to Millertown. It was a false alarm, but the young girl sure thought she was deliverin' any minute. That baby won't be here for some weeks yet, unless I miss my guess."

As Katherine Ingle busied herself boiling coffee and cutting big slices of last night's cake, Gracie pulled a tattered newspaper to her. While news was often hard to come by on the mountain, Algurial Ingle brought a paper home everytime he visited any store that carried them. The papers were read and shared until the print was practically worn from the pages. Once illegible, the paper found additional uses around the farm. The date on this paper was nearly a month ago.

"Was there any worthwhile news in this paper?"

Katherine's back was to her as she spoke over her shoulder, "Well I don't know, I looked at it, but Jury is the one that could quote it back for you. You and him are the biggest readers I've ever seen."

She glanced over the headlines bringing information from around the country. "Well Grandpa Elmore always told us to read anything we could get our hands on. Reading was really hard for him, I think, so he always wanted me and Lottie practicing…" Here voice trailed off as an article engrossed her.

She skimmed over a heading about "Riots in Haymarket Square" with little interest. However, as she read down the page, she realized this Haymarket Square was in Chicago and she immediately began paying closer attention. The paper reported that a bomb had been thrown at police during some kind of public meeting, and several people had been killed. No names were given and the exact number of deaths seemed unclear.

At some point in her reading, the coffee and cake had appeared in front of Gracie.

"What caught your attention child?" Katherine questioned Grace when she finally looked up.

"Some kind of trouble in Chicago."

"Oh, you don't think your father could be involved?" Katherine lifted her pewter mug prompting Gracie to test the hot coffee herself.

"Well, I have no way of knowing. I would think the old man would stay at home and out of trouble, but I know so little about him that I wouldn't know whether to expect him to be involved or not. And there must be an awful lot of people in Chicago."

"When have you had word from your father?"

Still holding an empty fork, Gracie stared off into space as though she were looking at a calendar in her head. "I really don't know. But I tell you what, I think I should go over to Lottie's and see if she's had word. I haven't even seen her in more than a week."

"You go right on, a good visit with your sister will probably rest you anyway."

Gracie planted a quick kiss on her mother-in-law's cheek and took a last gulp of coffee. "Thank you! Can I borrow this paper?"

"Take it. We've read it front to back."

Gracie realized how badly she needed a good visit with her sister when she saw how quickly her feet crossed the field to the little house by the branch. She found Lottie rocking Ida Frances on the front porch. Her face lit up when she recognized her sister.

"I'm awfully glad to see you Gracie, but land sakes you're movin fast."

Gracie took a deep breath as she pulled a split bottom chair closer. "I saw this paper at Mother Ingle's and thought I should bring it over."

"What's it about?"

"Well, it's this article about Chicago that caught my eye. They've had some kind of riot there and some people got killed. 'Course, like I was telling Mother Ingle, there must be an awful lot of people in Chicago so maybe it's silly to be concerned about our father, but somehow I am."

"I don't think that's silly. He's really getting on in years – how old would he be now? Up in sixty?"

Gracie took a moment to calculate his age, based on her own. "I'll be twenty-two in September and Grandma always thought he was about forty-five when I was born, Law' that would make him sixty-seven now. Am I countin' that right?"

"It sounds right. Surely a man that age wouldn't be out in a mess like that. But who knows. I reckon he's still running his own business and living there by himself."

Both ladies sat silently for a moment, the only noise the steady rhythm of the rocker and the chirping of birds. Finally, Gracie decided what must be done. "I'm going to write to him. Without Grandma to remind me to do it every few weeks, I've hardly written a line to him since moving to Martha Washington. Did we even tell him about Ida Frances' birth?"

Lottie abruptly stopped the rocker as her jaw dropped open. "Oh Gracie, you know I didn't. Why that's unforgivable. My own father and he doesn't know about his granddaughter! I'll write that letter for you and we'll kill two birds with one stone."

Gracie agreed and they turned the visit to more comfortable subjects. Lottie wanted updates on all of Gracie's babies – she always said every baby her sister delivered was a little bit Gracie's. In turn, Gracie wanted to know about all of her niece's recent accomplishments. The jingle of harness as Daniel drove his team in from the field reminded them of both the time and their evening responsibilities. After quick good-byes, Gracie hurried back across the field to her own home.

Weeks passed with no word from Philip Berai. Gracie and Lottie rarely passed each other's house without sticking a head in for a quick hello. But at this time, they were ever more likely to stop by, hoping the other had received the much-anticipated letter.

"Would we have gotten word if he was hurt?" "Did you ever try to figure how long the post took to reach Chicago?" Each sister questioned the other and surprised herself at the level of concern she felt for this relative stranger.

Gracie finally posed the unspoken question, "Would you ever have thought we'd be so worried about him? I mean, we don't even know him."

"But he's still our father. Don't you guess it's just a natural response when your kin are in danger?" Lottie had clearly asked herself the same questions before.

"I know that you are right, of course. I guess I never wondered so much about him until I was afraid he'd been hurt, or even – well, you know a lot of folks were actually killed in the rioting."

"Oh Gracie, don't even say that."

"Well Lottie sayin' it won't make it any more or less true. Whatever has happened is already done, we just have to learn the truth and deal with it."

Lottie turned her eyes out the window and seemed to scan the horizon as though their distant father would suddenly appear as the story went when he first arrived at Grandpa Elmore's farm and met their mother. With a deep breath she turned back to her sister, "We'll surely get word before long – one way or the other."

It was three more weeks before the letter finally arrived, written in the same crude script they had always identified as their father's. Perhaps his pen was a little shakier now, but the tone was as strong as ever.

I am unharmed by the recent unrest but very much annoyed. These people have ridiculous demands wanting shorter work days and complaining about the police. I could tell them a thing or two about police brutality - the Chicago officers are like your favorite uncle bouncing a child on his knee compared to the law enforcers in Italy. You know, I've seen them beat a boy mercilessly for taking a piece of bread and him about to starve....

Philip's letter was longer than any the sisters could remember. After reading it several times, Gracie realized she had probably learned more about her father in the last few minutes than she'd ever known before. It became clear that he'd done a lot of hard work and seen much trouble before coming to America. His letter mentioned working to make a fortune in America and Grandma had sometimes mentioned that wealth was his primary goal. Looking back, Gracie realized that her grandparents hadn't really approved of his staying in Chicago where he thought there was more money to be made while his daughters grew up a world away in Tennessee.

Two crisp dollar bills fluttered into Gracie's lap as the letter unfolded and they were only mentioned in a short post script. *'Money for the child and Gracie's new home',* their father wrote.

Chapter 19

Mandie Ingle pecked the doorframe as she called out, "Aunt Gracie, are ya' home?"

"Oh yes, come right on in. I'm just turning this ol' straw tick; I'll be right there."

Mandie walked right into the bedroom, "Well, let me help you. You never will get it smoothed out by yourself, will you?"

With a deep breath, Gracie smiled her thanks, "It sure is a lot easier with four hands instead of two. How are you today Mandie? I'm surprised Aunt Bithy could spare you today with that big field of beans ready to pick, and I know she's got all of y'uns pickin' blackberries."

Mandy giggled, "I's tryin' to sneak away from all that work. My fingers will be purple till kingdom come if I keep pickin them berries."

Gracie patted her shoulder as she ushered her back toward the kitchen, "Well you're not gonna' work here, let's get a glass of cool water and sit in the shade."

"Sounds good to me. Only I wanted to come by and tell you that me and Jack went over to see those Wilson girls yesterday."

"Mandie, thank you so much for caring for them. How did you find Georgie?"

"Her time's a-comin' close; I just know it is."

Gracie nodded as she led her guest out the back door. With her free hand she dragged a split bottom chair off the low porch and settled it under the big maple tree that cast deep shade over the neatly swept dirt yard.

"I figured I'd be hearing from them before long."

Mandie pushed the chair back on two legs and starred up into the tree. "It's not the baby that worries me Aunt Gracie."

"What then?"

"Well you told me and Georgie told me that she gave her life to the Lord and I'm just tickled to know that. But she's not goin to church and I don't see how she could stay away from God's house if she was really his child."

With a deep breath, Gracie closed her eyes and asked God for wisdom. "I'm sure it's very hard for her to go to church. The people in Muddy Pond look at her and just see the wild ways of her past. It will take time for them to realize that she is a new creature – that's what the Bible calls her, ain't it?"

Mandie smiled as the chair plunked back onto four legs, "Yes it is, and Aunt Gracie I can see that new creature. Georgie is really a sweet girl – oh she don't know to say 'Yes ma'am' and, 'Praise the Lord' the way me and Jack have always been taught, but she's purely thankful when we show up. And she don't really want to take the food and clothes that we've brung with us."

"Well once the baby comes she will find her way in the community, I'm sure."

"You know she talks about raisin' that baby in church. Do you reckon they'll let her in?"

"Oh, I'm sure the church will do more than let her attend. God will do a work in the ones that truly believe in him."

"Thank you Aunt Gracie. You know it always helps me to come talk to you."

"Well, Mandie, you can come talk to me anytime especially if you turn-in and help like you did with that straw tick." She grinned at the young girl, "When will you see Georgie again?",

"I think I'll walk over there now."

"Now! Child you'd never get back a-fore dark."

"But I won't have to pick no berries today! Wait, I'll take a basket along with me and pick a few on the way to give to Margie and Georgie."

Gracie wrapped the girl in her arms, "I don't think Aunt Bithy will have a thing to say against that idea."

As she watched Mandie from her front gate, Gracie breathed a prayer for this budding friendship and for Georgia's growing faith in the Lord.

Thank you Lord for giving Mandie Ingle this servant's heart. Please open other hearts to this young girl in Muddy Pond; she's going to need so much help with that little baby.

Suddenly Gracie felt strong arms around her waist and she gulped air in surprise.

"What're you lookin' at out on that distant hillside?" Stephen whispered against her neck.

She swatted at his arms, "Stephen Ingle you liked to scared the life right out of me. Now if you're hungry, that's no way to get dinner."

Laughing he stepped back and gently laid an arm across her shoulders, "Matter of fact I was looking for something to eat. But you made such a picture against the green of the fields that I couldn't help myself."

"Hmm, it is a beautiful site. Pappy Ingle chose well when he came to Tennessee."

Stephen turned back toward the house, "I think the land chose him. It was hard, real hard, to leave Virginia so when we found this plateau without many neighbors nearby I think we all knew it was home."

"It's not like Virginia, is it?"

"I was so little when we left, I can't say that I remember much of it. But they've all talked so much about it that it seems that I can see it in my mind. I guess it's this place I really see though; our land was right on the river in Virginia. Of course that meant there were times of flood and we never have to deal with that on this mountain, do we?"

"Thankfully no. Would you run down to the spring and bring up some buttermilk? I'll stir up some hoe cakes and I can have them frying before you get back."

With a nod Stephen was out the door. Gracie pulled a few coals to the front of the fireplace and dropped a handful of wood shavings on top. Even before they caught she set her iron skillet on top and dropped in a spoonful of grease. She began humming as she usually did as she worked in her home.

Stephen stood a moment in the doorway enjoying his wife before he spoke, "It's about time we got you a stove. You've squatted to cook at that fireplace far too long. Pappy told me that you know."

"Pappy? What's he know about cooking on a hearth?"

"Well, Mama had to do it when they first came to the mountain and maybe she fussed about it more than you do."

Gracie giggled, "I would appreciate a stove. Can we afford it?"

"Actually, Pappy offered to buy it for us. I don't know if we'll let him do that because I think we can swing it now. We've got a good crop of corn comin' along and I'll drive a load into Isoline to sell."

The skillet clanged against the wooden tabletop as she dropped it to hug her husband. "Thank you Stephen. You take such good care of me."

Grinning he sat at his plate, "Ummm hmmm. Yep, this is me taking care of you."

He took her hand and bowed his head, "Lord, we thank…"

"Graaaaacyyyyy!"

Both Stephen and Gracie jerked their heads up and turned from one side to the other trying to determine the direction of the call.

"It's out front," Gracie cried as she bounded toward that direction.

Again she heard the cry, "Graaaacyyyy, Aunt Gracie!"

Shielding her eyes against the mid-day sun Gracie looked toward the sound. She could see a running figure, the dress that billowed behind her told her only it was a girl. Several more seconds passed before she recognized Mandie.

"Stephen! It's Mandie runnin' as hard as she can."

She cupped her hands over her mouth to call back, "Child what's the matter?"

Mandie grew closer by the moment and soon stood panting before Gracie and Stephen.

"Stephen won't you get her some water. Mandie, how far did you run?"

"I uh-huh-uh-huh, I met Margie this side of Camp Ground. Uh-huh She said Georgie needs you."

"Georgie? The baby?"

Mandie nodded frantically.

"Mandie, you've got to tell me is something wrong or is it just time?"

Shaking her head she took the water from Stephen's hand, "Don't know."

Gracie turned to her husband but he had disappeared. "Mandie, I've got to go. You will be okay."

"Yes, yes, don't worry 'bout me."

Gracie ran to the back door to grab her basket, calling Stephen. "Stephen where'd you get to? I've gotta go to Muddy Pond."

The words had scarcely left her mouth when she heard the harness jingle as the wagon rolled from the barn.

"I'm ready, are you?" Stephen called from the seat.

As she climbed up on the wagon, she smiled and began to pray.

Lord, thank you for this man who helps when I ask and when I don't. Thank you for putting Mandie in Margie's path. Help me now please Lord.

The trotting horses drummed up a cloud of dust as they hurried toward the Camp Ground community. She could hear the trickle of water to her right as the road began to drop away in a steep descent. The temperature dropped and tiny bugs flew around her sweat drenched face. The couple were mute as Stephen concentrated on driving and Gracie prayed.

The sounds of the land were interrupted as Stephen calmed the horse, "Easy now, Red, you know this road. Watch your step girl, there's a lot of rocks here."

More to himself than either Gracie or Red, he commented on the condition of the ford, "Waters real low right now; it won't be hard to ford the creek at all. We'll have to stop for a few minutes at least before asking the horse to pull that hill."

He pulled back on the reins and stopped the horse on the rocky shore of the little creek.

Gracie had just taken a deep breath when something caught her attention on the other side of the creek. Halfway up the long hill was the folded figure of a young girl. As Gracie squinted her eyes to focus on the shadows the head raised.

"Mizz Gracie! Is that you?"

"Yes, it's Gracie and Stephen."

"Miss Gracie, it's Margie. Mandie found you! I was tryin' to git back to Georgie; she's all alone you know."

"You left her alone? Didn't you stop at your grandmother's house?"

Margie just shook her head.

Stephen picked up the reins again, "You can ride with us the rest of the way child."

"I'll meet you at the top of the hill. No sense making that poor horse pull my weight up it."

Stephen clucked and Red slowly picked her way across the water and leaned into her collar to pull the load up the hill. Margie was waiting just as she'd said when they reached the top.

"Climb on in here; we'll let her blow just a minute. We'll be there in no time."

Margie sat with her back against the board seat Gracie and Stephen occupied and found a hand hold on the low side boards. She was ready when Stephen called on Red to step right into her running walk.

An old man sat on the porch of the elder Wilsons home as they thundered by. Stephen didn't slow the wagon until they were abreast of the little shack Georgia and Margie shared. No words were needed as Gracie hopped from her seat and charged into the house.

She was speaking calming words before her eyes could adjust from the bright sunlight to the darker interior. "Georgie, I'm here. It must have seemed like eternity since you sent

Margie on her way, but we got here just as quick as we ever could've."

She peeled off her straw hat and turned back to Margie, "I'm going to need some good clean water to get this road dirt off my hands."

Margie nodded and hopped from the porch grabbing a bucket from the corner.

Gracie could hear Georgia panting as she turned toward her bed but she stopped short when she saw a withered little woman hovering over her. The lady looked up as Gracie froze in the room, her breath unconsciously held.

"I'm Arseny Wilson, the child's grandma. I heard Margie tear outta here and something just tol'e me I needed to come in here."

"Mrs. Wilson, it's a pleasure to meet you. How is our Georgie doing?"

"She's a hurtin' bad; I guess that's normal enough. I done had five young'uns and the pain don't get no better with each one."

Gracie smiled at her, "Well they always tell me you don't remember the pain when you're holdin' your little bundle of joy. Georgie, can you hear me?"

Georgia nodded her head as another pain started and she gripped the bedframe.

Gracie heard Margie returning, "Let me get washed up good and we'll see what we can do here."

Gracie went to Margie and tried to read the mixed emotions in her young eyes. "Margie, can you get a little fire going? We surely don't need to heat this place up but we'll want to clean the baby with warm water and I'll wash again when the water's hot. Also, I have some lavender that we'll make into a tea for Georgie to help her with the pain."

Arsena had eased close to them since Gracie spoke her instructions softly.

"Lavender? Who ever heard of the like? You've just gotta face the pain."

Gracie spoke as she washed in the cool water. "Mrs. Wilson, I want to do everything that I can for your granddaughter."

"Hmmf, I'm a-thinkin' she needs all the pain the good Lord will hand her in this."

Gracie took a deep breath and crossed to Georgia's bedside. There she stayed throughout the evening. Between Georgia's howls, Gracie heard crickets begin to sing; a light appeared in the room and she looked toward it in time to see Stephen's back as he retreated to the porch.

The sun lit the horizon promising a new day as Georgia lay drenched in sweat. Gracie spooned more lukewarm tea into her mouth and the girl blinked a weak thank-you.

The east-facing doorway was bright and the temperature of the single room was quickly rising when the mother's howls changed to a baby's whimper. Gracie heard a whoop from the front porch and Margie hopped up from her corner. Even Arsena Wilson's harsh face broke into a broad smile as Gracie wrapped the baby and lay him in his mother's arms.

"Georgie you're work is done for today; feed your son then we'll take care of him."

Margie and Stephen had kept a small fire outside through the night minimizing the heat of the cabin. Now Margie brought in a warm bucket and Gracie cleaned herself and Georgie. With more water she prepared a washpan for the baby and moved to take him from his sleeping mother. Arsena stepped up beside her.

"I'll do that for you Mizz Gracie," she smiled – a genuine smile of appreciation both for the baby and for Gracie's help.

"I'll wash up these rags and such."

"No child, you've really done enough. Me and Margie can tend to these things. You've done what we couldn't."

"It was really Georgie and the good Lord what did all the work."

"Mizz Gracie you're an angel among women. I know your God has sent you to us."

"Mrs. Wilson, he's not just my God. Do you know that Georgie accepted Jesus as her savior?"

She shook her head very slowly as the truth sank into her heart. "I did not know that. Do you reckon it will change her wicked ways?"

"Yes, I do. She won't be perfect, none of us are. But she is forgiven and if she can cling to that and grow with it then Georgie can walk with God just like the Bible tells us the prophets of old did."

"I used to walk with him you know. Only I let all the grief of the world steal the joy of the Lord away from me."

Gracie laid a hand on the little woman, "That joy is still there waiting for you to live in it."

A smile grew on her wrinkled face until she fairly beamed, "Living in joy – I thought that would happen in heaven." Looking down at her new great-grandson she said, "Maybe today is a good day to start though."

Arsena looked up at Gracie as a tear trickled down her cheek, "We gotta get him bathed here. You and your man need to eat. Margie, you take Mizz Gracie and her man over to my house and stir them up some corn pone and eggs."

Margie jumped when her grandmother called her name and turned to stare out the open door at the other house as though she feared the building.

Arsena urged her, "Go on now, they've got to be 'bout starved to death."

"Uh, uh, Gram, you want me to go in your house?"

"Yes child I do. There's probably not a bite to eat here and we'll need to get something together for your sister so you go on now and don't sass me."

Margie kept looking back at the little woman even as she moved toward the door.

Gracie opened her mouth to refuse the meal but Arsena rebuffed her before she could form the words, "Now it's your turn to let us take care of you Mizz Gracie. You go on over quick as you've settled things here. I'll stay with Georgie and this fine boy – we're gonna have to come up with a name for him. Can't give him his daddy's name I don't guess but, well, what about my daddy's name? Oh we'll wait till Georgie wakes up to talk about that. You go on now or Margie may burn the house down."

Stephen stood in the doorway and gave Gracie a nod and she stepped out to join him. Hand in hand they walked the short distance to the neighboring house. The same old man sat on the front porch, seemingly unmoved since they drove in yesterday.

As Gracie and Stephen approached the porch the old man's chair dropped onto all four legs and he stood. "Baby come?"

Stephen spoke to him, "Yes sir. It's a healthy baby boy. Georgie's fine too. Ain't she Gracie?"

Gracie nodded.

The old man leaned against a porch post and stared toward the rocky hillside, "Arseny got the boy?"

Gracie answered with a smile, "Yes, she took right to him. Wants to name him after her daddy."

"Hmmf, Lewis Wilson, don't know 'bout that although he was a good enough feller. Margie in the kitchen yonder?"

"Yes sir, she's putting together some breakfast. Georgie will need to eat."

He nodded, "Then come on in here. She ain't much of a cook but I reckon she'll keep us from starvin' today."

The trio entered the sparsely furnished house and were greeted by the warm smell of baking bread and the sizzle of frying meat. Gracie stepped into the kitchen to help Margie.

"You're fast Margie."

"Grandpa had a fire built so the oven was hot. And he had this side meat on the table so I reckon he meant for us to eat it. I never even thought I'd ever be in this house again."

Gracie smiled, "I think God's working on some hearts here."

Margie nodded, "He sure is. I been talkin' to him about my own heart, you know."

Gracie squeezed her shoulders as she praised the Lord for the work he was doing right before her eyes.

Chapter 20

Gracie was growing accustomed to the frequent and unexpected visitors who beckoned her for help and she now kept a basket sitting behind the kitchen door with clean rags, strong lye soap, a sharp knife and herbs she had learned would help with pain, slow bleeding and calm nerves. She had even wrapped pieces of Pappy Ingle's dried beef jerky so she could make a strong broth for exhausted mothers.

She rarely knew the people who knocked on her door and she'd stopped asking them how they knew about her or why they chose to come to the little shack that sat among the other Ingle family dwellings. Stephen usually knew the men and would greet them by name, asking after the condition of both family and stock.

Hot bread sat on the table and Gracie was just taking up a skillet of gravy when a heavy knock sounded. Stephen opened the door and greeted the stranger, "Mornin', how're ya' doin'?"

The tall man dipped his head in lieu of greeting, "Needin' the midwife. Woman's been hurtin' all night; says the time's come."

Gracie sat her iron skillet on the hearth rock and wiped her hands on her clean apron. "Le'me get my things."

She stepped to the back door, wrapped a light shawl around her shoulders and tied on her straw hat. Slipping the waiting basket over her arm, she started for the door. Stephen surprised her by picking up his own hat and coat and announcing, "Won't be but a minute and I'll have the horse harnessed."

Gracie looked up at her husband but held her questions, "I'll wrap up the biscuits, you'll git hungry before this job is done."

The stranger stepped out the front door and Gracie followed her husband to the barn. This began a model Gracie could never distinguish. Frequently, for reasons he could never fully explain, Stephen would choose to follow behind the messenger and drive his wife himself. Many other times, he bade her good-bye and continued with his own work on the farm.

Today's trip to a little one-room cabin perched on a hillside overlooking the Hurricane Creek was a false alarm. "I b'lieve she'll be a few more weeks. Sometimes the pains come like this, makin' you think the baby's on his way but it's just kindly the body's way of getting ready I think."

The gruff man had said little since he stood in her doorway. Now he handed Stephen a small burlap bag. "Had a good springtime for the corn so it's come in early. These are past roastin' ears but ought to make fine gritted bread."

With a big grin Stephen took the bag in one hand and extended the other to thank him. He helped Gracie up and clucked, telling the horse it was time to go home.

These calls were so numerous at times that Stephen's farm work would have indeed suffered had he abandoned his chores for every expectant mother. Some trips seemed fruitless when an inexperienced mother summoned Gracie far too early. Other times he would have to leave her for the hours-long birthing ordeal.

Gracie came to enjoy these quiet drives with Stephen. Somehow the relationship she had considered perfect was growing stronger and sweeter by the day. She pondered why this was happening; had she been doing something wrong before? It was Stephen who explained it to her on a drive to Roslin.

The buckboard creaked loudly as they hit ruts too deep to measure and too numerous to count. The road was well-traveled but poorly maintained. Gracie thanked God that Stephen was with her for this was her first trip across the Clear Fork Creek which lay east of the Slate Creek which the Ingles relied on so heavily. She watched the landscape as they seemed to be heading into very wild country, but Stephen was as calm as always and Gracie drew strength from him.

Stephen took her hand as he tried to share the thoughts in his head. "I've been thinking Gracie, doesn't the Lord seem to be blessing us more and more all the time?"

"He is good all the time. In what way are you thinking?" She asked him.

"Well, we never have been a bickerin' pair like I know some married people are. But it just seems like it's been all the sweeter in the past few months."

Gracie smiled, amazed that they seemed to be thinking the same thoughts. "I've been feeling the same way. Stephen, I can't help feelin' that it's all changed since I gave up myself."

"What do you mean?"

"Well, I had a certain picture of how our life was supposed to play out, and when it didn't seem to be going that way, I found myself questioning the Lord. Actually, I was a little angry with him – as scary as that is to even say."

Stephen just nodded, his eyes watching the road in front of his team.

"Then, that day I went to the bluff and prayed, I surrendered to do things God's way. And he's surely sent me a lot of work to do. Have you noticed that every few days somebody's knockin' on our door? Of course it's awfully nice when you come along with me."

"I like to be with my wife. And sometimes it seems like maybe I could be a help – oh I don't mean with the women-folk. I guess just a help to you."

She smiled and snuggled in close to his shoulder, "You are Stephen, you are."

"I really admire you, Gracie, for comin' into Marth-y Washington and just throwin' right in to help."

"Your mother gave me a talkin'-to about that you know. Said that if God called, how dare any of us question that calling. I try really hard not to question it, but you know that it's hard sometimes when I see other women getting' what I'm longing for."

"Babies. Yeah, you see them every week, don't you? I know our babies will come in God's time."

He couldn't see her but he felt her nod agreement against his shoulder.

Chapter 21

"Hellooo the house," Lottie called as she stepped onto Gracie's front porch.

Gracie called back as she made her way around the corner, bread pan in hand.

"I was out with the chickens; you go on in, I'm right behind you."

Lottie threw her a broad smile as she turned to open the door, "I didn't know if you'd recognize us, it's been so long since we've seen you."

Gracie smiled with her sister who was always teasing, just as she had when they were children. She waved away her chiding with a single hand then reached to take Ida out of her mother's arms, "Go on with you. Have you come just to fuss at me or do you want to sit down and have a hot cup of coffee and catch up a little while I play with my favorite niece."

Lottie tried to look disinterested despite having come for this very purpose, "Oh I suppose I could sit for just a minute or two."

Both sisters dissolved into laughter setting the baby cackling at them. With Ida on one hip Gracie reached with her free hand to pull the coffee pot forward, and then turned to the baby, "Well, Ida, you're going to have to play in the floor till I get this coffee boilin'. Lottie, I'm not as talented as you to be able to cook a whole meal with just one hand."

Lottie ignored the compliment and made herself comfortable at the head of the table setting a basket on the corner. "I've made molassy bread brought you half. I was teasing you before but I really do know that you are running from here to yon helpin' everybody else and I can't see how you ever have time to do all the things that fill up the days for me – cooking, cleaning and keeping the wash done up."

Gracie joined her at the table. "Lottie look around you, my home is not what Grandma Elmore taught us to keep, is it? Mother Ingle and Betty help a lot bringin' in a pot of beans or a loaf of bread. Speaking of that, did Uncle Bill bring you any flour?"

Lottie nodded as her eyes widened, "He sure did and what a blessing. Why do you think I've got molassy bread to share?"

They laughed together loving the time and watching as Ida scooted and crawled among the legs of the table, bench and chairs.

"Have you heard from any of the Elmores?"

Lottie was nodding even as she reached for the basket, "Oh yeah, that was one of the main reasons I wanted to come over here. Daniel brought home a letter just yesterday. Hettie's had a baby, another boy. And Gracie, they've named him William Julius – after Grandpa. Don't you think that's just the sweetest thing?"

Gracie reached for the letter, "I sure do. We could never forget Grandpa but that little boy will never know him so maybe they can always tell him, 'Your name is Julius the same as your daddy's daddy.' I'd love to be able to do that too."

For just a moment, a wave of sadness swept over Gracie. She tried to hide it by dropping her head seemingly to study the letter from home. However, she could hide little from Lottie.

"Gracie, you'll have babies in God's time.

Gracie's eyes involuntarily darted to Lottie's thickening waist. "I know Lottie. And I'm really content with that, there are just moments…you know?"

"I know Gracie. We all have our moments. Do you think it's doubt? When we have those moments are we doubting whether God will keep his word to us, whether he will be faithful?"

"It is surely a lack of faith but I don't like to think I'm doubting God. How could I when he's given me so much?"

Lottie smiled and reached to clasp Gracie's hand. "You have always been good at counting your blessin's, and that in itself is a blessin' to me. Well, did you see in the letter how Grandma is wantin' to come see us. She says she knows we're settled and happy but she just thinks she can rest better in the hereafter if she's seen it for herself."

Gracie laughed and tried to find that part of the letter she still held. "I'd love to see her but that's an awful silly way to think of it. She's going to rest in heaven, that's a promise, I think. Is that in the bible?"

"Yeah I think so. It says, 'rest from their labors,' don't remember where it's at though. I should ask Daniel. That man has more scripture in his head than I can even count."

"Like Stephen's mother. Lottie she is such an inspiration to me. It seems like half of everything that comes out of her mouth is straight from God's word."

"Grandma will enjoy spending some time with her and the other Ingles. Do you think she'll stay with us for a while?"

"I don't know, I guess I had only thought of a short visit. Let's write her and tell her we want to keep her for a while."

"She would surely be a blessing to you, and your house is better fixed to keep her."

"Gracie, that's a shame because I think you need the help more."

"Why in the world would you say that?" Gracie asked as she reached down to snatch Ida, "You have this precious little explorer to keep up with."

"Yes, but you have to be away from home so much and like I was sayin' before I don't know how you keep up with the house. Let's don't argue about where she'll stay until we can get her over here. I'll write to them today and ask them to come as soon as possible. Uncle Jesse should have his corn laid by so he might have a little idle time."

Bessie Elmore was eager to see her granddaughters because Lottie's letter was answered with Grandma, Uncle Jess and six year old James rolling into her yard just a week later.

"Gracie, Gracie," James called, "We've finally come to see you."

Gracie pushed open the screened door just as Uncle Jesse's oldest son bounded from the still-moving wagon and ran directly to Gracie's open arms.

She could hardly speak, she was laughing so hard. "James, you'll break a leg jumpin' from the wagon that way. Then what would we do with you?"

"I waited so long to come to your house, Gracie, and then it was such a long ride."

She squeezed him hard, "I know it was, James, and I'm glad you're here. Come on, let's go help Grandma."

Bessie Elmore was gathering baskets and packages from all around her feet and behind the seat. Jesse's arms were already full.

"Grandma, we hoped you'd stay with us for awhile but it looks like you've moved lock, stock and barrel."

"Hush that up, I've just brought a few things. Some of them are old, but you know I'm about to the end of my row, and I need to hand off things to folks what can use them."

Gracie reached up to take her hand, "Let's get you down from there and then we'll worry about the packages."

She stepped down from the high wagon without the slightest stumble and turned immediately back to get her packages, which she promptly piled into both Gracie and Jesse's arms.

"Well come on in everyone. We'll see if we can get Stephen in from the field and send for Lottie and Daniel."

Uncle Jesse emptied his arms into a porch chair and straightened with his hand on his back. "Is Stephen anywhere you can point me to? I need to walk after sittin' in that wagon so long."

"Yeah, I b'lieve he's just at the bottom of the hill there. And that's on the way to Lottie's house anyway so maybe he could walk on over there after you've seen him." She wrapped her arms around him before he could move away, "Oh Uncle Jesse, it's so good to see you and thank you for bringing Grandma to see us."

Jesse smiled and dipped his head, "James why don't you walk with me and give the ladies a chance to catch up."

"Ah, I wanted to catch up with Gracie." James obediently followed his father, albeit with his head down.

Gracie called after them, "James maybe you can go with Stephen to Lottie's house. She always has something baked!"

Gracie turned back to hug her grandmother, "And I guess I'd better get in there and stir something up too. I know yu'ns are hungry."

"There'll be time for all of that later. We've been eating along the way. Hettie wrapped up biscuits with tenderloin. They got cheese in at Isoline, and we splurged to buy a half a wheel! So we've had some of that, and I brought you a slice as well."

"Cheese! What a treat. You know Stephen's mother makes cheese but it really only works in the fall and winter. It's just too humid in July. Let's do sit down and talk. We won't have long to be alone here." She turned to look at the seating choices on her front porch, "Do you want to sit out here where there might be a little breeze? There's a wing on the back porch if you think you might prefer that. Eith er one will be nice until the very late afternoon when the sun's pretty hot out here on the front porch."

With a deep breath Bessie fell into the closest chair. "Child these ole' bones can't take much no more. 'Bout to the end of my row, I'm a'tellin' you."

"Grandma, that's the second time you've said that. Is something wrong with you?"

"No no, I'm just old and stuff starts to wear out. Like a plow point that won't take an edge, just wore out."

"Well this is not like you at all, and I don't like it. You even wrote about resting in the hereafter."

"Gracie, there's a time when you start to think more about the hereafter than about the here and now. And I just think I've gotten to that point. Your Grandpa has gone on and I miss him. 'Course, I know the timin' is in God's hand. And who knows, Jesus may step out on a cloud and call his children home before then. Either way, though, my time is short. But I din' come to make you sad. I came to see that you are settled in and that Stephen is treating you well. How about the Ingles?

Bessie looked around and could see the three houses built closer than most farmsteads. She looked back to Gracie for an explanation to her unspoken questions.

"The Ingles are a great family Grandma and they have taken me in just like I was born to them. They are clannish though, and that's why they've built so close together even though they own quite a lot of land. Land is important to Pappy Ingle and Daddy-Jury as well."

Her grandma squinted at her, "Daddy-Jury? Is that Stephen's father?"

Gracie laughed softly, "Yeah, my sister-in-law calls him that and she's got her sons using the same name. So it's kind of stuck I guess. Do you remember that his name is Algurial? That's kind of a mouthful, especially for the little ones."

Bessie nodded and looked out over the land. "They've got a good lookin' farm. Corn's so dark it's nearly black and they've got all their hay'n done I see cause the fields are short and neat."

"Oh yes, Stephen wants everything on the farm to be just so. He loves working with his father and little brother, but he longs to have his own farm you know."

"Every man wants his own land. I reckon that somethin' the good Lord puts into 'em. Your grandpa stayed on his daddy's farm, and of course we kept the Elmores until they passed. Still Julius always talked about his own land. That old farm was his daddy's until the day he died off and left it. Even though Julius worked it another ten years, I don't guess he ever really felt like it was his. Still it's been a good place to live, and no other place would be home, would it?"

Gracie just shook her head, sensing that Grandma wanted to talk and unwilling to interrupt.

"Of course it's not the same anymore. Nothing stays the same. With you and Lottie married off and gone, now there's another generation coming up in the old place. James and Pearly keep things alive there and now with the new baby you know the kind of noise we've got.

Gracie smiled, "Where is Pearly by the way?"

"Hettie thought she'd better keep her home. You saw James jumpin' out of the wagon, well, Pearly would've jumped ten times by now. That child is on the go non-stop let me tell you. Jesse was like that when he was little. Of course him bein' the baby, I had a houseful of grown kids to chase him. Thursey, she was a little mama by then, just waitin' for the time when she'd marry and raise her own kids. So I guess she practiced on Jesse."

"Jesse is still on the move. Just like him barely gettin' the wagon stopped before he's off walkin' the fields."

"Mmmhmm," Grandma answered as she stared off toward the horizon.

Gracie wondered if she was looking for a sign of Jesse and James walking in the field or was she looking back over the years to Jesse's childhood.

Chapter 22

As the sun crept toward its zenith and the temperature steadily warmed, Gracie and Bessie sat rocking and chatting on the porch until they heard the chatter of their family heading in. Whether it was James, Lottie or Daniel they first heard, there could be no doubt the whole group was together and already enjoying the visit.

"So you found Stephen?" Gracie asked as James worked at opening the leather latch holding the front gate.

"Oh, yeah. He was workin' hard but he quit straight away when he seen we'd come to visit. Then we all walked down the hill to Lottie's house and Dan'l come along with us. Did you see me ridin' way up high on his shoulders?"

By the time the little boy had finished his tale, he'd made it through the gate and bounded onto the porch. Gracie smiled, thinking how right Grandma was in saying he ran everywhere.

Lottie and Daniel weren't far behind him and soon joined them on the porch, Daniel hugging Grandma before taking a seat on the steps.

Lottie held Ida out to kiss her great grandmother and the baby reached her chubby fingers into Grandma's neat hair, pulling tendrils loose from their bun and erupting in giggles.

"That baby's silly," James exclaimed.

Lottie smiled at him, "No more silly than you were when you were not yet two years old! I guess you're glad you're never silly anymore."

"Sure am. I'm a man on the farm, you know. I can plow and fork hay and – well I can just about run that farm."

They all laughed before Gracie drew him to her in a warm embrace, "I know you are a real blessing to your daddy. And speaking of your daddy, where do you reckon he's gotten to?"

"Oh he and Stephen had to put the horses up. A man's gotta take care of his stock you know."

Gracie nodded, looking just as serious as the boy, "He sure does. And I've gotta take care of my man so I better get up and get after some dinner, don't you think?"

He nodded, "Guess so. I'm pretty hungry."

"Then you run out to the barn and see if you can get those two in here and I'll go in and see what we've got to eat."

Lottie and Grandma followed her in while Daniel carried Ida to a patch of grass surrounding the big oak tree in the front yard. Lottie grabbed the basket Daniel had left on the edge of the porch and Grandma directed both girls to carry in some of the packages she'd brought.

"I don't have any loaf bread, but I'll stir up a big pone of cornbread and that will be good with the cheese you brought, Grandma."

Lottie's eye's popped wide at Gracie's mention of the rare treat. "You've brought cheese?"

Grandma nodded and began opening one of the paper wrapped packages.

"Where did you ever get it this time of year? Daniel's mother makes cheese and I'm tryin' to learn how but we just don't have any luck in the hot summer. It always molds."

"Well, several crates of cheese come in on the train, and Jesse just happened to be at Isoline when they was unloadin' it, so he bought a half a wheel."

Lottie took the wedge in her hand as though it were wax covered gold. She went straight to the block of knives and began slicing thick portions.

By the time Gracie had the corn bread in a skillet, the wood stove had heated the room to a near unbearable temperature. "Girls, I'm gonna sit for a spell out here on the back porch. I just can't stand the heat no more."

"Just rest yourself Grandma, I'll ask Stephen if he'll go to the spring and get some water there. It's so much sweeter than the well water. And I think it's cooler too."

As Grandma went out the back door Gracie stepped through the front room to the porch and called over to the yard where Stephen, Daniel and Jesse were visiting. "Stephen, will you please go to the spring for a bucket of water? We'd all enjoy it, and Grandma is needing a cool drink."

"I'll be happy to run down there. Let's see if James can beat me."

Gracie hadn't even seen where James had gotten to until he came running up to the other men at the first mention of his name.

Gracie stepped back into the kitchen where Lottie was busily working. Gracie poured the cornmeal mixture into a hot skillet and slipped into the oven. Lottie had about a dozen eggs she'd brought and she dropped them into boiling water.

"The hens are layin' really well right now and boiled eggs will be good with the cheese."

Gracie nodded and began slicing up what meat they had cooked. By the time Stephen and James were back from the spring and Bessie rejoined them in the kitchen the food was waiting on the table with an apple pie Hettie had sent along for their dessert.

Gracie called out to Jesse and Daniel, "Y'uns come on in and don't forget little Ida. I guess you'll have to wash her hands off since you've been lettin' her play in the dirt."

Daniel picked up his daughter, brushing at her long dress with one hand as he walked.

Gracie was back on the porch with a wash pan filled with warm water before they could get into the house. She took Ida's hands in her own while Daniel held her up and Gracie scrubbed the dirt off with the lye soap that always sat by the back door.

With hands cleaned and the men seated around the table Stephen bowed his head and prayed, "Father God, we thank thee for this bountiful meal. We thank thee for this family you have seen fit to bless us with and who you've brought to our home. We pray your protection and blessings on those who cannot be with us and please bless the hands that have prepared this meal. In the holy name of Jesus we pray, Amen."

Everyone around the table echoed his "Amen", James loudest of all with even Ida attempting an "A-a-a".

Gracie took a piece of the warm cornbread and a slice of cheese in her hand and turned toward the back porch. "Grandma, can I make you a plate and you go on out to the porch and wait for me?"

"No child, you've cooked the meal, I'll be out there in just a little bit."

"There wasn't much cooking to it. We can talk out here where it's cooler."

In a moment Grandma joined her in the porch swing. Gracie looked at the tiny portions of food on her plate then looked into her grandmother's wrinkled face.

"Is that all you're going to eat? Do you not have any appetite?"

"The young ones need the food more than me, and the men that will have to have strength to work."

"Grandma, we are not short on food. Are y'uns having trouble at home?"

"No no. Jesse is doing well I b'lieve. Remember, he had the money in his pocket to buy the cheese. I just don't like to take too much."

"Grandma I'm going to say just what you would say to any of us. So long as the good Lord leaves you on this earth he's got work for you to do. If you starve yourself down to where you can't do that work then you are just disobeying our holy God. Now, what do you think about that?"

"I think I taught you all too well. I'll have a piece of the pie."

Gracie smiled, "I'll get it for you."

"No no, let me eat this meat and bread first and you tell me what keeps you busy of a day."

Gracie dropped her head, feeling that she only asked because there were no children in the home to fill her days as Aunt Hettie's days were surely filled.

Lottie answered for her, "Her days are mostly filled with servin' all the women-folk around Martha Washington. There's somebody at her door every day or two."

Grandma looked at Gracie, "Is that right Gracie? You never write so I don't know all that's going on with you."

"Oh Grandma, I know I'm awful at writing and I'm sorry about that."

"Don't you worry about it, Lottie fills in the gap with her letters."

Lottie beamed for a moment before turning her attention to Ida in an attempt to not look boastful.

"She is a good letter writer, I know. If she could get to the post office everyday she could run a ministry with her letters."

Grandma nodded, "Now tell me about servin' all the women. Are you catchin' that many babies?"

Gracie nodded almost reluctantly, "Yeah, I go whenever I'm called for and that seems to be quite often."

"Gracie, I knew way back that you had a gift for midwifing, you're just so young still."

Gracie nodded. "You're not tellin' me anything I don't already know, Grandma. However, the granny woman they had before was…well I don't want to talk mean about her."

Lottie spoke up, "Mean's a good word for her. She was there when Ida was born and Gracie was a whole lot more help. That ole' woman just acted like …well, I don't even know like what. She just plain didn't want to be there."

"And there's no one else around?"

"I don't know. Mrs. Reeder sent a man from down in the Baldwin Gulf to get me right after little Ida was born and then the word just kind of got around and they keep comin' to me."

Grandma smiled and patted Gracie's hand. "Stephen's okay with this?"

Gracie nodded, "I'm not sure how he might've felt except that his mother has really pushed the idea. It's not that she wants me out runnin' all over the country catchin' babies, it's more about obeying the Lord. She says I've got to do what I'm called to and Stephen won't argue with that."

"He ever go with you?"

"Yeah he does, sometimes. Of course there's lots of times that he's got to work. He says he can't explain it; there's just times he feels like he needs to go along."

Again Grandma patted her, "Then the good Lord's a'leadin' him, too, so that means it will all be okay. More than that, y'uns will be blessed for your obedience."

Again Gracie's eyes darted to Lottie's now obviously pregnant belly. She closed her eyes and took a deep breath to force back the tears.

Bessie felt the tension suddenly build in her hand, and she caught the swift look at her younger granddaughter.

"Gracie, just how God blesses you is not your choice you know."

Gracie looked at her hoping for an explanation.

"The good Lord may yet give you a houseful of children. Or he may give you a long, long life with this man you love. He may bless the farm or he may send hardships you cannot understand and if that's the case, you will know that you are blessed even in those hard times because you are drawn closer to the Lord, and maybe you can draw other people to him too."

Gracie smiled up at her grandmother, "I miss your wisdom Grandma,

I really do try not to waste my time counting the things I don't have."

"That's right child, you spend your time counting the blessings God has poured out on you and you won't have any time left for evil thoughts."

"Is it evil to wish for something you don't have?"

"No, I didn't mean that. It's only evil when you accuse God of not loving you enough to give you what you're a'wanting. And that's really what we're doin' when we complain, ain't it?"

Gracie reluctantly nodded her head. "Yeah, I guess it is. And I've gotta asked for forgiveness for some of that."

Chapter 23

Bessie stayed with Lottie for nearly a month. Gracie walked over to see her every day she could. Lottie had to continue putting by the fresh produce Daniel had grown for them and Grandma and Lottie helped her with everything she worked at. Still there was time for them to piece quilts and work together in Gracie's garden when Lottie and Grandma walked up the hill to her house. And they spent endless hours talking. They reminisced about their childhood years and Grandma told stories about their own mother Margaret as wells as the whole Elmore family. She talked a lot about Grandpa and it was ever more evident that she longed to be with him in heaven. She shared here heart with the girls in a way she never had.

Gracie began to realize that Grandma no longer saw them as children she was raising; now she related to both Lottie and Gracie as friends. It warmed Gracie's heart to be able to spend such sweet time with her and she prayed they could repeat this, maybe next summer.

Gracie sat on the steps of Lottie's front porch breaking beans while Grandma peeled apples well before noon when they heard a horse approaching.

Grandma never looked up as she offered her idea of who was approaching. "Jesse will be comin' any day now. Reckon that could be him?"

Gracie couldn't help but squint into the sunlight as she tried to make out the form sitting high on the wagon. "It looks like Stephen's wagon. I wasn't expecting him to go anywhere today though."

Sure enough, Stephen pulled the team to a stop just a few minutes later and called to his wife, "Gracie, there's work for you to do."

Gracie looked up at her grandmother, trying to both apologize and explain with her eyes.

"Child, you must go where you're needed." Looking up Grandma asked Stephen, "Is it a baby?"

"I reckon. Up past Campground, it's that Mrs. Lowe. Didn't you go up and see her once?"

Gracie nodded, "I did talk to her. You know, Mrs. Reeder is much closer to her, I just can't figure why they didn't go for Mrs. Reeder."

Lottie stepped out of the house in time to hear Gracie's pondering. "They come for you Gracie 'cause you're so kind to them. Don't no woman in that condition want somebody fussin' at them about how messy their house is or how they're not havin' that baby fast enough."

Gracie nodded slowly with a sad smile on her face, "And this girl's just real young and I think she's scared."

Grandma added, "It's a scary thing, especially the first one."

Gracie stood, wiping the bean strings off her apron and into the yard. "I guess I'll have to leave this job half finished."

Lottie was already picking up the bowls. "I can have these beans broken and cooked before you can finish the job that's in front of you."

Lottie had them all laughing, including Stephen who was trying to hurry Gracie to get on their way. "I've got your basket in the wagon. I hope I got the right one."

"I'm sure you did, you know where I always keep it. Are you driving me then?"

He nodded and grinned, "If I'm ever to amount to anything as a farmer, we're gonna' have to get you a horse to ride."

Bessie looked up more serious than the rest of the group, "Gracie, that's a real good idea. It would free up Stephen as well as the horses I know he needs in the fields. And on top of that, ridin' time is good prayin' time."

Gracie stepped up onto the porch and hugged her grandmother, "Leave it to you to find time to pray in any situation."

"There's always time to pray child. And all of your work will go better if you use that time for prayin'."

As Stephen and Gracie drove up toward the Martha Washington Road Stephen was unusually quiet.

"What are you studyin' about Stephen?" Gracie finally asked him.

"A horse."

"You thinkin' we need a different horse? Both of these seem to be doin' pretty well."

"Oh they are just fine. I was really just teasing you about riding and I know you've done a little of that, but your Grandma got me to thinkin' back there. Maybe we need to get you a good little horse that can just be yours and you can ride it anytime the weather is fit. It would give you a lot of independence because you wouldn't have to wait for anybody to drive you home."

Gracie nodded, "And it would free your time, too, because you wouldn't feel like you needed to leave your work and hitch the team up."

"I don't mind, Gracie. I'm happy to help you, and if God called you to both be my wife and to be the midwife in Martha Washington, then he surely meant for me to help you."

"Thank you Stephen. I like the horse idea, too. I just don't want us spendin' money we need to be saving."

"We won't. I'll put the word out that we're lookin' for one and see what turns up."

She smiled and looped her arm through his. "Until we find one I'm going to enjoy riding with my husband."

He smiled and sat up straighter, proud to help in this work Gracie was doing.

When they arrived at Joe and Emmy Lowe's house, Joe's horse stood at the front still lathered from his hard ride with the saddle in place.

Stephen stopped beside the horse that didn't budge with the noise and movement beside him. Lifting Gracie out of the wagon he volunteered, "Go on in and Ill get Joe's horse wiped down. You can't leave a lathered horse standing, it's liable to kill him. When I've taken care of the poor nag I'll head back home. Joe will bring you when things are finished here."

"Of course, that'll be fine. I'm sure the poor man was just nervous or he wouldn't have left the horse like that."

"Uh huh," was all Stephen uttered as he led the horse toward the barn.

Gracie stepped inside to hear Emmy moaning and Joe trying to comfort her. She gently called, "Hello, it's Gracie Ingle. Can I come in?"

Joe hopped up and rushed to the door, yanking it from Gracie's hand. "Yes, ma'am. Please come in. We need your help. Emmy, she's hurtin' awful. I guess I should'a gone to get her Ma, except I couldn't leave her again. It was the right thing to come get you, wasn't it?"

"Oh yes, it was right. My husband is tending to your horse out in the barn. Why don't you go see if you can help him because he won't know where you keep your feed and such."

"Yes, ma'am." He turned his head without letting go of the door, "Emmy, ever-thing's okay now. Mizz Gracie is here."

Chapter 24

It was morning before Gracie was able to leave Emmy. The labor was long and both Emmy and Gracie were exhausted. In the end Gracie left a sleeping mama and baby girl. Joe Lowe had gone out to find a young milk cow that he feared was also in labor, and Gracie chose not to wait on him so she started walking toward home.

She hadn't walked long before a wagon drew up beside her.

"Is that Gracie Ingle?" A man's voice called down.

Gracie turned toward the road, always wondering how so many of her neighbors knew her name. This time she found Stephen's uncle Willis smiling down at her.

"Oh, Uncle Willis, I wasn't expecting to see you this early in the morning."

"Well, I've got a turn of corn, and I'm headed to Bill's."

Gracie nodded remembering the road to Uncle Bill Ingle's grist mill was well traveled, especially by the family. Ever since moving to Martha Washington, Gracie had felt particularly blessed to have such easy access to the mill, and while the Ingles didn't usually grow much wheat, whenever Uncle Bill got a share of wheat, as his usual fee for grinding, he almost always shared it. Uncle Bill's generosity also amazed and inspired Gracie, for he had such a large family that she wondered how he could ever feed them all even if he kept everything for his own household. Yet, his philosophy was always 'Give and it will be given to you; a good measure, pressed down, shaken together and running over.'

Gracie drew her attention back to her driver. Uncle Willis was talking about the need for rain and Aunt Margaret's aching legs despite the dry weather. Gracie was fighting to hold her eyes open and found she could barely say, "Oh, I'm sorry to hear that," and "Yes it is dry".

Finally the wagon bounced off of the rough Todd road and onto the relatively smooth Martha Washington Road. Gracie was truly thankful she had not been forced to walk the whole way home and she was equally as grateful for a good excuse to get down.

"Uncle Willis, you just make your turn toward the creek and I'll hop out here. I don't want to delay you."

"No trouble a-tall. Jury would no doubt skin me if I let any harm come to you, so I guess I'd better see you right up to your door."

"Nah, Daddy-Jury won't have a word to say to you besides thanks. And please accept my heartfelt thanks for the ride. I've had a long night, and I might have fallen asleep even while I was walking if you hadn't come along."

He smiled down from the wagon seat, "I think you nodded off a time or two on me. I's worried you'd fall right down off the wagon, but I's ready to catch you."

She smiled at him again and reached up to clasp his hand, "Thank you, Uncle Willis. You've been a real blessing to me today." With that, she turned and headed back up toward her little house.

As Willis pulled away, she heard him whistling and hoped his service to her had blessed him as well.

As she walked around the corner of the house, she heard the back door squeaking open and soon saw Stephen as he maneuvered his way inside with a full bucket of milk.

She called to him, "Oh good, I'm home in time to take care of the milk."

Stephen jerked his head toward her, "When did you get home Gracie?"

"Just this minute." She began to untie her straw hat and sat on the porch swing to untie her high topped shoes. "If you'll bring me out a clean dress, I'll come in and strain that bucket of milk."

He smiled at her and kissed her lightly on her head, "That's a deal."

He was back in a moment with one of her house dresses in his hand. "I didn't hear a wagon," he commented.

"No, Mr. Lowe was tied up with his stock so I headed home on foot. Then, your uncle Willis came along with a turn of corn and gave me a ride. I got out down at the Todd Road and walked up the hill. There was no reason for him to have to make that turn when he was really headed the other way to Uncle Bill's."

Stephen smiled, obviously glad to have his wife home, "He wouldn't have minded and I'm sure glad you didn't have to walk the whole way after sitting up through the night. Did everything go okay with the baby?"

"Oh, yes, she had a healthy baby girl. They both seem to be doing well, and her mother was coming in this morning. I gave her broth around dawn, and she was asleep when I left."

"I'm glad you were there for her Gracie. I know you're anxious to get changed. Don't worry about the milk, I'll get it strained."

"But we had a deal."

"How about you make us a pot of coffee when you get in the house and I'll sit on the porch and drink a cup with you. Do you want me to put the milk in the crock for butter?"

"The deal is gettin' better for me. I don't think we need butter. You go ahead and put it in the pitcher and I'll check the milk hole to make sure there's still plenty of butter." Gracie skipped off toward the little smoke house where she always changed out of her birthing clothes, just as Grandma Elmore had taught her.

As the couple relaxed on their wide front porch, looking out on the neatly clipped hay fields of the Ingle farm, Stephen talked of what work was ahead of him. Gracie mentioned Uncle Willis' family and wondered how he had corn to grind this time of year. Then she thought of Grandma Elmore at Lottie's house.

"Oh Stephen, I left Grandma and Lottie in such a rush yesterday, I have to get down there right away."

"Don't you think you should rest a little?"

"I'll be okay. Maybe I'll lie down for a little bit after dinner when things are so hot." She smiled at him as she added, "But not before I cook you a good dinner. We don't have any meat left, do we?"

He shook his head, "I need to go fishin' don't I?"

She smiled, "Fish would be wonderful. Tonight we'll have new potatoes and corn bread. If I can find a cabbage head in the garden I'll cook a pot of that too. That will make a fine meal, won't it?"

"Mmhmm. I won't complain about it."

He drained his coffee down to the dregs and dumped them over the side of the porch. Handing the cup to Gracie as she stood, he headed out to the fields.

It took Gracie only a few minutes to replace and lace her shoes and head down toward Lottie's house where she found her sister and Grandmother just as she'd left them.

"Have y'uns even moved since I left you yesterday?"

Lottie laughed at her, "You silly thing, of course we've moved. In fact, we've been all over the place. Grandma decided we'd better look for blackberries."

"Grandma decided? I'm thinking it was you; you're always lookin' for berries weeks before they're ripe."

"Ha! Well this time I know better than you. We picked near a gallon and there's a blackberry pie in the pie safe if you'll have a piece with us."

"Lottie! You were right." Turning to her chuckling grandmother she acknowledged, "Grandma don't I remember you telling me that a long time ago that some years when the season is just right the berries will be in by Independence Day?"

Grandma nodded, "I don't exactly recall sayin' it, but it's certainly the truth. And this season appears to be just right. They are juicy and sweet, too. I hope Jesse will be along soon to take me home and I can get to pickin' over there."

"Home?" both Gracie and Lottie said in unison and disbelief.

Grandma just nodded.

Lottie looked heartbroken, "Grandma, aren't you happy here with us?"

"Oh sure I'm happy. I'm about as happy one place as another. But that ole farm is my home and I reckon I need to stay there till the Lord calls me to my eternal home."

Gracie chimed in now, "Please don't talk that way Grandma. I still need to learn so much from you. And if you'd stay here in Martha Washington, I'd have the best chance to learn."

Bessie reached a wrinkled hand out to her beloved granddaughter, "Gracie, you've passed me in learning. If I stayed here, I'd have to learn from you – and I'm too old to learn much more."

Gracie wiped away the tear that trickled down her cheek and she reached out to hug her grandmother.

As though he'd been summoned, Jesse arrived at Lottie's two days later. Daniel walked over to Stephen and Gracie's house with the news and they all hurried back to say their good byes.

As the loaded wagon made the turn out onto the Todd Road, Lottie and Gracie looked at each other and knew they were thinking the same thing but neither was willing to wonder aloud whether they would ever again see Grandma Elmore alive.

Chapter 25

Sometimes everything worked smoothly, and Gracie was summoned to an expectant mother in perfect timing. In those cases, she was back home in no time at all. Other times the hours dragged slowly by, and Stephen just knew she'd be home as quick as she could. She caught up on her own rest whenever she had a chance and both of them often commented how God enabled her to work long hours without sleep. Still when she returned after nearly two days at a bedside, she was so tired she could hardly bathe and dress. It was her custom to immediately change her dress in the smokehouse and then leave the soiled clothes on the back porch to await laundry day. When questioned about this habit she simply told Stephen, "It's hard to explain some of the houses I go in."

Stephen was looking out the little kitchen window with his second cup of coffee; each day he looked over the land and mentally planned his day. Gracie stretched as she voiced on her own plans, "I know it's still early in the day, but I'm already dreading to wash the clothes tomorrow. I'm so weary I couldn't possibly do it today."

Stephen turned and looked into his wife's dark eyes; he was rarely concerned about this strong and energetic woman, yet today she was not herself at all. "Was it a really tough one?"

"Not particularly, just long is all. Both baby and mama are doin' fine. I don't know but what I might be gettin' sick because I just don't seem to have any strength at all. Been feelin' this way for days."

Stephen left her to rest saying he was headed back to plowing. On his way to the field he stopped to ask his mother to check in on Gracie.

Katherine arrived just after noon and rushed to the back of the house where she heard her daughter-in-law retching. "Child, what's the matter? Stephen said you were plumb tired out, but he didn't say a thing about this."

Katherine took her by the shoulder and helped her up. "Mother Ingle, I'm so sorry. I was tired, more tired than I think I've ever been in my life, and I slept; just woke up feeling sick a few minutes ago."

Katherine cocked her head to one side as though she were measuring the girl. "How could you not know?"

Gracie sipped at a glass of water catching a drop on her wrist as she looked up to answer her friend, "Know what?"

Katherine's smile spread across her whole face as she stepped to embrace Gracie.

As realization settled on her, Gracie took a quick, deep breath, "It's been four years. I'd given up."

"Don't ever give up on God. We've been saying all along that it was God's timing."

Gracie's hand clasped her skirt below her waistline, "A baby!"

"Mother Ingle, I've gotta find Stephen."

"No child, what you've got to do is rest. You will be miserable for the next nine months if you don't take it easy, especially right now. You know all this far better than I do."

Dropping her head, Gracie took a deep breath. "Of course you're right, and it's exactly what I would tell any girl who came to me. He's just waited so long – and Mother Ingle,

Stephen has been as good and kind to me as he ever could've, but I've let him down not givin' him a baby these four years."

"You hush that nonsense Gracie Ingle. If my Stephen can't trust this to his God, he ain't much snuff, now is he?"

A little smile crept across her face, "No ma'am, I reckon not."

She turned back to her bed, certain of the futility of arguing with this strong woman. "I'm going to need you Mother Ingle."

"Shhh, you rest and I'll stir up some cornbread. A glass of milk and bread will do wonders for your stomach. I've doctored a little myself you know, you just let me take care of you now."

Gracie did allow the care; she soon fell back into a deep sleep and woke later to the faint scent of baking bread and the soft click of dishes in the kitchen. She swung her feet over the bed's edge and kicked around till she found the knitted slippers that always waited there.

Katherine stuck her head around the chimney corner, "You awake Gracie?"

"Yes ma'am, just now. Do I smell bread baking? I'm suddenly starving."

"Not bakin' child, done baked and nearly cold, I'd reckon. But it will be just fine crumbled in sweet milk. In fact Stephen has brought in the milk so that'll be good 'n fresh for you."

"Okay, I wish I had some buttermilk though. My stomach feels just fine right now, but buttermilk is good medicine."

Katherine's head bobbed up and down, "Don't I know it. I've got my churn full at the house and I'll send somebody over with the buttermilk just as soon as I can pull out the butter. I've put the kitchen in good order for you – now I know you're a fine housekeeper but you ain't home enough to do much keeping, and I'm glad to have a chance to help."

She placed her hands on Gracie's narrow shoulders and held her at arm's length, "Gracie Ingle you done run after and cared for half the women on this mountaintop. Now it's time for some of us to help you."

Gracie's eyes popped wide, "Oh Mother Ingle, what will I do when they come to fetch me? What if I'm sick or too weak to help? Oh, and who will help them now? Who will help ME?"

Her eyes widened as the only alternative she knew of occurred to her, "Mrs. Reeder?"

"Gracie I never knew of you to be so flighty. Now there's help to be had. It's just that you've been the one willin' to help ever'body. Rhodie England come from over toward Roslin and they're livin' down toward Campground now. She's birthed twelve of her own children and I hear she's a good hand to help the sick. So I'm thinkin' she's the one we'll see 'bout helping you when your time comes. But now that's a long while off yet so we've just got to keep you close enough to home that you can rest and give that little Ingle baby the chance to grow the way he needs to."

Her mother-in-law's simple logic gave Gracie great peace. She smiled and stepped into the embrace. "Thank you Mother Ingle. I think I'm ready for that bread and milk now. It sounds like it will hit the spot."

As she stirred the bread into her tall glass she suddenly remembered Stephen had brought in the milk, "Stephen! Did you tell Stephen?"

Katherine smiled and moved toward the chair where she'd laid her bonnet, "Twasn't my news to tell. I'll send the buttermilk along soon, but right now I need to see after the other sickness. Jury's not well today; he woke up aching all in his chest and arms. You rest."

Katherine left with a gentle click of the front door. Gracie looked down realizing she still wore her long nightgown despite the late hour of the day. The house was warming and she looked with longing to the swing on her back porch.

Well it's too late to get much done today, but I guess I can at least get out of my night clothes.

After a quick change to her work dress she snagged the milk glass and stepped onto the little porch. The heat of summer's Dog Days hit her face and her stomach did a quick flip. Closing her eyes she eased herself into the swing and sipped at the milk. She didn't realize how long she'd been there until she heard Stephen's footsteps crunching on the dry grass.

"Gracie, you been sittin' out here long? Mother was here when I brought the milk in and she said you'd been sleeping. Are you feelin' any better? You've got me awful worried."

Gracie smiled at him feeling love well from deep within her heart. She couldn't contain the smile or the joy and it blossomed on her face.

"You laughin' at me worryin' over you?" Stephen feigned a frown as he fell into the swing beside her.

"A'course I'm not laughing. And you sure don't need to worry and fret over me."

"So you really are feeling better? I guess it was just pure exhaustion."

"No Stephen, I was tired and I've been working really hard but that's not what's wrong."

"Well what is wrong Gracie, do you know?"

Again the smile that she could not hold back stretched across her lips. "Nothin's wrong, everything's right. Stephen we're going to have a baby."

Stephen opened his mouth to speak, but his voice failed him. He mouthed the word, 'baby', his brow crinkled as he tried to work through the information. He froze for a brief moment before he found his voice and whooped so loud Gracie jumped setting the swing in wild motion. Stephen wrapped his arms around her and pulled her onto his lap before instantly setting her on her feet.

"Law, I didn't hurt you did I Gracie? I got carried away."

She laughed and sat back onto the swing. Stephen laughed too. He took her hand in his then he took her face in his hands. He seemed to have no way to express this joy.

"I never thought…I mean I wasn't expectin'…Gracie, I didn't think we could…," with a deep breath he finished, "I don't know what to say."

"You should say – no, WE should say Thank God."

He closed his eyes and nodded, "Yes, thank you Lord Jesus you have blessed us beyond what I could even imagine."

They were still on the swing when Martin wandered into the yard with a large jar nestled in the crook of his arm. He walked a few steps, then kicked at a rock, then moved on until he found something else to move with his bare foot.

"Martin, you got nothin' to do better than wander around aimlessly?" Stephen called to his baby brother.

"Nah, Mother's done sent me over with buttermilk. Reckon you ain't milkin' enough for Gracie to make her own." Martin ducked his head to hide the grin that would give away his joke.

"You good for nothin', you come up on this porch and let me whoop you."

"Ya' ain't big enough no more Stephen."

Gracie giggled as the boys bantered and Stephen feigned a lunge at the teenager. Martin shouldered by him and then offered the buttermilk to Gracie as though it were a prized gift presented to royalty.

"Thank you Martin. Did you have to churn it, too?"

He nodded and again tried to hide a sheepish grin. "Didn't care to churn, at least the porch was shady and it got me out of the corn field early."

"Well I thank you for the work and the delivery. Have you had your supper? I'm afraid I've not made anything, but I think there's some cold side meat, and Mother Ingle made cornbread just a little while ago."

"No Ma'am, supper'll be waitin' by the time I can get back. Dad's sick too you know, he vomited while Mother was here with you. Do you reckon he's got the same trouble you do? Anyway, I hope the buttermilk helps your belly. I always drink a little of it when I'm feelin' poorly."

Gracie smiled and patted his shoulder, "I'm feeling much better, Martin, and I know the buttermilk will help."

As Martin ambled back toward his own home Gracie stretched and stepped into the warm kitchen calling back to her husband, "I'm so sorry Stephen, can you eat this side meat? If you want to stir up the fire I'll scrub some new potatoes and slice you a ripe tomato."

"Never would a man argue with that offer. Stove'll be hot before you know it."

Gracie bent to pull the potatoes from a basket on the floor and said a silent prayer of thanks that she wouldn't have to cook in the fireplace as she grew larger carrying this baby.

Lord, there's just so much to thank you for; how can I ever say it all?

Chapter 26

Martin returned to Stephen and Gracie's door at the crack of dawn. However, his usually happy face was lined with distress this time.

"Martin, what's got you over here so early? Something happen to the milk cow?" Stephen questioned as he buttoned the shirt he'd thrown on to answer Martin's banging at the door.

"It's Dad, Stephen. He's gone on to heaven in the night."

"What? What are you talkin' about boy? Dad's as fit as a fiddle."

"No, no he's not. Please come. Mother is sitting with him, but I don't think I should leave her there."

Stephen turned toward the bedroom door, "Gracie! Gracie, did you hear him?"

Gracie stood in the doorway with her hands still at the buttons of her housecoat, her face blanched white. She could only nod.

"Don't get out, I'll go see what's going on." Stephen moved about the room shoving his feet into his boots and grabbing his hat from its peg on the kitchen wall. He was out the door before Gracie even found her voice.

She looked around her house thinking it was deathly silent. *Well that's because death has come to our happy family. Oh, Lord, what will Mother Ingle do? How will we manage?*

No answers rang out from the pale morning light. She stared into the empty room another minute before turning back to dress for the day. She soon followed Stephen next door to Algurial and Katherine's house where she was met with the same unnatural silence.

The door squeaked as though announcing her entrance; the lamp burning in the kitchen led her there, where she found Martin sitting with a chipped cup in front of him.

"Martin, are you okay?"

He nodded, but she wasn't convinced.

"Where are Mother Ingle and Stephen?"

Martin raised his head to look up and she knew they must be upstairs. She turned silently and went up the stairs to join them.

Gracie slipped into the room and laid a hand on Stephen's shoulder. He smiled an acknowledgement of her presence and looked right back to his mother. The ever-practical Katherine was planning their day.

"We need to send word to Bud and Betty."

"I'll ride over there now and stop to tell Pappy on the way. Do you reckon he'll take it hard?"

She nodded, "Yeah, but he's strong. Pappy's lost a lot in this world but he knows where your daddy's at now, same as me. It sure makes the passin' easier."

Now Stephen and Gracie nodded.

"I'll go now."

Gracie reached for her mother-in-law to draw her from the room, "Mother Ingle, let me get him ready."

"No! Whatever you do, don't touch this dead body, you'd lose that baby for sure."

Gracie bowed her head, "I forgot."

"Gracie, Jury's gone from this world, but that baby you are carryin' is the promise of another generation of Ingles. He would not want you to sacrifice it.

Gracie shook her head, "Of course not. Let me walk down to Lottie's, I'm sure she will get him ready."

"Don't you worry about it, me and Betty can take care of it. Gracie this is such a shock. He didn't feel 'xactly right yesterday, but I never dream't he was nigh dead."

"We never know, do we?"

"No child, we don't. And none of us are promised tomorrow. That's why we've got to get ready with the Lord early on. You be ready to teach that little'n about Jesus from the day he's born."

"I promise."

The Ingles moved through the day scarcely knowing it had passed. The boys went out to care for the stock that were hungry and helpless regardless of the family's mourning. Word spread through Martha Washington and well before noon people began to file in with dishes of food, hugs and sympathy.

By nightfall a coffin had been built, although Gracie never quite knew who took care of that task. Daddy Jury was laid in the pine box and set over stools in the front parlor.

Betty and Lottie joined forces to convince both Stephen and Gracie to go home while they sat up with the body. The couple had little energy to argue and found their way home to pass a restless night.

The morning saw the entire Ingle clan walking and riding to Clarkrange where Daddy Jury would be buried in the cemetery at Bruner's Chapel where so many of the family members had already been laid to rest in the two decades since they trekked from Virginia.

Gracie was sure it was a miracle handed from God that no one arrived at her door for two full weeks following the funeral. She rested - she didn't have any choice with both Stephen and Mother Ingle hounding her every time they saw her standing.

"Goodness Lottie, they'll hardly let me walk to the privy."

Lottie chuckled at her sister as they sat breaking beans.

"You be thankful for the care. Dan'l scarcely notices when I'm big with child anymore."

"Well honey you've been pregnant more than not since you've been married."

Again Lottie chuckled and immediately looked into the yard where Ida Francis shepherded her little brother as he toddled from one flower to another.

Gracie's hands never stopped grabbing, stringing and breaking the beans as she watched her niece and nephew play. Her heart swelled as she thought how much she had loved them and wondered how she could love her own baby any more.

Lottie interrupted her thoughts, "You been such a comfort and blessing to me in those two births, I sure hope this England woman will be as good for your time."

"Well Mother Ingle thinks highly of her and she's seein' after her own daughter's birthin's so those are both good signs, don't you think?"

"Like I said, I hope so. More than that, I'm praying it'll be so. Did I tell you that Armildy Baldwin's in the family way again? You know she's gonna' be sendin' for you."

"Don't you think Mrs. Reeder will attend her?"

"No, Gracie, I don't think Mrs. Reeder's one iota willin' to catch a baby anymore."

"Even with me expecting? Surely when she hears."

"Well she's gettin' on up in years, and I don't think she ever liked midwifin' – in fact I don't know why she ever started it."

Gracie giggled, "You don't start it; midwifin' starts you, sort'a like a big rock rollin' down a hill."

Lottie laughed with her as the pan of broken beans grew fuller and the children in the yard grew more tired. Lottie looked at her beautiful sister and said a silent *Thank you Lord* that they could be so close.

"Lottie do you ever think what a blessing God has given us that we can live so close together, and be married to cousins so our families are intertwined?"

Lottie began nodding before Gracie even finished the question. "I was just praisin' the good Lord in heaven for that very thing. I know it's a comfort to Grandma that even though we can't live real close to her we still have each other."

"Hmmm and I imagine it would've been a comfort to our mother as well."

"Guess so, 'cept she was willin' to go way off to Chicago and not live anywhere close to her people."

"Lottie, we can't judge her by the willful and disobedient girl that ran off from her family. Never forget that she gave her very last ounce of strength to save us from that life. She had surely realized where she needed to be."

"I don't know, Gracie. There are so many questions that we won't know the answer till we see her in heaven, will we? Maybe one day our father will come to us and give us some answers."

Gracie nodded, "Maybe. Right now I'm just thankful. I need to write him and tell him about the baby though."

"Yep, would be the right thing to do." She stood as she called, "Ideee watch your brother. That cat's gonna' try and steal his breath."

Gracie watched as Ida Francis pulled the big tabby into her lap and began jabbering at him as she stroked his back. She marveled that neither child nor animal was too rough with the other.

"Gracie, now that you've got started, I'm guessing you'll have a houseful of youngins before you can even catch your breath."

Gracie smiled and closed her eyes for a deep breath, "I will take whatever blessing God has in store for me." She looked straight into her sister's eyes as she continued, "I'm really learning, Lottie, that God has a plan for me, and every time I try to make that plan a little better I just make a big mess. Somehow I've got to be willin' to sit back and let him love me and heap blessin's on me, just like little Idy is lovin' on that cat. I often wish I was as smart as the animals that just let us take care of them without worryin' about whether we're going to be faithful or not."

"Sister you a'plannin' on preachin' this week? Because there's a good sermon in that."

Again the sisters shared a hearty laugh and they continued laughing and chatting until Daniel appeared on the steps a while later. "You two been a laughin' and carryin' on till I could hear you way down to the barn."

Lottie tossed a bean tip at him, "Go on now; look at all these beans we got ready to can. Now don't act like we've not accomplished anything."

Daniel laughed as he always did and said no more as he collected their scraps and slowly walked back down the worn path leading to the pig pen.

"That was a hint that he wants his dinner now, you know."

Gracie smiled and stood, "Yes, I know. Daniel Ingle is never too hard to figure."

"No he is not and his needs are simple. He's a good man, Gracie, and a fine husband."

Gracie laid a hand briefly on her sister's shoulder, "I know. Let's get these inside and I'll scald jars before I have to get back home. Do you have the rubber seals soakin' already?"

"Yeah, I do. Daniel got me another dozen jars you know. He said if we're gonna' have a houseful of children we'll need to be putting by plenty every summer."

"He's got big plans for sure. How many jars does that make you?"

Lottie tried to quell her pride and ducked her head as she answered with a simple, "Six dozen."

Gracie smiled too thankful her little sister had such a valuable resource. "Well I'll bet we've got enough beans broke up here for nearly three dozen." Working while she talked, she pulled a kettle of warm water from the stove, "Where are your soap flakes?"

"There's a tin on the shelf by the dry sink. I think there's enough but I'm going to need to shave some more off soon."

"Lottie, I'm out of soap, I just remembered. Do you reckon it'd be safe for me to make a batch?"

"Hmm, we won't chance it. I'll send you with some of the bars I have made and I'll tell Dan'l we need to be savin' the ashes for another batch soon. I should've been doing that for you all along seein' as how you spend so much time running from one house to another helping people."

"Lottie I could never see after these women if you and Mother Ingle didn't help me out so much. I guess I'll have to get myself used to doing for my own household instead of running around like you said from one house to the next."

Chapter 27

The weeks flew by as Gracie sewed clothes and knitted blankets for the baby while still running her home. Word spread through the community that she was in the family way and would not be able to attend other births and mostly folks respected it. Stephen reveled in the attention she was able to pour on him cooking his favorite foods and sitting on the porch through the hot summer evenings then before their fireplace as autumn spread across the mountain. He hunted and rarely failed to return with hands filled with rabbit or quail and a proud grin. Every time Gracie immediately turned to helping him skin or pluck the game and then applying the skills Grandma had taught her from an early age to create delicious dishes Stephen bragged about to all of his brothers and cousins.

Two times through the winter months the familiar knock sounded and each time Gracie looked to Stephen. Whether for permission or advice neither knew but each time Stephen reached for his coat without a moment's pause and personally drove her to attend the women in need. They talked on these trips and found they were in complete agreement that their own baby must be the top priority. Still neither Stephen nor Gracie could turn away someone in need, and, with each passing month of her own pregnancy, Gracie developed a better understanding of how needful these women were. Time and again she thanked God that Grandma Elmore had taught her this midwifing skill and she clung to the hope that her skill, would see her through her own travail.

It was Christmastime when she stepped onto the porch after Stephen had waited for hours with an anxious father and she read in his eyes that it was time for her to stay home. She gave the new father a reassuring smile and nodded to the door behind her, "Allie has something to show you inside. She said her mother would be over to see about y'uns once she'd taken care of the mornin's work at her own house. So, I'll head on home with my husband."

The young man was shaking his head and took her hand to shake it too, "Yes, Ma'am, Mizz Gracie. We shore 'preciate you, I don't know what we'd have done without you. Oh, I should've got somethin' for you – I've got plenty of chestnuts and Allie, she kept several pullets back for the winter – let me go see what I can find."

By the time he'd finished his excited speech Stephen was returning from the barn with the little wagon. Gracie gently pulled her hand from his and gave another of her warm smiles.

"No, no Mr. Delk, you need to see about your wife right now. Now I don't want her up much, her mother'll know when she gets here, but you just watch her till then, okay?"

"Yes, yes. I'll do just what you say, Mizz Gracie. And I'll be over ta' your place in a day or two with your pay."

Stephen called from the wagon's side as he lifted Gracie onto the seat, "Thank you, Rosco. Come on by anytime you want to."

As they drove away Gracie tucked the blanket around her thickening waistline and asked, "Now Stephen, why didn't you tell him that there was no need to bring anything?"

Stephen never turned his head from watching his mare as he raised one side of his mouth, "Because I wanted them chestnuts."

She swatted at his arm with the back of her hand, but couldn't stop the smile.

"It's time to stop, ain't it?"

"Yeah, I just got the feelin' real plain sitting out there that we need to keep you at home now. Of course, you're the expert on babies, but maybe the Lord gives a husband an idea or two along the way."

"He surely does. And I won't argue with my husband."

Several minutes passed with only the plodding of the horse's hooves and crunch of wagon wheels.

Then Gracie added, "Only I'm gonna' let you answer the door so you can tell them 'no'."

Stephen grinned again and just nodded.

The winter started out cold, but the snows were scarce. The Ingle men kept busy mending harness and building furniture or feed bins; they cut firewood and hewed out a few cross ties along the way to bring in a dollar or two to buy coffee and flour. Stephen kept the kitchen woodbox filled and Gracie was never expected to step out the door except as her own needs demanded.

She smiled as she watched her husband push the barn door against a stiff wind and balance a bucket of milk while trying to secure the button latch. *Lord, he has spoiled me terribly this winter. Please help me to show him how very much I appreciate it and how thankful I am that you have given me such a wonderful life…*

She was still praying when the screen door squeaked ahead of the thump of the wooden door made as Stephen placed a foot against it to push his way inside.

"Whew, that lil' heifer is takin' all the milk, or maybe our brown Guernsey thinks it's just too cold to give up her milk."

"Stephen, I ought to be milking for you. I can, you know."

"You can milk after the baby comes. Right now, I want you to take care of yourself."

"Would you have pampered me so much if I'd had a baby the first year we were married?"

"I doubt it." He turned back to add, "Maybe that's why God made me wait. I had to have time to really appreciate this blessing."

She smiled and reached to stroke his back as he headed out again to tend to the feeding of his father's animals.

As she spread the cheesecloth over her milk pitcher she resumed her prayer, *I have tried to be faithful to the work you gave me Lord and I surely hope I've pleased you. I do not deserve these blessings, of course I don't even deserve the attention of a heavenly Father. Thank you Lord for your care of a sinner like me. Lord please protect this little baby I'm carrying, and Lord if you could allow me to survive the birth and live to see him raised – if you could give me that blessing, I would praise you everyday. And I won't fail to tell this child that he is a gift sent straight from you Lord…*

Gracie had long been in the habit of talking to her lord whenever she was alone. In fact, she remembered her grandmother talking to God aloud.

A realization hit her, *Hmm, was she doing that to teach us to pray? I'm going to have to ask her that. Surely we'll go visit in the early summer. As soon as I'm able to make the trip after the baby comes…*

The blustery winter blew right into spring with little green buds dotting trees and deep green crocus blade peeking through the hard ground. It was an early Easter and Gracie wanted so badly to attend church. They even had a preacher, and that was a special treat for the celebration of the Saviour's Resurrection. Stephen sat by the front window with the bible on his lap, his back bent to see the words more clearly.

"Stephen will you ride with your folks up to Bruner's Chapel?"

"No, I won't be going today."

"What? But, it's Easter Sunday. Why ever would you miss church on this of all days?"

"Because I need to stay with you."

"Oh, no, you don't. I will be just fine. Now you get on your white shirt – I've not stood over that flat iron pressing it for nearly an hour just to let it lie on the bed and get wrinkled again."

"Gracie, please don't send me away. I wouldn't have a moment's peace in that service if I knew you were home alone when it's so close to the time for our baby."

"Stephen Ingle, the good Lord is going to watch over me and this baby. And I've not seen the first sign that he's ready to come. Get your shirt on."

He smiled and lifted his hands in surrender. "You're the expert, not me."

Gracie was pouring a cup of water over dried mint leaves when she heard the rattle of harness and chains. "Stephen, do you hear them?"

He stepped from their bedroom pulling his good coat on as he walked. "You sure?"

"Yes, of course I'm sure. Anyway I want to read the bible and you were hogging it from me."

He answered her smile with a tight embrace. "I love you Gracie Ingle. I'll be home as quick as I can. If they aren't driving fast enough I'll walk and beat 'em."

She waved to the Ingles as he stepped from the porch "Tell everyone I miss them."

With the door closed tight, she grabbed her cup and just as she'd promised Stephen went directly to the rocker by the front window where he'd left their bible.

Chapter 28

Gracie opened her eyes and pushed with both her hand and her foot trying to shift her weight. "Oohh," escaped her lips involuntarily. Her head jerked to see if Stephen was still in the bed beside her but the covers were flat and his pillow empty.

What time is it? She wondered.

Then she heard the squeak of the stove door and the raking of the fire poker against wood chunks. She shifted her weight again trying to find any position that would relieve the ache in her back. Finding none she swung her legs over the side of the bed and located her shoes waiting there.

She stood slowly as the aching spread from her lower back to her hips. With shuffling steps she moved into the kitchen still kneading her back. No light could be seen through the windows, yet there was coffee boiling on the stove and Stephen had one hand full of a cast iron skillet and the stove's eye lid in the other.

"What time is it? It feels like the middle of the night but you're going strong."

He smiled and positioned the skillet over the open flame. "It's well after five. I've got to get to plowin' at the very first light."

"Why didn't you wake me? You shouldn't be cookin' your own breakfast when you're gonna' spend the day behind a mule and plow."

He cracked an egg streaming egg white onto the gleaming black stove. "You didn't sleep well, kept tossin' and turnin' – well, that's not exactly right 'cause you can't turn much these days, can you?" He grinned and winked at her.

"Hmmph, no I cannot turn much."

She dipped a glass of water from the bucket and sipped it staring into the darkness of the early morning.

"You gonna' have some coffee? I made plenty."

She looked at the pot then down at her water glass that she'd emptied without realizing it. "No, that doesn't sound good to me this morning."

"Okay, well would you push it over to the cooler side of the stove?" He carried his heaping plate to the end of the table and dug right into it.

Mechanically she moved the coffee pot and closed the dampers on the stove. Again her hand went to her back.

Finished with his food, Stephen stooped to tie the laces of his low brogan boots. Tugging his pants over the tops, he stood and turned to Gracie, taking a good look at her for the first time that morning. "Gracie, you don't look good. It was a rougher night than I thought, wasn't it? It's getting really hard for you to rest."

"I'm fine Stephen. You worry about the mules and plow points, not me."

He smiled and drew her to him in a warm embrace.

As they stepped apart he reached one hand for his hat and the other for the doorknob.

She smiled and said as he stepped out, "Are you goin' to take Martin with you?"

"Well he or Daddy one will plow beside me."

"Will you tell your mother to come by whenever she gets her work caught up?"

"Sure will." And he was gone, fading into the morning's twilight.

Gracie looked around her home, one hand still on her back. She saw the skillet left on the stove, crumbs on the table. Tilting her head to one side she took in the condition of the parlor and judged it acceptable.

"I've got work to do," she said to the empty house.

She filled the skillet with water and pulled it back over the still-warm stove. Grabbing a rag she cleaned the table and went for her broom to remove any crumbs that had made their way to the floor. In no time she had scrubbed the skillet clean and left it upside down over the stove's reservoir.

Thank you Lord for giving me a good stove. It was an oft' repeated prayer.

She pulled her Grandma's big basket from the corner and took out a tiny white shirt and several new diapers. The diaper pins were in a small basket waiting on the dresser and she put them all together. The bottom of the basket was filled with clean rags she'd collected from several of Stephen's cousins as well as Lottie. She pushed the basket under the foot of the bed.

Gracie had drawn several buckets of water and was filling her last big pot when she heard Katherine call to her, "Gracie what in the world are you doing? Didn't Stephen draw your water this morning? You're not fixin' to wash are you?"

She continued into the house with the bucket in her hand as she answered her mother-in-law. "No Mother Ingle, but we're going to need this."

"Why'd you fill that washtub?" Suddenly she realized. "It's time?"

Gracie nodded, her big eyes disclosing her fear and the growing smile proving her excitement.

"I'll send Martin for Mrs. England."

"Don't rush him. It'll be a while I think. I was hurting when I woke up and I don't really remember it but Stephen said I was fretful all night long so I guess it kind of started then."

"We better get word to her anyway." Katherine turned and was gone in an instant.

Gracie smiled realizing Stephen's family all shared her joy and looked forward to their first grandbaby.

Absently she rubbed her bulging belly as she looked around again trying to anticipate every need. *Why is this so easy when I walk into a stranger's house?* She wondered.

She cracked open the stove's damper and added a couple of pieces of wood. Then she went to her favorite seat by the window and rocked, and prayed.

Mother Ingle returned with a basket over her arm and a jar in the other hand. "Do you have plenty of eggs Gracie?"

"Yes ma'am, we only set the one hen, so I've got a bowl full."

"Well I've brought a jar of pickled-relish and I'll just put some eggs on to boil and I've got fresh butter here so I'll mix up some mayonnaise. Oh, and I brought bread too. Does any of that sound appetizing to you?"

Gracie was smiling at this precious woman's kindness. "Mother Ingle, you think of everything. I was only thinking of myself."

"As you should be. But how many times have you stood by a laboring woman for hours only to be offered cold cornbread and water afterward?"

Again, Gracie could only smile and wonder how Katherine Ingle could know these things. She had no chance to ask the question aloud for a strong cramp began to spread down her stomach. She reached for a chair but caught it unevenly causing it to topple.

Katherine rushed to her side before she fell. "That means it's time to put you in the bed."

"It will be a long time yet I think. I can't lie in the bed while you're cooking in my kitchen."

"I don't suppose you can give me a good reason for that, now can you?" She turned Gracie around still holding her arms and gently pushed her into the bedroom.

"You try to relax and get a little rest. You know you're going to need it. My goodness child you'd think I was the midwife here."

Gracie heard the tinkling of the boiling eggs and before they were cooked the shuffle of feet on the front porch announced Mrs. England's arrival ahead of her knock on the door. Gracie heard Mother Ingle greeting her.

"I've put her in the bed. The pains got strong enough that she nearly fell out."

"How long?" asked a strange voice.

"I'm not sure. My son said she didn't rest well all through the night."

"Well, this is a very polite baby to come early in the morning. My babies were never so thought-y; they mostly came in the middle of the night."

"We sure are thankful to have you helpin' us. She's the one what knows about catching babies around here."

"Yes, I've heard a lot of good things about your daughter."

"Thank you. She's actually married to my son and a great blessing to our family."

They entered the darkened bedroom and Gracie started to sit up. Together both women reached arms out to stop her. "No, no. There's no need for you to get up."

"Mrs. England, thank you so much for coming. I sure hope we've not called you too…" Another pain stole her voice and Gracie fell back on the bed without any more urging.

"You can call me Rhod-y, there ain't no need to be formal here. We – well, I's about to say we 'Granny-women' but you sure ain't no Granny-Woman. I've been hearin' all over what a blessing you've been when all these women in the Martha Washington community have needed you. Then when they asked if I'd help in your delivery I thought you must already have a houseful of youngins. Is this your first?"

Gracie could only nod as another pain built like a sea wave.

Rhoda continued to speak softly about everything and nothing at all. Soon Gracie realized her tactic and smiled, hoping she would remember it the next time she attended a birthing.

Even as the pains came more and more quickly she chided herself, *What do you mean the 'next time'? You will only be attending your own births now that God has started giving you children.*

Gracie heard Stephen come in the back talking to her as he walked. There were hushed words then the sound of the door clicking closed again. She never saw Stephen and wished he were there to hold her hand. *He always makes things better… but it wouldn't be fair to make him see what a woman has to go through…*

Then another pain.

Rhoda left the room and then came again.

"How long…," Gracie tried to ask.

Unsure of the exact question, Rhoda began again in her diverting chatter. "Oh honey it won't be too long now. You're doin' real good. That man of you your'n come by earlier wantin' his dinner I guess. Mrs. Ingle she sent him along to her house only she gave him some of that good egg salad. She sure is a good cook, don't you think? I hope she's taught you only I guess your own mother taught you before you married. I sure learned about everything I would need about keepin' house at my mother's knees. And I've tried to give my own girls the same thing. You know I've got three girls, and little bitty boys. A'course there's one boy waitin' on me in heaven…"

Gracie tried hard to focus on the words, wanted to know all about this woman who was caring for her, wanted to be able to relate to her in a calmer moment. Another pain stole that thought from her.

William Burton Todd finally made his much anticipated appearance just before five o'clock. Rhoda handed him to Katherine who stood by with a big white cloth to swaddle him in before wrapping him in a new quilt. She beamed as she nestled him in Gracie's arms.

"I can't see him."

"That's because you're crying," Katherine said through her own smiling tears.

"Where's Stephen?"

"Not yet. Mizz Rhoda will be finished in a bit."

Rhoda leaned over to Gracie, "Feed him and let Katherine get him cleaned up. You've still got a little work to do here."

The next piece of time blurred to Gracie, in fact she could scarcely remember most of the day as she thought about it later.

Soon Stephen stood at the door with their baby in his arms. He smiled first at his son and then at his wife.

Chapter 29

Gracie wrapped the blanket snugly around Burton's pudgy shoulder and silently prayed, *Lord keep him in your care this night. Thank you for my Baby Burton.*

Her hand was still on the lamp's wick regulator when she heard the rushing feet, panting and in the next instant, a pounding on the door. "Hello the house, please help me," came the frantic cry.

Stephen hopped from the bed and practically jumped into his overalls. He was still reaching for the galluses as he opened the door. He never had the chance to greet the man.

"My wife, she needs the midwife. She's been a'laborin' the whole day and now she's bleedin' and my mother done sent me to fetch your woman."

Stephen was nodding with his hand on the man's shoulder. The familiarity of the request coming back to him after the months of quiet.

"Gracie, can you come out here?"

She stepped around the chimney, cinching her housecoat and looked from the stranger to her husband.

"Looks like you're needed."

"But Stephen, what about Burton? I can't…"

"Honey, you can't *not* go, can you?"

Her head was already shaking, "No, I guess you're right. But what about Burton?"

"He's had his late night milk, and he'll be fine till mornin'. If you're not back, I'll bundle him up and go over to Mother's. She can handle one little baby boy for a few hours."

Gracie formed a dozen excuses, perfectly good reasons why a mother ought to stay right in that house. Then she looked at the strange man who kept looking at the door as though he might bolt any minute.

Stephen saw him too.

"Gracie, get yourself together." Turning to their visitor, "Do you have a wagon?"

"I run. I run all the way. Never even thought to harness the horse. I mean, I got a good sled that would've carried your woman just fine but I never even thought of it."

Stephen again placed a strong and calming hand on his shoulder, "Come help me harness up my ole' mare and then Gracie will have that to drive back in the morning."

Before Gracie had her boots laced she heard the harness jingle and brakes squeak as the little wagon stopped at the front porch. The stranger stayed on the wagon with reigns in hand as Stephen stepped inside.

"They live up toward Clarkrange, ain't been around here long. Don't know much of anybody."

"Clarkrange? Why didn't they get Dr. Lydick?"

"Don't think they trust a man-doctor. Anyway, he said the old man was off somewhere doctorin' or tradin' or something."

Gracie nodded as she stood and grabbed her basket. "Well, if you're sure you're okay with little Burton I'm ready."

He wrapped her in his arms as he reassured her, "Gracie, it's your callin' and I've got no right to hold you back from the work God's given you to."

A tear threatened to escape as she nodded and stepped into the darkness. After a moment her eyes adjusted and she situated herself on the hard wooden seat. As the wagon lurched forward, she began preparing herself for the ordeal before her by questioning her driver, "I'm afraid I didn't get your name, and I'll need to know your wife's name. It helps if I can talk to her like we're old friends…"

By the time Gracie returned, the springtime sun was creeping toward its noonday apex. As the mare stole into the yard, the reigns lay limp in Gracie's hands and she sat stone-like before the barn until Polly neighed, jolting her from her trance.

"Whoa girl…oh, I guess you already stopped." Gracie talked to the horse as she climbed from the wagon and took hold of the bridle leading the rig into the barn. Her hands fumbled with the trace chains and dropped them to the ground. She was working with the shaft buckles when Stephen found her.

"Gracie, you sure do look tired."

"Oh, I…" the tears overwhelmed her words as she buried her head in the horse's coat.

Stephen crossed the distance from the door in two long strides and turned her into his embrace. "Shh, what's happened? Did you lose them?"

"Huuuh," she sobbed trying to form the words to answer him. "Just the mama. Stephen she was bleeding before he ever came to get me and by the time…huuh…it was just too late by the time I got there."

He gently caressed her back, speaking gentle words of comfort until she could go on.

"I shouldn't have gone. I can't do it anymore. What's happened to me?"

"You? Gracie, you had to try. There was a chance, there's always a chance you might save one of them."

"Oh, the baby made it. She's a strong beautiful girl." A smile crept through the sobs, "Lungs like a wild cat."

"Gracie, see what you did? Would that baby have made it without you? God put you there just for her."

She couldn't face him as she revealed the name, "They named her Grace. Why am I ashamed of that?"

"I don't know, I really don't. They named her after you 'cause they knew you were that baby's only chance at life. Don't be ashamed. You be proud."

"I need to hold my baby." Suddenly she realized Stephen was in the barn. Was Burton all alone? "Stephen, where is he?"

Stephen tightened his hold on her, "Mother's in the house with him."

With another deep breath Gracie began to slow her frantic breathing, "Of course. I knew you would take care of our baby. Let me get my dress changed and get in there to him."

As she walked away from her husband's work with the horses, her shoulders began to lift.

I dread confessing this to Mother Ingle. She's goin' to fuss at me for leaving my own baby.

Gracie smiled as she saw the clean dress laid out on a bench in the little wood hut. *Did Stephen remember to put this out here? Who would think of a man being so thoughtful? Or maybe it was Mother Ingle.*

Again the thought of her mother-in-law gave her a shudder. *Nothing to do but get in there and face the music. Burton will be needing to nurse and I sure am needing to hold him and know he's okay.*

She dropped her soiled dress in the basket by the back door and pushed open the screen door. As though he sensed her presence, the baby began to fuss and she could hear Katherine Ingle's deep alto humming a wordless tune. She walked directly to the front room and put a hand gently on Mother Ingle's shoulder.

"He's sure missin' you." Mrs. Ingle stood and handed the warm bundle to his mother.

When their eyes met, tears welled in Gracie's.

"Child, what's happened?"

"I'm just waiting for you to tell me how awful I am for leavin' my baby."

"Awful? What are you a'talkin' about Gracie?"

"I left him, just walked out that door with some stranger, I didn't even know his name. And I left my baby!"

"Gracie, you're not makin' any sense. You ain't left nobody. Burton is just fine. Stephen said he slept real good through the night and just woke up early. I's able to get a little warm milk down him but of course he's needin' to nurse. So you take care of him and dry your eyes. I'll get you some coffee boiling."

Gracie took her place in the rocker and began to feed little Burton. She ran her finger over his soft brow and when he wrapped his own tiny fingers around hers she prayed. *Lord thank you for this baby. Thank you that I'm healthy and strong and able to care for him. Please Lord let me live to raise him. Please help Mr. Bradford and help him raisin' that precious little girl. Lord I know you have a plan for him and for his children but it's always so hard to see when they've lost their mother.*

Gracie jerked her head at a noise and opened her eyes as Mother Ingle lifted Burton from her arms.

"I must have drifted off."

Katherine smiled down at her, "You need to rest."

"I guess we ought to talk first."

"Let me lay this boy down and then we sure can. Go on in and pour yourself a cup of coffee."

Gracie smiled, trying to look braver than she felt. Mother Ingle joined her in the kitchen just as she finished stirring thick cream into the strong coffee. She picked up a slice of bread slathered in butter and used her toe to scoot out a straight-back chair from the table. Katherine slid into a chair across from her and cocked her head as though she were trying to read Gracie's mind.

"Well I'm ready Mother Ingle."

"Ready for what?"

"Ready to hear whatever you've got to say to me about runnin' off in the night."

"Gracie Ingle, I don't know what you're talkin' about. Are you so tired you're out of your mind?"

"No, it's just that I was sure you'd be mad at me since you were here keepin' my baby – the baby Stephen and I waited so long for. Now he's just a few months old, and off I go to catch somebody else's baby."

Mother Ingle placed a warm hand on Gracie's trembling hand, "Gracie, I can't be mad at you without bein' mad at God Almighty and I ain't willin' to do that. He sent you that man last night, and I know you've gone and been a blessing to that family so, I've just gotta' be a blessing to you – my very own family."

Tears tumbled down Gracie face now, "Why are you always so loving to me?"

"Because God first loved me."

Gracie smiled. "And you've always got a word from the scripture too."

"I've got to be ready always to give an answer."

Both ladies burst into laughter and Gracie pulled a handkerchief from her pocket to dry her face.

"Now Gracie, I want you to tell me about your night. Who was this stranger?"

"Well I don't know too much. Their name is Bradford. They come from way off, and all over. He said they'd been out in California and their first baby was born there. They've only been here for a few weeks and it was just too late for her to be travelin' you know. They first went for that doctor that's moved in up in Clarkrange but he was off somewhere. I don't know but what he might have been able to save her."

"Was it because of the bleeding?"

"No, that wasn't the trouble. She was just worn out. It's almost like the birthin' took the last of her strength. She had been laboring for hours, maybe days because she couldn't tell me when it had started. To tell you the truth, she couldn't tell me much of anything, even her name. It was almost like her mind had done passed on from this world and it was just her body there. That sounds crazy, too, don't it?"

"No, I've heard of the like before this. Back home in Virginia there was a neighbor girl. She weren't too old and everything seemed to go fine until right before the baby came. It was a long labor, and she just quit talkin' and they said her eyes seemed to die even while she was still moving and laboring."

Gracie's head slowly moved from side to side as she tried to make sense of the sad story even as she remembered similar tales from her Grandmother. "It's always hard for me to understand. I know I can only do what the good Lord lets me do but you know I can't help but feel like I've done somethin' wrong when I lose someone."

Katherine patted the hand she still held and nodded gently. "What about the baby?"

"Oh the baby's fine – strong even. Of course it's always hard to raise one without her mama."

"You know, one of our milk cows should be calvin' any day. I'm going to take some of the first milk and send it over to them. Will do Martin good to make the walk and that first milk will sure help start that lil' baby off right."

"Oh Mother Ingle, you always think of the best thing to do."

"Well now, I've had lots of lil' orphaned animals through the years and I've learned a few things you know. Well I'll mosey back up the hill – unless you need me to watch the baby while you get some sleep."

"No, I'll be just fine. I'm going to spend some time in God's word and then when he's up we'll get ourselves out to pullin' weeds in that garden before they plumb take the peas and little potato plants."

With a final pat of her hand Katherine rose and slipped out the back door, tying her bonnet as she walked. Gracie returned to her rocking chair, pulled it close to the window and opened her bible. She turned to the Psalms knowing she'd find there the comfort her soul was craving.

With Burton's first waking sounds her eyes popped open and she had to lunge to keep the precious book from falling to the floor. Immediately she realized she had fallen asleep before she'd read three words. With great care she returned the book to its place on the little table, and said a silent prayer to thank God for providing His word and to beg His forgiveness that she had not managed to read it.

At this rate, I'll never have words from the bible spring to mind the way Stephen's mother does.

However, her time and attention were now demanded by her son. After a diaper change, she did walk out to open the squeaking gate into the vegetable garden where she sat Burton down on a tattered blanket to play while she pulled weeds and talked to him.

"Burton, you'll have to help with the garden in just another year or two. I'll teach you which plants we keep and which ones need to be thrown out. Weeding is good for the soul…"

"Gracie, is Burton answerin' you yet?" Stephen called as he painted grease on his double shovel.

"How long you been over there without saying a word?"

"Not long. Just enjoyin' you workin' on your knees."

She threw a clump of weeds his direction, "You keep talking like that and you'll be doin' this weeding yourself. Anyway, if I don't talk to Burton how will he ever learn to talk? And he is learning, you know, so he might as well be learning about godly work."

Stephen grinned as he picked up the grease can, "Can't argue with that. He won't learn nothin' but foolishness from me, I reckon."

"Burton, you have a lot you can learn from your father. He's a good man and I hope and pray you will be just as good when you have a family of your own."

Chapter 30

Gracie spent the rest of the afternoon cleaning out her garden and chasing the patch of shade where Burton would lay kicking and coo'ing on his blanket. Between talks to her son, she talked to her Lord. Still uneasy about her decision to go with Arthur Bradford last night, she thanked God for Mother Ingle's wise counsel, yet still she begged him to know whether he agreed with her mother-in-law.

She's proven to me again and again that I can always trust her to point me toward you Lord. And even today it was your word that she quoted to me. And I felt comfort while she was here but now I feel guilty again. Lord, I thank you for giving me this precious child. And I want to be the mother you mean for me to be and I can't do that if I'm a'runnin' all over creation catching babies.

A fragment of a sermon popped into her mind, for an instant she could see the little church house in Elmore, could smell the lilacs she'd put in the windowsill the day before. "GO! God has called everyone of you to go…"

Now that preacher was tellin' us to go out and tell people about the Lord. To spread his word all over the world.

Even as she made the argument a still small voice seemed to whisper, *I told you to go and help these women and tell them about my love.*

Lord, I always pray and I always tell them that You are the only one who can help them. Oh Lord, did I tell Marie Bradford in the wee hours of this morning? Did I even tell her that she needed you to forgive her of her sins?

She looked up, ready for God's judgment to fall on her as it had when Lot ran from Sodom. Instead wispy clouds glided through a tranquil blue sky and the sun settled just a degree lower on its pathway to the horizon. Somewhere a bird called. Gracie let out a deep breath and her memory flashed Arthur Bradford's whispered prayers as his wife slipped across the divide into eternity. His words came back to her, "…she is your child…" This man had known his wife and he had known she was a believer.

Thank you for giving me that, Lord. Now if I could just know what's the right thing to do.

Again her mind flashed a memory, the gulf so deep she stood above birds as they flew along the creek far below, the hard rock she sat on and God's voice. So real was the memory that she turned her eyes toward the furthest edge of the Ingle farm as though maybe she could see that ravine from here. She cocked her head wondering if she would hear from God as clearly now as she had then. She only heard her memory but it was enough.

I'm sorry, Lord. You promised me a great blessing – more children than any woman on this mountain if I would only obey and serve you. Please don't take that blessing from me because I doubted. You were faithful in your promise to Sarah even after she laughed at your angel. I'm no better than her, am I? Well I will obey. If you want me to keep helping the women of Martha Washington, I will surely do it. Only please care for my own little Burton.

The sun had again shifted leaving the baby's blanket exposed and she stepped over to him, holding him close and taking in the sweet baby scent. Wordlessly she praised God for his goodness to give her this son.

When the sun finally touched the western horizon Gracie was mashing potatoes with a heavy steel spoon, carefully folding in sweet cream. The door squeaked as it always did when Stephen stepped inside, his hands still damp from the wash pan.

"Sure smells good Gracie."

"The potatoes don't want to mash smooth this time of year."

"I won't complain about a few lumps." He bent his head to lay a kiss on her cheek.

She smiled up at him. "I stewed a chicken. I know they're a little small for it. It was just what I was craving."

"So long as you're the one plucking 'em and cookin' then I won't complain about that either. You've worked hard today on little rest. Gracie, you must be sure you're taking care of yourself."

She smiled at him, "You work hard every day."

He grinned as he turned toward the blanket where his son lay, "Not too hard to play with this boy."

Little Burton stretched and coo'd in his daddy's arms.

Stephen turned back to Gracie to ask, "You were surely takin' something out on them weeds today. Do you want to tell me about it?"

Again she smiled, always wondering how he could read her so clearly. "I guess I was. I needed to talk to the Lord and out there under his sky seems to be the best place."

"Yep, that's where you always go."

"Hmm, and he never fails to answer me."

"You lookin' for a pillar of a cloud like the Children of Israel followed in the wilderness?"

"You're makin' fun and I've been nearly broken under a burden all day."

He smiled at her and wrapped one arm around her waist as he held Burton in the other.

Reassured that he was serious again, she went on to tell him how she was struggling with her decision last night.

"You're mother says that if the good Lord sends me women to help, I've got no choice."

Stephen stooped to return the baby to his blanket in the floor, "Ain't that what I said last night?"

"Yeah, I guess it's about the same. Then why do I feel so awful – I feel like I abandoned my baby and for what? That poor woman died anyway."

"Gracie, the baby lived. Do you think that man would have his little daughter without you?"

She closed her eyes and bowed her head, "I don't know, but what will become of him widowed with a new baby?"

"God has a plan for that. Look at Uncle Bill. He's lost two wives and the second one left him with twelve children. I'm sure he wondered what he was going to do until Vandora agreed to marry him and raise all those children."

"And now, she's going to add to the brood. Do you think that's a blessing?"

Stephen smiled, "Well, I sometimes wonder how he'll feed 'em all, but life is always a blessing from God even when it's a baby calf or little chick born. How much greater is a son or daughter – a baby that has a soul?"

Oh Lord, please forgive me for questioning whether something that only comes from you would be a blessing. You've told us that every good gift comes from you so surely every gift you give is for our good. Lord, Lord, Lord, when will I get it all right?

Stephen interrupted her prayer, "Is somethin' burning?"

She jerked her head to the stove where she'd laid the potato masher and the remnants of potatoes were scorching on the hot surface.

"Just another thing I got wrong," She dropped her head as a tear welled in her eye.

Stephen was at her side with a pot holder and a clean spoon to scrape away the burned potatoes. "Sit down, I've got this and we need to eat – and pray."

He sat and reached for her hand, "Lord, I keep asking you to lighten the load on my dear Gracie. I know you are listening and I believe you are faithful to answer. Could it be that Gracie keeps pickin' that burden back up? She says she keeps getting things wrong. Lord, won't you please show her that we all do and that you know we're gonna' mess up until we get to heaven? She knows how you've called her and she knows that you don't repent of your callin's – you told us that in the book of Romans, but you said in that same place that you won't take your gifts away either. We all know that you've especially gifted our Gracie with a healing touch and a wisdom beyond her years when it comes to these babies. Now you've given us our own dear boy, and we thank you ever so much for him. Except, now, Gracie don't quite know what to do with both a calling and a baby. It seems that you've made it clear both to me and my own mother that we need to support Gracie in this work. Maybe that's why you made me a farmer and not a circuit preacher or some long hunter that went wandering for months at a time. Please make it clear to Gracie that you've given her the baby, and you've also given her people to help with him whenever you send someone for her to help?

Now, Father God we thank you for this good meal you've provided. I ask you for a special blessing on these hands that have prepared it. Please bless this food to strengthen our bodies that we might serve you better and longer.

In the name of your Holy and precious son, Jesus Christ we pray, Amen."

Gracie had not raised her head since Stephen sent her from the stove. Now the tears flowed unheeded down her cheeks.

"Why you cryin' now?"

"Because I love you so much. Thank you Stephen for understanding; and thank you for walking so closely to the Lord that you see when I don't."

He squeezed the hand he still held, "When a team pulls together, one can see a hole before the other and move the whole rig out of the way. When the good Lord yoked us together we both took that responsibility. Sometimes you're the one that sees things clearer than me."

"Well I can't think of any of those times right now." She passed the bowl of potatoes, "Lumpy taters?"

"Thank you kindly," he grinned and took a double portion before handing them back to her.

"I guess we need to think about what we do when the next knock comes on the door. We'll have to have a plan. Did you get bread?"

Stephen was silent for a moment as he spread butter atop his cornbread and added a pinch of pepper to the potatoes.

"It's hard to plan when you don't know when anybody is coming or what we'll be into at that time."

"Yeah, this work I do is hard to plan for."

"We need to talk to my mother I guess. She sure is crazy about our little Burton so I know she'll help anyway she can."

"But Stephen, she has work of her own to do, and Martin still at home. We can't rely on her all the time, can we? It's not her place to raise our son."

"You can ask her that question, but I'm pretty sure she'll tell you something like, 'Everybody needs to be serving the Lord'."

Gracie smiled and nodded as she continued to eat.

After a few more bites Stephen had another thought, "He will always be okay with me if you get called away in the night. And then in the morning me and Mother can decide how best to handle things. If it's a day I don't much need to be in the fields then I can just keep him around the house here. Or if I'm out hoein' corn then he can be on a blanket there the same way he was at the garden with you."

Gracie could find no argument with his plan.

"There's more to do in the house with a baby. Just the washin' takes nearly twice as long what with diapers and clothes he soils."

"Hmm, I'm not too good at washin'. But God has a plan."

She tried not to laugh as she said, "You think the Lord's gonna' give us a magic box that will clean the clothes?"

Stephen laughed too, "He could, you know."

Chapter 31

Just as it had before Burton was born, life settled into a familiar rhythm. Most days, Gracie tended to the house and garden while she watched her baby boy move steadily toward manhood. Stephen worked his father's farm and dreamed of owning land of his own. With every passing year, Burton spent more time in the fields with Stephen as well as his Pappy Ingle learning the skills of the land that had been passed down for generations.

Five years passed and Gracie attended an untold number of births. Dr. Lydick was sometimes called and he very soon realized the gift Gracie brought to a woman's bedside.

"You won't need me with Mrs. Ingle attending," he would sometimes say and disappear into the night in his shiny black buggy.

More often than not someone in the home bid 'good riddance' to his departure as many mistrusted the man who came from the north, talked a little different than the local folk, and spent too much time with the bottle and women of questionable character. Still Gracie realized he had a different kind of knowledge than she did and she tried to encourage her neighbors to give him a chance, especially when serious injuries were involved.

The day Gracie realized her energy waned early in the day and everything she cooked smelled foul, she set out to see the good doctor herself, telling Stephen only that she needed to walk up to Clarkrange and asking whether he needed anything from Peters' Store.

"Mrs. Ingle, how good to see you in my offices today. Are you finally here to learn the modern birthing techniques?"

Gracie couldn't help but laugh, "Can't see how birthin' could have changed much since the Hebrew midwives delivered Moses' generation."

Dr. Lydick too chuckled, "Well we are making great strides in medical knowledge with every passing year. So I suppose the body doesn't change but our minds must."

She nodded at him but the anxiety in her eyes caught his attention.

"You are here with a medical need of your own, aren't you?"

Her voice was quiet, barely above a whisper as she answered, "Yes, I'm afraid so."

"Would you care to step up here on these little steps so you can sit on the table? That way I can take a look at you" He turned his head toward the open door that led into his home. "Francie, come on out here if you will."

He stepped to a small cabinet filled with glass bottles of all sizes and on the bottom shelf a tray of medical instruments. Gracie's heart leapt as her imagination flashed thoughts of what he might be planning to do to her.

A woman about Mother Ingle's age stepped into the room and smiled a greeting at Gracie. Dr Lydick turned at the sound of her entrance.

"Ah, Francie, thank you for joining us. Mrs. Ingle, do you know my wife?"

Gracie smiled and nodded her head toward the older woman, "I'm afraid I don't know her, but I'm pleased to meet you Mrs. Lydick."

"You can jist call me Francie, honey," the woman smiled at Gracie, rather shocking her by the familiar accent.

Gracie's surprise was evident because Francie Lydick explained, "Frank's from up north but I's raised right down in Burrville so I talk more like folks in Martha Washington than he does. I've got a boy about your age, Wiley, do ya' know him?"

"No Maam, I don't b'lieve I do. 'Course you know I was raised over in Elmore."

"Well yes, and your husband, his family come from Virginny after he was near grown, din' they?"

"Well, he was still a baby when they left Virginia but they stayed a time in East Tennessee before comin' on to this mountain. So he was a good sized boy by the time they settled here."

Dr. Lydick stepped between the ladies, "We'll have to do the historical research at another time ladies. Francie, Mrs. Ingle is having some health problems that we need to look into. Now, why don't you tell me what's been going on."

Gracie took a deep breath, "Well I can't just 'xactly put my finger on it. I'm able to keep all my work up and such but I just don't have any strength beyond that. And I'm cookin' for my family of course but everything smells bad to me."

Dr. Lydick shook his head while she talked as though he already knew everything that she was about to say. "Open your mouth please."

Gracie opened her mouth.

Dr. Lydick held out a tool, wider on one end and about ten inches long. He placed in on her chest and turned his head to stick the narrow end to his ear. Gracie held her breath until he prompted her, "Just breathe normally please."

"Have you had trouble with your stomach?"

"No Sir, except for not being able to eat much."

"Trouble with your bowel?"

"No Sir."

"How is your menses?"

Gracie cocked her head to one side trying to understand, "My what?"

He smiled, "You woman's cycle."

Gracie blushed slightly, she'd never discussed this with a man. Then she tried to figure the answer, "Come to think of it… Oh."

The confusion cleared in her eyes until a spark spread over her face in a broad smile.

Dr. Lydick watched as understanding dawned, "I see you didn't really need me at all."

"It's funny because I couldn't figure it out when my son was coming either. Stephen's mother had to tell me."

"I would think you would be more attuned to the cycle of birth and life than anyone else around."

"Well I'm usually called on much later in the process, you know."

Francie stood in front of her and took both hands to help her off the examination table. "You take good care of yourself. I hear how you run all over tending to laboring women. Why don't you let my husband take some of the burden from you in these next months."

Gracie nodded at the kind woman, "I only go when they call on me, you know."

Francie nodded, "And I know they appreciate you. 'Aunt Gracie' is known far and wide."

Gracie smiled, a hint of pride shining through. "It's just the callin' the good Lord has laid on me you know."

The woman smiled and patted Gracie's back as she opened the office door for her.

Dr. Lydick called from inside, "Come on back if you have any trouble at all – or if you decide to listen to my lecture on modern medicine."

Gracie couldn't help but chuckle as she pushed open the yard's gate and looked down the long Stock Road. *Well the walk home will take just as many steps as it did to get here but at least I don't have to carry that heavy heart.*

Chapter 32

Gracie kissed Burton's soft cheek and pulled the patchwork quilt over his shoulders. She began to pray aloud as she did each evening, "Lord, keep my boy through this night. Please give him the rest that he needs to grow strong and wise. Please always make him to know that his Mama loves him very much."

She straightened and looked down on the angelic face. He'd fallen asleep before she got past 'Lord'.

"Amen," she whispered and stepped out of the room.

The screen door squeaked as though announcing Gracie as she joined Stephen on the back porch where he sat with a cool glass of water.

"Hot night, ain't it?"

Stephen scooted over in the swing to make room for her, "Not as hot as the corn field was today."

"I'm sorry I couldn't help you. I'll get out there tomorrow. Was Burton any help or just under foot?"

"No, no. He's getting to be a big help. I don't think he cut down more than a dozen stalks of corn today."

They laughed together as Gracie leaned into his strong embrace.

"Did you see anybody you knew in Clarkrange?"

She took a deep breath knowing this was the time to share her news. "No, but I met Francie Lydick. I'd heard of her, but never knew her before today."

"Don't b'lieve I know her. She's that doctor's wife ain't she?"

Gracie nodded, "Uh huh. He ain't from around here but she was raised down toward Glades. Don't I remember hearing that England man was from that area?"

"I think that's right."

"Stephen, I met Mrs. Lydick because I was at the doctor's office."

Stephen jerked away to have a better view of her face, "What're you doin' goin' to the doctor?"

"I just haven't had any energy, and I can't find anything I want to eat. I've just been makin' myself get some food down so I can keep going."

Stephen nodded, "Yeah, just like you 'bout got down before…" He paused before he finished the sentence, "…before Burton was born."

He craned his neck to see into her eyes in the dim light.

She smiled and simply nodded.

"You mean…?"

She kept nodding.

Stephen wrapped her in his arms, "I never dared to hope. Ah Lord God, there is nothing too hard for thee."

She pulled away to ask him, "What's that mean?"

"Well it just seemed like after all these years – what, it's been five years since Burton was born – and no babies came, well, in the stock you'd decide there was somethin' wrong."

"Well this is God's timing and we aren't animals."

He smiled and hugged her again, "No, we are not. We are God's children and he is surely in control of our lives."

"You were the one who told me to take my eyes off what I can't do and see what God will do – well this is what God is doing in our lives."

"What he's doing is blessing us. And you haven't had many birthing calls lately either, have you. Do you reckon he's moving you away from that calling?"

"I don't feel any particular moving but then I guess I never really *felt* the calling. It was just sort of there before me and it was up to me to obey."

"Well if no one is knocking on our door…"

"It comes in waves you know. Harvest time in the fields is often birthing time too it seems. We'll just have to see what happens. I think I'm finally surrendered to doing whatever God puts in front of me – you can remind me of that the next time you see me wrestling with God. Maybe I'll never learn."

"Maybe none of us do."

"What? I never see you struggling. You're as steady as a spring rain."

"Not really, it's just my job to be strong for you."

She smiled as she nestled back into the crook of his arm and enjoyed the sounds of the nighttime.

The hot summer months melted into the rains of the fall. And the rains came early, before the corn was shocked. "Everything's been late this year. Didn't have the corn laid by early enough in July. Now I've not got it shocked up and it's already a'rainin' – just a mixed up season all the way around," Stephen complained. Still he headed out to the field leading the big mares, Martin riding on the sled and little Burton running circles around the whole rig. Cutting the corn stalks and tying them in big bunches to dry was rarely women's work and especially when the rains fell and the mud caked on everything that hit the ground. By the time the men came home they were carrying ten pounds of dirt on their shoes.

Just as Gracie had predicted babies began to arrive and she was called away three different times during that autumn, and every time she was called, it was raining. She bundled Burton up and hugged him before he ran giggling into Katherine's waiting arms, each time searching her mother-in-law's eyes for approval and always finding it there. The only concern anyone voiced was for her health. "Wrap up Gracie," they always cautioned. Even the families she attended warned her to pay attention to her own health.

Just as her grandmother had taught her, she bathed religiously after these visits, often to strangers' homes. Stephen always had a good fire in the front rooms' fireplace with the rocking chair scooted close. "My feet are aching with this cold rain so I can only imagine how you're feeling," he reminded her.

While Gracie was happy to do the work the Lord placed in front of her, she recognized the wise counsel she received was sent from him as well and so she tried to pay close attention and obey.

Soon the rains turned to snows and Gracie paid even more attention to safety. Every day she lay a hand on her expanding abdomen and said a quiet prayer, *Thank you Lord for this blessed miracle.*

Gracie had always known life was a miracle of God and since she'd watched Grandma tend to Nelda Turner when Gracie was sure she was watching death itself, she had known for sure that only the hand of God could bring mother and baby safely through the ordeal of childbirth. Still, to carry a child herself seemed ever more miraculous. The promise of another baby five years after Burton's birth was more than she would ever have dared ask of the Lord. All she could say to her heavenly father was *thank you*, and she said it often.

The winter was always a quiet time, calmer after the bustle of the harvest. It was a time for the land to rest and prepare itself to grow another crop in the springtime; and it was a time for men to rest and mend harness and tools and weary muscles. Very few people visited and Gracie wasn't making the trip to Bruner's Chapel all the way up to Clarkrange whenever the circuit preacher visited. So her heart leapt when a knock sounded at the door in the early evening.

Stephen opened the door to his cousin Jack. Burton dashed to the young man who he well knew from family gatherings as well as prayer meetings. "Jack-ee, Jack-ee, you've come to play with me."

Jack scooped up the boy in one arm and dropping his hat began to tickle him with his free hand.

After a moment he set him down, "Not today Burton, I wanted to talk to your folks." Looking up to Stephen he added, "If it's okay with you Stephen."

"A'course, it's okay with me Jack. Let's go in the kitchen, it's warmer in there." Stepping through the doorway he pointed to the straight backed chairs around the table, "Pull up a chair."

Jack swung a chair around to face the stove and Gracie asked, "You want me to put on the coffee?"

Stephen looked to Jack who shook his head.

"Well what's on your mind Jack. Uncle George and Aunt Bitha are doin' okay aren't they?"

"Oh, yes, everyone is just fine. I just wanted to come tell you, well that is that Margie…" He looked to Gracie as he stammered to find a way. "You remember Margie Wilson don't you Aunt Gracie?"

She smiled and nodded, knowing that Jack had continued to visit Muddy Pond and wasn't surprised if a romance was budding.

Jack stared at the cast iron cookstove still hot while Gracie cooked beans for their supper. Finally he spoke again and the words tumbled out in a single breath, "Well Margie really wanted me to let y'uns know that we're a'plannin' to marry just as quick as the weather breaks and a preacher comes through over there."

"Marry?" Gracie exclaimed.

Stephen stood slowly and simply extended his hand to his cousin, "Congratulations Jack. If you're feelin' the Lord has led you to this girl, then I know you'll be blessed."

The young man smiled now, "Oh Stephen, I just know that he's a'leadin' me. And it was Aunt Gracie's doin' of course. I mean I never would'a met Margie way off on the other side of the Hurricane Creek if Aunt Gracie hadn't sent me off over there after Georgie had that lil' baby. And you know they all, even Margie's grandparents, say that Aunt Gracie changed their whole lives. They're the most faithful family at the Muddy Pond church now and Georgie, you know she married a boy from Cliff Springs. They're doin' real good, got another boy of their own and they're faithful to church, too."

Gracie beamed, more from the news that the young girls, whose lives appeared so hopeless just a few years ago, were now walking in such close fellowship with the Lord, rather than pride in the credit Jack gave her.

"Jack, I'm so happy to hear that they are doing well. And I just know that Margie will make you a fine wife. What are your plans? Will you come back to your Daddy's farm?"

"No, I don't think so. Mr. Wilson has a pretty good piece of land over there – on a hillside of course but he says he can make a good crop on it. And Daniel's still tillin' some of Papa's fields and there's still Bruner and Arra comin' along. There's just too many sons in our family."

Stephen laughed and clapped him on the back, "No such thing as too many sons. Remember our grandpa had seven sons and nine daughters."

"Yeah and he had to leave Virginny to feed 'em all."

Stephen smiled at the joke and didn't bother to correct his cousin on the political strife that drove the Ingles to head west after The Civil War.

"Well I'm sure you'll do just fine over in Muddy Pond. Mr. Wilson has lived there a long time and he'll teach you what you need to know."

Jack stayed until Gracie opened the stove's dampers to bake cornbread for their supper.

"Well I've wasted your whole day I reckon," Jack declared as he stood and moved his chair back to the table.

"Was not a waste a'tall Jack. We don't visit much in the cold winter so it's a blessing to see your face today."

Gracie called from the kitchen as the two men headed toward the front door, "Be sure to give my love to Margie and tell her we'll be waitin' for the two of you to come visiting."

"Yes Ma'am," Jack called ahead of the click of the closing door.

Stephen returned to the kitchen grinning at his wife, "Well, we can add matchmaker to your many talents."

"Oh hush, that had no more to do with me than it did with the man in the moon."

"You sent him over there. And you surely knew Margie was huntin' a man."

"I knew no such thing. And you just be serious. Ain't it a blessin' to hear how those two girls have turned their lives around?"

Stephen nodded, "The girls and their grandparents as well. All kiddin' aside, you will always be well-remembered in that family."

"The glory's the Lord's!"

Chapter 33

The springtime sun seemed to smile on the land after a hard winter. Bits of green burst through the dark ground and Lottie appeared at Gracie's door with a big dishpan under her arm. "Let's go sallet hunting, Gracie!"

Gracie looked at her house with broom in hand, and she clasped her apron vainly trying to cover the protruding stomach. Still she paused only a moment before she propped the broom against the wall and headed toward the back door, "Just let me get a basket."

Lottie looked around the unusually quiet room, "Where's lil' Burton?"

"He's gone out with Stephen today. They're picking up roots in some new ground and Burton will have all kinds of fun and come home absolutely filthy."

The women laughed together as they set off toward the split rail fence that separated Algurial Ingle's property from Uncle Bill's and attempted to keep the roaming hogs and cattle away from the corn crop. In the V formed by each opposing rail they looked for signs of poke sallet, plantain and dandelions. They chattered along like two young girls and both reveled in the childhood memories they discussed. Grandma Elmore had taught them what plants to look for and this first mess of green salad always tasted better than anything else they'd eat all year.

"Have you got any salt pork left Gracie?" Lottie called down the length of a fence rail.

"Yeah, matter of fact, Stephen brought me in a good sized piece of ham this morning. I've got it cookin' on the back of the stove now."

"Oh law, it won't boil dry will it? I didn't even give you much chance to settle things in your house when I just showed up and said, 'let's go'."

Gracie laughed at her sister, "Of course it's okay. Like I said, it's on the back of the stove and it's got plenty of water. Plus, there's not enough wood in the stove to cook it too terribly dry."

"Well in that case, you're ahead of me. You're meat will be ready as soon as you've got your sallet parboiled."

Gracie nodded and knelt to get a sprig of sour dock. "It's not easy pickin' greens when you're this far along."

"Tell me about it."

Gracie nodded, her sister had seen every season of pregnancy after six babies.

Lottie was still talking when Gracie hoisted herself up, holding onto the rails. "Don't guess I'll have to dodge my belly picking greens next spring though. This one will come about time to pick the corn."

Gracie froze for a moment, "Oh Lottie, that's wonderful. I'm sure Daniel is beside himself."

"Of course. He wants to beat Grandpa George you know."

"What? More like Uncle Bill – his third wife has already given him two babies to add to the ten he already had and she's very young so there's just no telling how many children she'll have."

They giggled together until Lottie added, "Dan'l Ingle may have to get him a younger woman if he wants twelve children."

Gracie sobered, "Lottie, don't even joke about that. Now the good Lord has protected you through six pregnancies and I'm praying right now that he'll see you through this seventh one. But now it's not anything to take lightly, this curse that Eve brought on us takes the lives of an awful lot of women."

"Gracie, I'm sorry. You know there's no use worryin' – you are not worried about the baby you're carryin' are you?"

"No, I wouldn't say I'm worrying, it's just a serious thing. Lottie, you know that I've lost mothers and it's hard to think about those babies never knowing their mama."

"I know it is but don't you believe God has a plan even then? I mean, look at Uncle Bill Ingle, two times God saw fit to take his wife on home and still he provided another woman to mother the children that were left behind. And do you remember that family you helped more than a year ago now? They were from somewhere far away, California or something."

"Yes, I remember, the Bradfords. Poor man, lost his wife and left with a newborn baby and another young girl. He left the mountain, didn't he?"

Lottie nodded, "He left alright but he's come back. He never sold that place up there next to the Bledsoe Stand, and now he's come back with a new wife."

Gracie stood and as the news Lottie shared sank in her face lit with joy. "Oh I am so happy to hear that. I've really worried about him with those little children and no family around to help. Why Lottie, he'd be in about the same shape our father was when Mother died. Only she was able to get us home to Tennessee and to the Elmores."

Lottie was nodding even while she continued to stoop and cut greens. "But I'm not done with my story, Gracie. He's brought this wife back. She come all the way from Scotland."

"Scotland?" Gracie exclaimed.

"You heard me right. Dan'l saw 'em up at Peters' store and said she's got the funniest soundin' talk you ever did hear."

"Reckon where he found her?"

"I don't know except I had heard he moved to Nashville with his children. I think they've moved around a whole lot."

"Well, maybe they can settle now that he's found a mama for those babies. If he kept the place up there, that sure seems like he's wantin' to stay around here."

Lottie was still nodding her head agreeing with her sister. "I guess so. The next time we go over to visit Grandma we should stop in there. Their house is right on the way down to the swinging bridge at the Ferry Bend. I'm sure she'd be happy to see some neighbors even if we'll sound funny to her, too."

The ladies laughed again together before Gracie sobered and quietly said, "Wherever that woman is from I hope she'll love those children. I know raisin' someone else's children is never the same as raisin' your own."

Lottie was serious now, too, "You're right, of course. Just like having Grandma and Grandpa wasn't really the same as if we'd had our own mother and father with us."

Gracie nodded with her and they continued on along the fence-line sometimes darting out into the field where the plantain and sour dock was more likely to sprout up. They were nearly to the deep ravine that cut along the northern end of the property when Gracie froze with her hand at her side.

Lottie immediately recognized the movement and asked, "How bad was the pain?"

"Not too bad, but more than the baby kicking."

"We better head back to the house. I think it's too early for this baby to come, don't you?"

"Yes I do. He needs another month by my count."

"Give me that basket."

"No, no. I can carry it. It don't weigh much."

Lottie reached over and gently tugged it from her folded arm. "Maybe not, but you need to focus on walking right now.

They veered away from the fence and headed straight across the field. "Walking may be a little rougher out here where it's been plowed but I think we can make it faster. What do you think Gracie?"

Gracie just nodded her head as another pain crept down her body.

"Gracie, can you tell if the baby is really coming or is this the false labor you get called out for every once in awhile?"

"I think it's too early to tell. I sure am praying it's false. This baby needs a little more time to grow."

Lottie nodded her head and closed her mouth as she began to pray in earnest for her sister.

The walk back to Gracie's house passed quickly since they were no longer meandering wherever the greens might be found. As they stepped onto the back porch, Lottie asked Gracie, "How're you feelin' now?"

"Well I haven't had another pain in a several minutes. I think that's good."

"Yes, that's definitely good. Let me draw some water to wash these greens. You git in there to that rockin' chair."

She'd hardly made it to the chair before the door burst open and Burton came bounding in. "Mama, where've you been? We come in from the barn and you were just gone. Daddy said maybe you had to go help a baby, but I seen your basket was there by the door so he was wrong. A'course I didn't say that to him 'cause that wouldn't be 'spectful, would it?"

Gracie smiled at her sweet boy, "No son, it wouldn't be respectful. And I went out with your Aunt Lottie to pick greens for your supper. Now aren't you excited about that?"

He pursed his lips and wrinkled his brow trying to figure the answer to her question. "I don't know but Aunt Lottie always has good food."

Gracie sat for another minute but hearing her sister bustling in the kitchen drew her out of the chair.

"Lottie, you can't be doin' my work when you have plenty of your own."

"Well of course I'm going to help you. I put a stick of wood in the stove and opened up the dampers so that meat will cook a little more. I'll get the greens in water and then I'll head home. We got a'plenty for two messes."

"I sure hope you kept enough out for your family. Eight mouths need more than our three – and little Burton isn't even sure how he feels about them."

"He'll feel like they are his favorite thing when he bites into them. After months of eating dried leather britches and turnips, these will be about like a stick of candy from Peters' store. Any more pains?"

"No, nothing since way back up there in the field, so that means the baby isn't coming just yet. The pains just get closer and closer when it's really time."

"Don't I know that. Well, I don't want to think about it because Dan'l is so happy about this next child, and I can't start dreadin' the birthin' right now."

Gracie smiled at her and gently took the greens from her hand. "Have you already divided out your part?"

Lottie nodded as she wiped her hands on her ever-present apron. "If I can't help here then, and if you're pretty sure you're not fixin' to have that baby, then I'll be on my way home. It was awful good to spend a little time with you out today, sort'a like bein' a kid again, didn't you think?"

"That's just what I was thinking earlier."

Dropping the pan full of salad she turned and hugged her sister, "Thank you Lottie, you were just what I needed today."

As Lottie stepped out the front door both ladies were smiling.

Chapter 34

Tina Ervain Ingle did indeed wait a whole month to arrive. With the land safe from frost and the May Apples blooming the men were all in the fields getting their crops planted. Just as when Burton arrived, Gracie spent a near-sleepless night and she greeted the dawn with complete understanding of what her day would hold.

She sent Stephen on his way to the field and led Burton to his grandmother's house herself.

"Gracie, what are you doing out this early in the morning?" Katherine greeted her.

"It's time Mother Ingle. I'll leave Burton with you if I may because I have a few things to do to get ready."

"You'll do no such thing," Katherine's voice was rising in pitch and volume. "Martin's still in the barn, Burton, you run out there and get him right quick."

Burton was gone in a flash and Gracie was closer to being angry with her mother-in-law than she'd ever been. "Mother Ingle, I don't think there's any reason to scare the boy."

"I'm not try'n to scare nobody but we've got to get you some help. Did you tell Stephen? I saw him headed out with the plow just before you came knocking."

Gracie was completely calm as she explained, "No, there's no need to worry him and you know he can't do a thing to help me."

Katherine nodded, "You're right, of course. Well, let me send Martin to get Mrs. England; I'll have him take the wagon so he can drive her back. And then I'll take Burton to Lottie's. That's too far for you to walk. Can you get back to your house on your own?"

"Oh yes, I can get home just…" She grabbed the door-facing as the first real pain worked it's way down her body. Taking a deep breath she finished, "I can get home."

As Gracie left from the front door, Katherine flew out the back, grabbing a bonnet and shawl as she went. "Maaarrrtiinn," she called as Martin ambled from the barn. "You're a'moving like molasses boy! I want you to hook up that wagon right quick and go get Mrs. England."

"Who?"

"Rhodie England, on up past the school."

"In Clarkrange?"

"Martin, goodness! Why are you being so slow this morning? Up past the Martha Washington school, Gracie's baby is comin' and we've got to get her some help."

"Baby! Why didn't you say so?" He was gone, and she could hear the rattle of harness inside the barn as Martin no doubt slung it onto the poor horse's back from a few feet away.

Katherine Ingle was still moving as she called to Burton. "Come on Burton, we're goin' to Aunt Lottie's."

"Aunt Lottie's!" the boy screamed with glee. "I'll beat you, I know I can." With that Burton ran ahead of his grandmother and she let him go. She was just passing the little house Stephen and Gracie shared when she heard the squeak and jingle that told her Martin was on his way. Looking ahead she could barely see Burton's dark brown hair as he bobbed up and down running across the field.

Daniel was hooking his horse to the plow he'd left in the corner of the field yesterday when Katherine crested the hill.

"Mornin' Aunt Katherine," he called. "Did that boy get away from you?"

She called loudly to answer him, "No Dan'l, I sent him along to Lottie. I need to go help Gracie."

"That's fine, I'll run tell Lottie. Ever'thing okay?"

She turned and called her answer back over her shoulder, "It will be Dan'l. It will be."

Martin must have finally sensed the urgency of his mission for he returned with a wide-eyed Rhoda England in no time at all and he tore into Gracie's yard completely missing the rutted, dirt driveway.

"Martin, I should'a sent Burton to get her 'cause I think he would'a driven better."

Martin looked sheepish, "You told me to hurry," he answered his mother softly.

She smiled, "I reckon I did. Git on back to your work I guess. Me and Mrs. England can handle everything here."

Rhoda England waited for her at the head of the rig and smiled at her neighbor's confidence.

Katherine placed a hand on Rhoda's shoulder and turned her toward the house, "Come on in Rhodie, I'm glad to spend a little time with you today."

Rhoda chuckled, "Not much of a time for visitin' Mrs. England."

"You call me Katherine, we'll be good friends by supper I know. I'm just ashamed I've hardly visited with you a'tall since you helped Gracie deliver her first one."

"Nothin' to be ashamed of, time gets away, don't it? And with you going to church at Bruner's Chapel and us at Campground we don't much cross paths."

The two ladies stepped into Katherine's front room and Rhoda began untying her bonnet and shawl. She smiled as she looked around the homey room, complete with a roughly carved wooden horse Stephen had created for Burton.

Katherine stood at the bedroom door and invited Rhoda to join her, "I've put Gracie to bed even though she argued somethin' awful. She said she still had things she wanted to do this morning."

Both ladies chuckled, "Babies have a way of interrupting our plans when they're comin' and then for the rest of our lives. At least that's been my experience."

"Mine too Rhodie," Katherine answered. "How many do you have?"

"I've got eight livin'. We left three of my babies back in Roslin; well our Georgie he was sixteen when the fever took him. I reckon they'll always be my babies."

They'd arrived at Gracie's bedside and she heard the account, "Mrs. England, I'm so sorry that you've had to face that."

Katherine chimed in, "Me too. I only had three and they're all spaced out, seven years between each of 'em. But there was never any trouble in between. We've sure been blessed."

"You had your boys back in Virginny, right?"

"Yes'm, Bud was just newborn when Jury marched off to the war. He mourned leavin' his little family but he was sure they'd shoot every Virginian if we didn't resist. So he was gone over four years. Little Bud didn't even know he had a Daddy and to tell you the truth I tried not to talk too much about Jury during that time 'cause what if he never come back? I guess I thought it would be easier on the boy. Maybe that was wrong, I don't know. Anyway, then we had Stephen even as we were packin' up to leave Virginny. And Martin come after we got to Tennessee. In fact, I was havin' such trouble and we have some connections in East Tennessee so we stayed there till he was born and Jury thought me and him could travel, and that's when we come on to Marthy Washington. Gracie did you know that?"

"No, Mother Ingle, I don't b'lieve I did. I knew you had stopped somewhere along the way."

"You feelin' okay child?"

Gracie nodded, moving to swing her legs over the edge of the bed.

Katherine put her hands up to stop the movement, "Oh no you don't, you're stayin' in that bed."

Katherine looked to Rhoda for support.

Rhoda bit her lip before offering, "I want to do what y'uns think is best but I've found that walkin' some helped me. I'd need somebody to hold on to when the pains came but it seemed to speed things along. My Gustie and Georgie, they's twins you know, they were two whole days a'coming and it liked to killed me. After that the granny woman we had over in Roslin, she started walkin' me and the next ones come right along."

Katherine looked a little skeptical but nodded her head nonetheless and reached to take Gracie's arm and help her up.

Rhoda asked, "How far along you reckon you are Mizz Gracie?"

"I've been hurtin' through the whole night."

"Have the waters come yet?"

Gracie shook her head and took a deep breath as she felt a contraction beginning to build. No one spoke as she held onto the arms of both women waiting for the pain to pass.

In a moment they were able to start walking and they made their way into the front room then on to the kitchen. The long kitchen room which ran the length of the back side of the house, was where Gracie would spend the rest of her day. She walked from the stove to the wall where a peg rail held coats and hats.

"Mizz England, I b'lieve you're right and I'm wishing I'd known about walkin' when I was helping with birthing. The pains seem to be more tolerable this way."

Rhoda nodded and smiled as she walked beside her, Mizz Hall used to say that you walked right out to the pain."

The three ladies spent the entire day walking and waiting until the time drew near enough that Gracie was returned to bed for the final stages of her labor.

By supper time Gracie held her precious daughter in her arms.

Katherine beamed at her first granddaughter. "What are you gonna' name her?"

"Tina."

"Well, she is tiny, but you know she'll grow."

Gracie smiled at her beloved mother-in-law, "T-I-N-A".

"Yeah, Tiny. I think that's a fine name."

Tina was a healthy baby and grew off as well as any mother could hope for, yet her name was forever pronounced as though she were always a tiny baby.

Chapter 35

Gracie always tried not to take a single blessing for granted. She taught Burton and Tiny to thank God everyday – all through the day. She thanked him for the sunshine and she thanked him for the rain. She reminded her children to thank God for their food and their lessons – which were sometimes hard for little ones to appreciate. She thanked God for her husband and this big ole' Ingle family that surrounded her. And she certainly thanked God every time she was able to deliver a healthy baby and walk away from a quickly recovering mother. Even when the births were not exactly what she would've called a success, she thanked God for his presence and his comfort.

Gracie was in such a habit of praising the Lord that when hardships hit, she thanked God even before she fully realized that she was suffering. However, she did lift up her needs before the Lord as well. When Burton's temperature rose, Gracie prayed. When Tiny's throat hurt and the sunlight revealed an ugly red color in it, Gracie prayed. And the children came through their childhood aches and pains.

Gracie prayed for Stephen's work on the farm, for the crops he planted and the corn and wheat he harvested. Still sometimes the harvest was not what they hoped for and Gracie was always quick to remind him that God would provide.

"You sound like my mother, you know."

"Thank you, that is high praise indeed."

Stephen would smile and wrap her in his arms. She provided the comfort he needed when all of life seemed against him.

"I've gotta' sit down. Gracie can you sit with me by the fire?"

She looked at the supper dishes piled on the dry sink and the crumbs scattered across the table and floor. Then she looked at her husband, "Of course I'll sit with you, Stephen."

Stephen pulled a low stool close to the rocker and reached to pull his boots off. This was his daily ritual, especially when he'd spent the day behind the plow or hoeing the corn. He'd pull off his boots and prop his feet before the fire until he fell asleep.

"My feet are always cold Gracie, even in the heat of summer. That don't make much sense, now does it?"

Gracie could only shake her head as she brought him thick socks to put on and Tiny would often sit and rub his feet.

As the years passed Stephen began to complain that the coldness crept up his legs, and then he dropped the axe on his toe but never felt the pain he expected. The toe swelled and the nail turned black but there was no pain.

"Gracie, I hate to wish for pain, but I just know that it's not right for a foot that looks that bad not to hurt.'"

Gracie nodded, "Something sure ain't right. We need to go see that doctor up at Clarkrange."

Just a few days after the axe incident, they loaded up in the wagon and headed out. Francie Lydick opened the side door to them and gave them a sweet smile. "Mizz Gracie, how good to see you."

"Hello Mrs. Lydick. Is your husband at home?"

As she shut the door she turned to them, "You just call me Francie, I'm home folk and don't need no titles. I'm 'fraid he's not here right now. Fact is, I don't 'xactly know where he's got to. Are you needin' him right away?"

Gracie looked at Stephen who had remained quiet since stepping down from his wagon but he answered now. "No, I reckon it can wait."

Francie looked from Gracie to Stephen and must have read concern between them, "I'll send him down to you as soon as he gets home. Matter a'fact, I'll send my boy Wiley out to hunt him and try to get him down your way all the sooner."

Gracie smiled and took Francie's hand between both of hers, "Thank you, Francie, I would really appreciate that."

It was late evening, too late to be calling, actually, when Dr. Lydick's little shiny buggy pulled up to the hitching post outside Gracie's kitchen window. A near-grown boy sat beside him looking less than pleased to be there.

"Burton," Gracie called up to the loft, "The doctor's here. Run out and help him with his horse."

Burton bounded into the kitchen all legs and arms and willing to help his mother. She said more softly as he moved toward the door, "Looks like one of his boys is with him too so you stay out and talk to him, okay?"

Burton shrugged his shoulders and Gracie knew her request would be carried out as well as he could do it.

It was only a moment before Dr. Lydick stood in the back doorway knocking at the door Burton had left open for him.

"Dr. Lydick, I'm so happy to see you. Please, do come in. I hope my boy was cordial and is helpin' with your horse. Do you think he ought to get that bit out of his mouth?

The doctor squinted his eyes as though trying to calculate the time required to examine his patient until he finally opened them wide and said, "There's just no way to know. Your husband isn't injured is he?"

"Oh, no, no, nothing like that. And maybe we're just worryin' about nothing but come on in here. He's resting by the fire." Gracie put a hand on his upper arm and gently turned him toward the open doorway. A slight movement made them both notice the little figure sitting halfway down the stairs. "Tiny, you want to come down and say hello to the good doctor?"

She shook her head vigorously and raised a rag doll up to cover her face as her thumb popped into her mouth.

Gracie smiled at her then turned to the doctor and continued into the front room.

"Stephen, have you fallen asleep? The doctor's arrived."

Stephen raised his head with a jerk and started to pull his feet to the ground before he winced at the movement.

Dr. Lydick raised his hand and swept his Homburg from his head. Gracie reached to take the fine felt hat before it hit the floor. Even in her concern for her husband, her hand unconsciously caressed the soft wool of the brim and fine silk of the grosgrain ribbon. Dr. Lydick was the only man on the whole mountain to wear such a hat and whenever he rode on horseback you could always recognize him by the hat long before you could see his face.

"Mr. Ingle, you winced when you tried to put your feet on the ground. Can you tell me where the pain is located?"

Gracie opened her mouth to answer for him but quickly closed it back knowing the doctor needed a first-hand account of the problems her husband was having.

Stephen looked down as he tried to give a complete answer, "It's hard to say. My legs just ache, they've always given me some trouble but now it's nearly all the time they ache, no matter how much I've walked or what kind of work I've been doing."

Dr. Lydick nodded his head as he pulled the thick socks off of Stephen's feet. He looked at the toes, frowning at the black nail of the injured toe.

Gracie was watching him and wanted to explain, "He dropped the axe on that toe this week and that's when we really thought we needed to see you. It didn't hurt him."

Dr. Lydick threw an unspoken question at Stephen as though wondering if Gracie had her facts straight.

Stephen nodded, "That's right Doc, I kept expectin' it to hurt but it never has. Even when Gracie cleaned it and poked a needle to relieve the pressure, it still din' hurt."

The doctor continued his examination without comment as he pushed Stephen's heavy work pants up to his knees and looked at legs surprisingly red. He pushed his finger deep into the flesh, while watching his patient for any pained response, none showed on the patient's face.

Dr. Lydick stood, still looking at the exposed limbs with his eyes traveling down to the discolored feet. He reached a hand to feel Stephen's forehead and found it warmed by the nearby fire but no warmer than his own. Opening his black leather bag for the first time he took out the horn-like instrument he used to listen to people's insides. He placed the large end on Stephen's chest and the smaller end against his own ear.

"No need to hold your breath, just breathe normally."

Stephen took a gulp of air, suddenly realizing how long he'd held his breath.

Dr. Lydick stood upright again and looked directly at Stephen. "Tell me about any injuries you've had – I need to know everything, even if you think it's minor."

As Stephen began to tell of childhood falls and trips over logs Gracie grabbed a ladder-back chair and placed it behind the doctor who sat immediately unbuttoning his coat.

"Nothing in that list could have caused this. You said that your legs have always given you some trouble, tell me about that."

Stephen explained he had suffered after a long day's work since early adulthood, "But a good night's sleep always made everything right. It's not enough anymore though. I can't ever seem to get enough rest."

Dr. Lydick nodded his head and sat silently for a moment. "Tell me about the food you've been eating. Do you eat much away from your family?"

"Oh no, not much at all. Gracie," he reached up to take her hand as she stood behind his chair," "She's a fine cook you know. And she nearly always has something ready for me when I come to the house at dinnertime. A'course if she's off catchin' a baby, I might eat with my mother."

He looked at Gracie and seemed to assess her to be in the best of health before he asked, "Do your mother and father live alone now?"

"No, I still have a younger brother who's at home."

"And they are all healthy?"

"Oh yes. My Pa can work me out of the field. Martin of course works circles around the both of us."

"Have you ever lived away from them?"

"No, not more than a few days off huntin' or something. We came from Virginny, you know, but I was born in Clinton, Tennessee where they lived for a couple of years before coming on to this mountain to settle for good. I have one older brother that was born back in Virginny and the younger one was born here. The Ingles are a clannish bunch, you know. I guess we brought that with us from Scotland, nearly a hundred years ago."

Again, Dr. Lydick nodded. With a deep breath he delivered his diagnosis, "Sir, I fear you have a wasting palsy. I have read that sometimes this can come from poisoning but if no one else in the household is suffering any, and if you have all your family around you so you know their history then this must be something you alone have contracted or developed."

Gracie's mouth fell open and her hand immediately flew to cover it. She didn't need to ask questions, Stephen was way ahead of her.

"A *palsy*? What in the world? I ain't shakin' or nothing."

Dr. Lydick gave him a weak smile, "Not everyone does. It's a very broad term I'm afraid. Ultimately what I'm seeing in you is your feet are losing their blood. That's why they are always cold and now they are numb.

Gracie found her voice and asked, "Should we bleed him? Wouldn't that remove the old blood that's died in his feet?"

The Doctor raised his hand as though he couldn't bear to hear the request, "No, no. We know better than that. And let me tell you I saw the rebels let plenty of blood out of our Union soldiers during the war, and it came to no good end for any of them."

Gracie dropped her head, ashamed she had suggested something that could offer no relief to her husband. "What then? What can we do?"

He lifted his leather bag and rummaged for a moment, "I had thought Potassium Iodide would help, but if there's no hint of poisoning, that's not right."

Finally he pulled a green bottle from the bag and held it before his face as though he studied the single word printed on the label, *arsenic.*

Gracie prayed. *Lord God, please give this man wisdom. Make him to know what my husband needs. And Father we pray that you will attend him as the Great Physician we know you are. Help us Lord Jesus, help me…*

After a long moment Dr. Lydick replaced the bottle in his bag and pushed himself off the chair. Mrs. Ingle, how is your larder stocked?

Gracie's eyes popped open wide at the unexpected question. "It's stocked well Sir. We are eating quite well."

"You need to feed him generously, If he says he cannot eat, then make strong broths. We may try the arsenic later but I would like to see if he can regain some strength and stamina without it. Rub the feet and legs anytime you have a chance."

"One of us will rub them every day. And I will use the turpentine on him."

Dr. Lydick waved a hand as if to dismiss the folk remedy but said nothing. He turned one way and then another until he spotted his grey hat on an unoccupied chair. Reaching for it he promised another visit soon, "I will come back in a month to see how he has improved. Please come to my office if you find you need me before then."

Gracie led him the handful of steps to the front door and she stepped out ahead of him. On the porch she had another question, "What can we expect from this Dr. Lydick?"

"I'm afraid I do not know Ma'am. He may improve greatly with this treatment plan, or he may decline. I do not think he will ever be rid of this palsy, for it's lasted too long and come on him so gradually. But he may yet be able to return to some of his farming duties."

Gracie smiled at him.

The doctor had reached the cleanly swept front yard before she thought of payment. "Doctor, I failed to pay you. Please tell me what we owe you."

Dr. Lydick looked out to the wooded horizon for a moment then he turned his head toward her, "What did you earn for your last birthing?"

Gracie grinned broadly, "a bag of apples and a stewin' chicken."

"Oh no, that won't do. I dearly dread carrying chickens home in my buggy, although that is preferable to carrying them on horseback."

Gracie couldn't help but chuckle. "I've dried the apples, could I send them along that way?"

"That would be just fine."

"Gimme just a minute and I'll bring them to your buggy."

Chapter 36

The palsy grew worse and worse until Stephen was finally unable to pull himself out of bed. It was the dead of winter and Dr. Lydick felt it best for him to stay in bed, where Gracie could best keep him warm. "Under no circumstances must he go out into the cold, damp winter air," the doctor ordered Gracie.

"No sir, I'll keep him right there and we'll fetch him whatever he needs."

However, neither Gracie nor their beloved children could bring him the independence that he wanted. During these weeks she saw a side of her husband she had not known in their fifteen years of marriage, Stephen was mean. He complained about the food they carried to him, he disliked the water Tiny drew from the well, the quilts Gracie had so lovingly stitched were scratchy and uncomfortable. Mother Ingle walked in the backdoor one day as Burton tried to help his father get situated in his bed and she was shocked by the tone she heard.

Walking into the bedroom Katherine nodded for Burton to leave them. "Stephen, surely I did not hear you fussing at your boy when he's in here working to give you a little ease."

"Hmmf, there's no ease in this bed. Don't know where we ever got it, but it's the worst thing I ever thought of layin' on."

"Well it's the same bed four or five of us slept on when we first came from Virginny. Your Grandpa built it right in this room and we were glad to have it after sleepin' in wagons and on the ground when we traveled from Clinton. So I do not believe it is the bed that you're dissatisfied with."

"No Mother, of course you're right. It is so hard to stay in this bed, yet I hardly have the strength to get out. And Gracie is so insistent that I obey that Yankee doctor."

"*Yankee* you say? Why, Stephen, that war's long over and we're all Americans again."

He squinted his eyes, "You think so? I think that man's come to Tennessee to take out any Confederates his Union soldier-friends missed."

Her eyes popped open wide and she shook her head as she backed out the open door.

"Gracie, where are you?" Katherine called softly.

"Here, Mother Ingle, is something wrong with Stephen?"

"Yes, something is very wrong."

Gracie turned to rush into his bedroom when her mother-in-law placed a firm hand on her shoulder, "You can't help him in there. He's losing his mind stuck in that dark room. The sun is out today, I think if we wrap him up we can get him out on the porch."

"How will we ever move him? Me and Burton together can barely get him up and down to use the chamber pot."

Katherine's eyes darted around the room as though the solution lay somewhere among the family's meager possessions. As the two women tried to find a way to help Stephen a knock sounded. Somehow Gracie knew without seeing the caller that he would be summoning her away.

Katherine smiled at her, pride in this strong woman beaming from her eyes and an unspoken message of encouragement passed between them.

Gracie looked from the door to her friend unable to move to open it.

Katherine took control of the situation as she so often did; she gave Gracie a little half-hug and moved to the door. As the lifted the latch she directed Gracie, "Go get your wrap and bonnet and maybe say a word to your husband. I'll get the door for you."

The knock sounded again before Katherine could pull the door open to reveal Daniel Ingle. "Come quick Gracie. It's Lottie's time."

"No Daniel, it's too early."

"Don't know 'bout that, but Lottie said to get you right quick."

Forgetting the late winter temperature, Gracie grabbed her wool covered hat and managed to get it perched on her head as she ran down the hill.

"Gracie!" Daniel called behind her, "Ride my horse."

She heard him but didn't slow to answer. In fact, she didn't slow until the reached the edge of her sister's porch, and there she stopped long enough to take a deep breath and run a shaking hand up the back of her head attempting to reclaim some of the strands of hair escaping their bun.

Lord I need to calm Lottie, but I need you to calm me, please Lord.

Without knocking, Gracie stepped into the house and immediately turned into the front bedroom. Big windows let light in from the weak winter sun and Gracie breathed a prayer of thanks. *Too many times I've done this by lamplight; thank you for the sunlight Lord.*

Lottie sat on the side of the bed, a quilt piled beside her. She hadn't even heard Gracie come into the house.

"Lottie, tell me what's going on. Dan'l said it's time but that can't be right."

"No it's not right but something is happening. The pains are coming hard and fast." She lifted a corner of the quilt in one hand, "I was tryin' to put this ole' thing over the bed clothes and had one pain that put me down."

Gracie took the quilt from her and began doubling it to just the size she would need, "Here let me. Can you scoot yourself up on toward the headboard a little?"

Lottie complied with only a shake of her head. In a moment Gracie had her stretched out. "Where are the children? Your house is way too quiet."

"Dan'l sent 'em to his mothers." Lottie smiled despite her pain as she described the picture they made, "Idy took lil' Tom by the hand and Ruth in her arms; Marthy and Bithy each took Ovie and Dewey by the hands and off they went."

"Virgil?"

"He was in the barn when this hit me seein' after some chore or another. Dan'l will keep him out of this though, don't you worry."

With a nod Gracie sat down on a little stool beside the bed ready for a long wait and praying this was a false alarm. Within the hour Lottie was in hard labor and when Gracie caught the perfect little baby girl it only took a glance at the blue lips and a touch of the body warmed only by her mother's body heat and quickly cooling for her to realize she had lost this precious life. She bit her lip to quell the rising emotion and gently wrapped the soft blanket she pulled from her shoulder around the baby, laying it in a basket beside her. She blinked hard reminding herself that her sister's very life might now depend on her.

However, Lottie quickly delivered the placenta and showed no signs of abnormal bleeding. As Gracie packed the clean rags on Lottie the mother asked for her baby.

"Is it a boy or a girl this time?"

"Lottie…"

"I know Gracie. I've done birthed eight babies and I know this one ought to be wailin' by now." Her voice cracked despite her brave words, "I still want to know if it was a boy or a girl."

Lottie's voice was barely audible, "A girl. A perfect, beautiful little girl."

"Can I hold her Gracie?"

"Do you think you ought'ta?"

"Yes, just one time. That's all I'll ever get to hold my baby but I can't let one of them go without knowin' I've held her once."

Gracie nodded and stood to hand the little bundle to her sister. She had no words as a silent tear slipped from one eye.

Lottie took her baby and held her just as carefully as she'd held each of her newborns.

"I's thinkin' of callin' her Pansy if she was a girl. So we'll bury her with that name. What do you think Gracie?"

"I think that's just fine Lottie." She cocked her head to study the woman's face and wondered, *When did my little sister become such a strong woman?*

A noise on the porch drew Gracie's attention and she saw Daniel sitting on the edge of the porch, a piece of leather in his hand.

"I'll send Dan'l in to you."

Lottie smiled up at her still holding the motionless baby close. "Thank you, Gracie."

The front door squeaked as Gracie pulled it open and Daniel jerked his head toward the noise. Seeing Gracie he hopped up dropping the worn harness on the porch.

"How is she?"

Daniel read the pain in Gracie's eyes.

"Not Lottie?" he started to question.

Gracie shook her head gently. "Dan'l… the baby…" She couldn't find the words.

Daniel nodded an understanding and stepped around Gracie into the house.

From the porch Gracie watched as father and mother held and admired their lifeless child. She seemed glued in place. She shook her head trying to clear the fog and think of what needed to be done next. Still she stood in that one place on the porch, finally dropping her eyes to not invade her sister's private family moment. At long last she had the presence of mind to pray.

Lord God, why? Oh Lord, I know it's not my place to ask why, please forgive me for that. Thank you for the healthy children Lottie and Daniel have. Thank you for letting me glimpse my sister's strength. Please, Lord give me the strength now to care for her as she cares for everyone around her.

Daniel stepped out of the room, and Gracie took the opportunity to check on Lottie. "You doin' okay? You're not cramping too badly are you?"

Lottie shook her head and blinked away tears. "No, it came on me hard but tweren't anything compared to birthin' the twin girls."

Gracie smiled, "No I guess not. Well it looks like you are doing fine. I'll go in and get you something to eat. You'll need to get some strength in you."

"Gracie would you please go down to the barn and send my Virgil to get the rest of the family? It just seems like I need them close to me right now."

"Oh, yes, of course. I'll be right back."

"No honey, you've got plenty to do. You go on and Idy will get me some food."

Gracie hurried to the barn and sent her nephew on his way to his grandmother's house. She turned to head home but stopped and looked long back at the little house then back up the hill to her own home. She felt so torn about where she was most needed. In the end she went on home.

Chapter 37

When Gracie walked into the yard of her own home she was greeted by a smiling husband. He hailed her as she opened the front gate. "Gracie, I'm so glad you are home. Did you look at the sunset that was following you home?"

"What? Sunset? What are you talking about and what in this world are you doing out of bed?"

"You can talk to my mother about that but before you do, please look at that beautiful sky."

Gracie couldn't help but smile at the radiant look on Stephen's face. And she laughed out loud as she turned around to see the sky pained pink and orange.

Stephen said, "It's the end of a day, but that sky promises a new day tomorrow and new possibilities."

She stooped to hug him, "Thank you Stephen, you were just what I was needing. You do know that you're defying the good doctor's orders don't you? He told me you absolutely must not be in the cold, damp winter air for any reason."

"Well, I'll be in the cold damp ground if I can't get out of that bed. Gracie I've spent my whole life underneath God's glorious sky. Do you know how hard it is to look at that dark ceiling all day and all night?"

She took his hand, "Oh Stephen I do know and it has broken my heart to see you stuck in there but I want to see you well and isn't it worth it..."

Stephen held up a hand cutting her off, "Gracie, I'm not going to get any better."

She shook her head vigorously, "No Stephen, don't say that! Dr. Lydick says…"

Again he interrupted her, "Gracie, I know how I feel – or at least what I can't feel in my legs. It's getting worse and worse, not better."

Gracie had no more arguments, no more strength to argue. She dropped her head onto the top of his.

"Now I don't want to talk anymore about me or dark days to come. Look at that sunset and tell me why we would think sad thoughts. Tell me about you, where have you been?"

She did raise her head as she answered him, "Lottie's."

"You were just visitin? I thought you were out midwifin'."

She laughed again, with a pang of guilt for having joy after walking away from an unsuccessful birthing. She sobered as she explained, "I was midwifing. Lottie had her baby."

"What? I've been in that bed way too long, I didn't think it was time for Lottie…" He went silent when he finally recognized the despair on his wife's face.

"Gracie, tell me what happened."

She took a deep breath and pulled a split-bottomed chair close to his, "The baby was early. But I don't think that's what was wrong. She was blue as soon as I caught her. Oh Stephen, Lottie is being so brave, and I just want to sit and cry and cry and cry."

She dropped her head on his arm and he brought his free hand to stroke her hair.

"Shhshh, sweet Gracie. It's always hard on you, but this has got to be especially bad since it's your own sister."

"It makes me think I shouldn't be attendin' to her. But then maybe this will be her last one."

"Was the birth bad? You don't think she can carry anymore children?"

"No, no, I don't mean that. Lottie came through it all very well. When she kind of came to herself she knew without me even telling her that her baby wasn't alive. She was just real quiet and asked if she could hold her."

"Her? It was a girl?"

Gracie could only nod.

He smiled at her, "They have a houseful of girls, don't they? She would have fit right in with the crowd."

She sat quietly with her husband as the sun sank below the horizon; by the time Gracie stepped inside, the house had grown quite dark and Mother Ingle was lighting lamps. She remembered that she was upset Stephen was out of his bed, but could find no fire to fuss at his mother.

"Gracie, you saw Stephen on the porch. Doesn't the fresh air seem to have perked him up? But it'll get cold fast now that the sun is down, so we have to get him inside."

"How did you ever get him outside? And where is Burton?"

"Burton's out in the barn milking I think, or maybe feeding. Anyway, Bithie's boys Bruner and Arrie came and with Burton they got him right into a chair and carried the whole chair outside."

Gracie was looking at the door where she could see her husband still staring into the quickly darkening sky. "Did you think about how we'd ever get him back *in* the house?"

Katherine giggled as she gently pushed Gracie out the door where she pointed to a long piece of burlap wadded behind the chair. She pulled it past the door and into the house before she explained, "Bruner had this idea. I think by scooting his chair on this tow sackin', me and you can manage to get him in out of the cold. Then the boys said they'd be back quick as they got the evening chores done to help you get him back in the bed."

Together Katherine and Gracie tilted Stephen's chair back and slid it along the rough fabric. Just as Katherine had hoped the chair took very little effort to move. Gracie couldn't help but notice how much weight her husband must have lost over the past months. She looked at Katherine wondering if she noticed it too.

I was supposed to be feeding him really well but it doesn't seem like I'm doing a very good job at that. Lord, please help me get some meat on this man's bones.

As they pushed the chair back up on all four legs, Stephen reached up for her and she took his hand. "Gracie, this has been the best day I can remember. I've been layin' in that bed back there wishin' the good Lord would take me on home. If that's all I can do I don't need to be taking up space and wastin' your time fetching food to me. But if I could get out on the porch, then I really think that sunshine would start to heal me."

"Stephen that is not what Dr. Lydick said."

"Well, I do appreciate the good doctor. Mother, I think I said some evil things about him before. I didn't mean them really."

Katherine pulled a chair close to his and took his free hand. "Stephen, I knew that. But you talking bad about him sure made me realize that we were probably killin' you, sticking you in that room back there. We'll find a way to get you out."

"Well, I been sittin' out there thinking on that. What if we made me a sled?"

"A sled?"

"Yeah, we haul hay and seed and corn shocks and all manner of stuff around the farm on sleds, so why couldn't we haul a man? You can pull a big load on a sled you know."

Katherine was nodding with him even as Gracie looked puzzled.

"Well I wish your daddy was here; he could build anything you could imagine, as you well know. Still I know the good Lord did not take him home before he taught you boys a thing or two."

"Mother, you are exactly right. If my cousins can get me out to the porch tomorrow I'll have Burton bring up some curved saplings I've hung out there and I'll fix me some runners on one of the porch chairs. I'm actin' like I'm helpless and my two arms and hands are still working just fine, ain't that right Gracie?"

Gracie had caught their excitement by this time and eagerly chimed in her approval of the plan.

"Yes, Stephen, I know you can build that. I've seen pictures of chairs with wheels on them to move people around, but that would be real hard to manage here, wouldn't it?"

Stephen nodded, "And no tellin' the cost. I'll make it like we make most everything we use."

Chapter 38

Stephen really did improve as he sat on the funny-looking chair with bent saplings attached on the right and the left. Once Stephen's creative mind got to work on the issues he was facing, he contrived a way to get himself out of the bed, asking Burton's help to suspend a bar from the ceiling that would allow him to pull himself up with his arms. 'We can pull big loads of hay with a rope and pulley, why can't we pull up a man?', was his only response to Gracie's questioning look. And it worked wonderfully for him, returning a measure of independence.

Dr. Lydick still stopped in at least once each week and when Gracie explained to him how Stephen thought he was actually getting worse, the doctor proposed the strong medicine. "We can still try the arsenic or strychnine sulfate. They are strong and may have some side effects, but they are the accepted treatment for this type of palsy."

"Do you have any hope that it will help Stephen," Gracie asked.

Dr. Lydick squinted his eyes for a long moment, then took a deep breathe before finally answering her. "No Miss Gracie, I don't guess I do have any faith in it."

"Then we won't put him through it. I mean, unless he decides he wants to. Most of the time medicines bring on problems of their own, don't they? I think my husband has a bucket full of problems as it is. Anyway, Dr. Lydick, you say you don't have any faith in those medicines, well I do have faith in a mighty healer."

The doctor could only nod.

So they continued on following more of Stephen's plan for his care than the doctor's. Each day, first with Burton's help, and later on his own with his suspended bar, Stephen would get out of the bed and into his sled-chair, then Burton and Gracie would slide him into the kitchen or out to the porch if the weather permitted.

While he was in bed, he had refused to see much of anybody, but now family and neighbors would see him on the porch and come up to talk with him. Burton and Martin would even bring him pieces of harness that needed mending or small wood projects he could work on from his chair. As springtime passed Gracie always sat on the porch with him to shell sweet peas or cut potatoes for planting. Stephen was once again a working member of the farm and the family.

They were working together one mid-day as dark clouds amassed to the west. Stephen smiled at Gracie and said, "Sure am glad you're not out tending to a new mama on a day like this." He nodded toward the western sky without stopping the work in his hands, "That's lookin' like it's going to be a big storm."

"Mmmhmm. I'm always glad to be home. And I've been here a lot lately you know."

"Yeah, you have but three people may show up for you today askin' you to come catch three different babies."

She chuckled at his exaggeration before sobering to respond to him. "Well, I haven't been out in months now so maybe the good Lord has moved me on from that time of my life."

"What in the world would make you say that? You've had lots of periods where no one called on you for help, then along comes a deluge. You better rest, or mend, while you have a chance."

Just as Stephen predicted, it wasn't long before one of their familiar sessions on the porch was interrupted by a young man riding a beautiful black horse. He tore into the yard at such speed both of them jumped.

Stephen first recognized the young man. "Cordell Miller, what's got you so fired up?"

"I apologize for tearin' in here like that Mr. Ingle, I gave Goose her head and when it was time to turn she thought she was still supposed to be traveling." He turned his head to Gracie now, "Mornin' Mizz Gracie. I've come needin' help."

"Good mornin' Cordell. What kind of help you need?"

He cocked his head to the side as though he didn't know how to answer her question. "It's Gladys, of course. She needs you."

Gracie was caught off guard and it took her a minute to realize he needed her to catch a baby. "Is she with child Cordell?"

He blushed a deep pink and nodded his head, looking down at the hat in his hand.

"Is Gladys your wife?"

"Yes ma'am. She thought the baby wouldn't come for another month or more but she's been hurtin' and then the water come, and I ran to get you."

"Who's with her now."

"Nobody."

Gracie caught her breath, "Oh. Well, we need to get to her right away, don't we? Cordell, will you please step into the barn and ask my son to saddle my horse?"

"Yes ma'am, I'll run right out there." He turned and picked up the reigns of his own mount then turned back quickly, "Well, I should've brought my wagon, I guess. I'm sorry Mizz Gracie; I wasn't thinkin' too clear."

Gracie smiled at him, "It's okay, I can ride." She glanced to Stephen with her last statement, thankful that he had insisted on finding a horse that was just the right temperament for her with steady footing for the unpredictable locations she'd have to ride. "Go on and help Burton, and I'll get my things."

As Cordell trotted around the house, Gracie laid a hand on Stephen's arm, "God's not finished with me yet, is he?"

Stephen reached over to cover her hand with his and looked up into her face, "Don't want to say 'I told you so. You better get yourself together, he'll be back in a heartbeat. Now you don't try to keep up with him, let him race on ahead of you."

"I'll be very careful."

He patted the front legs of his customized chair, "We can't have both of us in one of these chairs, now can we?"

Gracie patted his back and went inside without further comment. It took her only a moment to tie on her straw hat and grab the quilted tote bag she'd made after Stephen started talking about her riding a horse most of the time. She knew the basket she'd always kept her things in was far too cumbersome to carry on horseback. By the time she stepped back onto the porch, Cordell was waiting for her with a horse in either hand.

"I'm ready, let's get to your wife and see what we can do to help."

He nodded and mounted, turning his horse to face the road in the same movement. Gracie smiled down at Stephen and mounted the little mare Stephen had hand-chosen for her. "Come on girl, we've got work to do."

Chapter 39

Just as Stephen predicted, Cordell Miller rode much faster than Gracie wanted. She'd ridden this little mare a few times. In fact, she'd taken her up to Clarkrange just so that she would feel comfortable when this call came. Gracie noticed that following Cordell made Bell, as she called the little bay, move faster than when Gracie rode alone. Gracie soon settled into the ride and by the time they arrived at the tiny house just off the Emory Turnpike, she was a little sad to stop.

When Cordell told her his wife's water had broken before he left, Gracie feared the baby would have already arrived before them. However, it ended up being near dark before she could leave Gladys with her mother rocking the baby and Gladys resting peacefully. Saying her goodbyes, she was a little surprised when Cordell rushed out to re-saddle her horse.

When did he have the peace of mind to remove her saddle? she wondered. Still she was thankful the little horse had been well cared for and she expressed her appreciation when Cordell handed her the reigns.

"Mizz Gracie, I b'lieve it's too late for you to start home. How long you had that horse? Will she know her way home in the dark?"

"Thank you for your concern, Cordell. I think she knows her way and I can get off and walk if we're having trouble. There's certainly enough moon out tonight that I can see to walk."

"Okay," he said but the concern on his face was clear.

Gracie climbed into the saddle and looped her bag over the saddle horn. There was already a bag there and she looked at Cordell, "It's half of a good, smoked ham. We sure appreciate your help with Gladys and I hope that will be enough pay."

Gracie smiled, "It's more than enough. You take care of your family now. Good bye."

In the fading twilight Gracie maneuvered the short distance on the Turnpike and made the turn onto the Sisco Road that would lead her on to the Martha Washington Road.

Maybe I'd be better off without the horse at a time like this, I could cut through the nigh way if I's walking.

She patted her horse's neck and spoke gently to her, "Bell, you'll get us home just fine, won't you?"

Gracie couldn't help but think that this was a time Stephen might well have driven her, or maybe come to pick her up as he sometimes would do in years past. It brought a single tear to her eye to realize that their life had changed so much and he could now scarcely climb into a wagon much less hook one up and go driving about the country with his wife.

Lord please forgive me for feeling sorry for myself. I want to thank you for giving Stephen the strength that you have. Thank you for all this family that surrounds us and helps us. Thank you that Burton has grown into such a strong boy, and he's so dedicated to his family. Lord, you have blessed me more than I can even count. You have been faithful to your promises, that's what it is and I praise you for it.

By the time she reached the Todd Road, it was quite dark yet Bell never stumbled once. Gracie spent the ride talking to her Lord in silent prayer. What started as mourning for

Stephen and what seemed the sadness of their life soon moved to rejoicing for their many blessings.

The horse sensed home well before Gracie could see the lights burning and she quickened her pace to close the distance. Burton waited on the back porch and stepped down to take the reins as soon as his mother was on the ground. As she reached to get her bag, she thanked her son.

"Thank you Burton, I know you're tired and yet you're waiting out here for me."

"Nah, I heard the horse and couldn't figure anybody else that would be riding at this hour."

She smiled, "There's a ham on the saddle horn. Will you bring it inside when you come?"

He nodded as he and Bell walked toward the little barn.

Gracie cracked open the kitchen door to call for Tiny, but saw the dress she was going to ask for already draped over a chair near the door with a low-burning lamp sitting on the table right beside it.

Tiny's already learned, just like I learned from Grandma, Gracie thought with a pleased smile.

Gracie was soon accustomed to riding independently to homes where she was called. And she truly enjoyed the independence. The little mare allowed her to return sooner to Stephen and the responsibilities of home that always drew her. And she spent the solitary time in praise and prayer. Time and again her mood was tugged downward, especially after long hours at a bedside. Yet every time she turned to God to plead her woeful case, she ended up thanking and praising him for her many blessings.

The longing for the times when Stephen accompanied her did not end, however, she remembered those times were mostly before she had Burton and then when Tiny was born

Stephen always needed to stay home with them or at the very least to take them to Mother Ingle's or to Lottie's house if he was needed in the fields. As she searched her memories she couldn't find a single time he'd driven her since they were born and that put her pining into a proper perspective.

If she was able to return home in daylight, Stephen was always waiting for her on the porch. In fact, Burton reported to her that he couldn't get him to come inside until it was very dark and long past time to see the road from their porch. When it was already dark, Stephen would be in the bed awake until very late waiting to see that she was safely home.

"I pray till you're changed and in the house," he once told her when questioned about not getting the rest he desperately needed. "Maybe I can't be with you anymore, but I can lie here and beseech the good Lord to stay at your side and shepherd you home."

And God faithfully brought her home each time.

Chapter 40

Gracie's days were filled with work on the farm and in her home, time spent at a bedside and going to church. There seemed little opportunity to visit with neighbors yet she very often heard from women she'd tended. She could no longer keep track of all the names of the babies, but the mothers never waited for her to guess, 'That's lil' Martha You were sure a blessing when she came,' or 'You see Amos runnin' ahead of me? We didn't even know if he'd live when you caught him.'

Gracie smiled when she thought of these women and Stephen noticed it as they sat in their familiar spots on the front porch.

"I'd offer a penny for your thoughts, but I'm hardly good for it. Still, I'd love to know what put that pretty smile on your face."

Gracie blushed slightly, "Oh Stephen, you are silly sometimes. I was thinkin' about seeing some women around that I've helped along and some of their babies are really gettin' big now. They always tell me the children's' names. I guess they just know I can't ever remember them all."

Now it was his turn to smile, "You can't even count 'em. How could you ever name them?"

"Hmm, well I don't know. I always wonder how I'll know when the good Lord is done with me." With one hand she picked up the worn pair of pants Burton had torn a knee completely out of, and a scrap of patching material with the other.

Stephen grinned down at his own work, "You'll die when the good Lord's done with you, that's how you'll know."

She smiled down at her work, "The same could be said for you."

A little snort escaped her husband, "It's lookin' like he'll be done with me about any time then."

"Stephen, that's awful. You are much stronger and you are helping…"

"I ain't helpin' nobody Gracie. I've wondered for all these years why God would let me hang on being a drain on you and a burden to our children."

"Oh Stephen, I don't think Dr. Lydick really thought you'd survive that first winter after the palsy hit you. And just look at how long that's been and there you sit in your chair workin' on – what is that you're workin' on?"

"It's a bridle. And don't you quote that ole' Yankee doctor. He don't know nothin' about the strength of a Virginny-born mountain man."

"More like the stubbornness of a mountain man."

"Maybe so but I get so tired of the struggle. And ever-time I think I'll just give up I hear that verse from the bible where the good Lord tells Paul, 'My grace is sufficient for thee: for my strength is made perfect in weakness.' Well I am the picture of weakness wouldn't you say?"

Gracie smiled and reached out to lay her hand atop his. "You've been my strength since the day we said vows before that circuit preacher at Clear Creek. And ain't you glad Mother Ingle has quoted bible at you till it's ringin' in your head?"

He nodded and his eyes trailed off to the western horizon.

"Stephen, God's grace has been sufficient for us, hasn't it?"

He nodded, "Of course it has. And I'm ashamed when I get to feelin' sorry for myself. It's just this is not the life I had wanted to give you."

"No doubt it's better."

Stephen cocked his head and squinted at her, "How could that be? I thought we'd have a farm of our own and a big family with stock and crops to spare so that you'd be at ease by this time of your life."

She giggled, "Well that's a pretty soundin' story but I mean that what God had for us was better than what we could've imagined for ourselves."

"I haven't been very faithful to God, I've complained a lot."

"Faithfulness is not about keeping quiet, it's about obeying."

"You're the very one to preach this to me, Gracie. You've spent your whole life obeying God and serving every woman around here."

"Huh? Stephen, I'm the one that's fought against the Lord every step of the way. I said, 'Why can't I have children?' He gave me Burton and I wanted more. There are still days I don't really appreciate all of the babies I've gotten to catch and hold and love just a little bit."

The rocker creaked as she slowly pushed it back again and again and Stephen worked quietly beside her. Finally she finished her thought, "It just seems like God kept blessing us even when I didn't deserve any of it."

Stephen nodded without looking up. "I guess that's the way God's blessings always work. We can't ever deserve 'em, yet understanding you are blessed makes you want to work that much harder for him."

Stephen, that's just where I've come to! After struggling against God time and again I finally understand that the Lord's been so good to us, I just can't help but serve him. I guess as long as folks keep coming for me, I'll keep catchin' babies.

Epilogue

Whether it was the warm September sunshine or the gentle squeaking of the porch swing Gracie couldn't tell but her mind was lulled near sleep, her thoughts drawn over the span of her life. She could scarcely believe she was ninety years old today. She'd lived through three wars although admittedly she could not remember The Civil War as she was born in the middle of that terrible conflict. However, she well remembered two world wars and the fear and uneasiness the whole world felt during them. The first war when they all worried her twenty-six year old son would have to fight. Then the second when her young grandson was sent overseas despite the family's best efforts to protect him. Gracie breathed a prayer of thanks that the good Lord had delivered him home again whole and safe – she offered thanks for that merciful act every time she thought of it these past nine years.

Gracie gave her head a little shake, "Old woman there's not a bit of reason to dwell on the troubles of this life. Here your kids are working on a celebration and you're thinking of wars and battles."

She smiled to herself; she found she was reprimanding her thoughts more and more these days.

Burton, Tiny and Ida Mae insisted that they have a little party for her birthday and then they ran her out of the kitchen when she tried to participate in the preparations. "Not on your birthday," they insisted.

Gracie, back unbent by the years looked them right in the eyes when she reminded, "I'm not here to be kept up by my children. I'll work so long as I live and I've got the strength to do a little." The stern look and the strong words did not work this time and she found herself idly swinging.

Must be nearing time for Daniel and Delcie to get here, she thought, peering at her wristwatch. She had bid goodbye to her sister and dearest friend six years ago. Now, Daniel spent all of his time between Gracie's house and each of the children who still lived in Martha Washington – so many of them had been forced to leave to find work. But sweet Delcie still kept her father's house just as she'd done most of her thirty years. Gracie wondered both whether Delcie would ever marry and whatever Daniel would do without her.

As she pondered the Daniel Ingle family, she heard the roar of Ernest Hall's big car. She could see from the faces peering out the windows that he had brought his father-in-law and sister-in-law. Lottie's youngest daughter, Cecil, couldn't have found a finer man. In fact, Gracie thought that of most of Lottie's sons-in-law and daughters-in-law, with just a couple of exceptions, she dropped her head as she couldn't help but grin at that thought.

The roar of the engine seemed awfully loud, I wonder if there's something wrong with his car? Gracie thought. But it wasn't a problem with Ernest's car, in fact it was the cumulative roar of many big engines as car after car began to fill the yard. As people disembarked from the automobiles, the din of chatter steadily rose and as she watched, she realized there were people walking in as well. Almost immediately children began to swarm the porch calling, "Aunt Gracie this" and "Aunt Gracie that", for the whole community knew her as 'Aunt Gracie'.

Gracie welcomed the children, wrapping her arms around as many as she could reach. As soon as one squirmed away to attend to some adventure, another would take his place. She knew their names – mostly. Somewhere in the throng, Ida Mae moved her from the porch to a padded chair under a shade tree so she could be more easily reached by more people. And the people kept coming.

Then a woman nearly her own age took her hand and began to thank her, "Gracie, I had lost three babies and the old midwife at that time had given up on me. She said, 'Child, you won't ever birth a live baby, I don't think.' Well, that near to broke my heart. Then when the fourth one was a'comin', they brought you in the door. Well, you looked to me no more than a girl, but I thought, 'she's all I've got'. And you was all I needed. You brought that baby out kickin' and screamin'. And if you'll look over yonder, you'll see three little towheaded boys that's my great grandsons – now, can you even believe that? I feel about like Sarah who thought she'd never have a baby, and then she was the mother of God's chosen people."

Gracie reached up to hug the frail shoulders and had barely turned loose when another woman no more than thirty took her hand, "Aunt Gracie, you know I'm your namesake. And I can't count how many girls are here named 'Grace' or 'Anna Grace' or 'Ella Grace'. Law there's so many Graces we couldn't count them. We're all named for you Aunt Gracie – named because our Mamas didn't think we'd be here but for your help. And then you helped me when my two came, and I thought the same thing, 'what would I have done without her?'"

Gracie looked across the yard and again heard that voice from so long ago, If you'll serve me I'll give you more babies than any woman on this mountain.

She praised him aloud now, and no one questioned her. "Thank you Lord."

Romans 8:28 And we know that all things work together for good to them that love God, to them who are the called according to his purpose.

A Note from the Author

Gracie had a vision for her life in which she would marry Stephen and raise a large family on his farm in Martha Washington. However, those plans did not come to fruition.

The bible tells of a young woman who no doubt had similar plans. Mary expected to marry Joseph and raise a large, traditional Jewish family. However, God had other plans; she and Joseph were given the distinct honor of bringing up the incarnate Jesus Christ.

Just as Mary had to submit to the divine calling of her Lord, Gracie knew she would have to surrender her life to the plans and the calling God had for her. You and I are faced with the same choice. If we surrender to the Lord, He will direct our paths, and on that path we will enjoy His blessings.

The very first step in surrendering is to understand that you are a sinner (Romans 3:23) and that God sent Jesus Christ to die on the cross of Calvary to forgive you of your sins (John 3:16). Jesus is eagerly waiting to forgive you of your sin, you need only to call on his name. (Romans 1:13).

God has a special plan for each one of His children. If you are serving the Lord, you can claim the promise of Romans 8:28: "And we know that all things work together for good to them that love God, to them who are the called according to His purpose.

About the Author

Author Beth Durham writes Christian Historical Fiction inspired by the characters of Tennessee's Cumberland Plateau. She blogs weekly at: www.TennesseeMountainStories.com where she shares legends and lessons from the region.

Beth's passion for preserving the history and culture of her homeland and the people of Appalachia shines through in each of her novels. She brings the legends to life on the pages and takes you back in time to this beautiful land.

A native of Clarkrange, Tennessee, she now makes her home near Chattanooga with her husband and two children. She enjoys reading, gardening, horseback riding and flying small aircraft.

Other Titles by Beth Durham

All titles available from Amazon
For Retail locations please visit www.BethDurham.com